AN ARTFUL SECRET

HOLLY NEWMAN

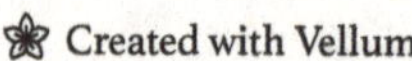 Created with Vellum

CHAPTER 1

A GOTHIC NOVEL, LATE JUNE 1816

The white-washed oak door to the writing retreat of Lancelot Nowlton—commonly addressed as Lakehurst or Viscount Lakehurst—flew open, bouncing off the bookcase beside the door with a loud, reverberating bang. The sound of books falling over and a cat's shrill, yowling protest added to the rude disturbance.

Lakehurst sighed and set his quill down. He knew without looking around that his twin sister, Lady Guinevere, had come looking for him.

He turned slightly, laying his arm across the back of his chair as he looked at her. "Yes, Gwinnie?" he asked in a long-suffering tone. His sister might be a lady by birth; however, she was no lady by behavior.

"Do you realize what time it is?" she demanded.

"And do you realize that you have once again barged in on me while I am working?" he countered, waving his hand at the pile of parchment spread on the desk before him. "You promised you would knock first after your last interruption."

"Yes, that was before I realized it takes forever for

you to answer your door!" she retorted, her hands planted on her prominent hips.

He nodded. "That happens when I need to finish a scene while it is fresh in my head," he explained with exaggerated patience. "Everyone else seems to understand that. Why can't you? Is the house burning down, or something equally dire? No," he answered for her before she could say a word.

Oscar, Lakehurst's large black cat, jumped down from his corner of the desk and sauntered over to Gwinnie to rub against her gowned legs.

"No, go away, Oscar," Gwinnie told the cat. "I don't want black fur on my dress—at least not this early in the evening." She looked up at her brother. "You were supposed to be downstairs before Ann and her fiancé, the Duke of Ellinbourne, and Ellinbourne's sister arrived."

"They are not expected until six o'clock, an infernally early evening hour for dinner visitors. And it is not—"

"It is!" Gwinnie exclaimed. She pointed at his clock on the small table next to his desk as she pushed Oscar away again.

Lakehurst turned to look at it. It displayed twenty minutes past the hour. "Bloody hell!" he swore, running his hand through his hair. Apparently, he'd been so deep into his writing that he'd never heard the chiming of the hour.

Rising to his feet, he grabbed his jacket from where he'd tossed it over an ornate hook hung on the wall.

Lakehurst filled the small room—what had been their childhood governess's room—with his presence. He towered a good five inches over his twin, who was herself an unusually tall woman, a good six feet in height. Taking after their mother's Scottish Highland forbearers with their broad shoulders and large-boned frames, they loomed over everyone in society. With his size, he might have appeared menacing to others if it weren't for his thick, wavy red hair that curled across his wide brow, his warm brown eyes, the cleft in his chin, and the sprinkling of freckles across his cheeks and nose. He often groused that he looked like an overgrown leprechaun.

Freckles. The bane of his existence. What man suffered freckles? That was a woman's characteristic, one that unfortunately bypassed his sister and blessed him instead.

"Grandmother, Ann, and Father are in the library with Ellinbourne and the solicitor. They are signing the settlement paperwork for Ann and the Duke of Ellinbourne's marriage," she explained. "I left Ellinbourne's sister in the Lady Margaret parlor to come up here and get you."

Lakehurst groaned. "I don't understand why she is here."

"Lady Darkford? And I'm not understanding your quibble that she is," Gwinnie declared, her brows drawing together.

Lakehurst ran his fingers through his hair again, his frustration habit. "It is probably more of Grandmother's matchmaking. She commented archly, in that manner of hers, that she saw me talking to Lady Darkford at Ann's betrothal ball. *Talking!* We were just talking. The woman looked so lost. I was just trying to put her at ease, not that I was successful—or ever could be at putting a lady at ease given my size."

Gwinnie chuffed and rolled her eyes. "That again?" she asked dismissively.

He shook his head, his gaze sliding away from hers. "You wouldn't understand."

"*Ha!* I don't know how you can say that. You know full well what it is like for me. I stand head and shoulders over all my female friends—the few I have. The others titter behind their fans about the giantess and wonder aloud how she can ever hope to snag a husband. '*Unless, of course, she trips the poor man in question and sits upon his back so that he can't escape her,*' they say."

To Lakehurst's dismay, he could see tears fill her dark, Scotch whiskey-colored brown eyes. "Gwinnie, I—"

"And they are not wrong," she declared, cutting him short. "How many men in society are as tall as I am? How many of them can look me in the eye? They certainly don't wish to look up to murmur their sweet nothings!"

"Yes, I grant you all that," he said. "And I'm sorry, I tend to forget that most people don't see beyond your size to your beautiful face and clever mind. But if it makes you feel better, I have a worse issue."

Her eyebrows and lips twisted into a doubting frown that only she could carry off. "And that is...?" she asked sarcastically.

"The women in society are afraid of me," he said simply.

Gwinnie made a sound of disbelief. "What? How can you say that? I have seen women flock around you at balls," waving her arms before her in large circles.

"They flock around the heir to the Malmsby Dukedom," her brother said disgustedly.

"Yes, and so what? That's perfectly natural in our society. That doesn't sound like fearful behavior to me," she scoffed.

He inhaled deeply. "Fine. Let me give you an example. Lady Mary Sudbury."

Gwinnie nodded and crossed her arms over her ample chest. "All right, what of Lady Mary?" Gwinnie prompted. "She is in this year's crop of debutants and has some distant relationship with Grandmother and to us."

"She slightly attracted me," he admitted, with a shrug of his broad shoulders. "I thought it was time I think about marriage and considered her a possibility."

She frowned slightly. "I don't care for your '*slight attraction*' as a reason for taking her to be your wife; however, choosing a wife would make Father and Grandmother happy," she acknowledged.

He nodded.

"But what? Why did you not pursue her?" Gwinnie asked, opening her arms.

"I overheard her speaking about me with some other debutants," he reluctantly admitted.

She shrugged. "Eavesdropping never pays toll."

"I know. It was not intentional, I assure you."

She sighed. "So what did you hear that has you all twisted up and ready to burst like a Christmas cracker?"

He felt a warm flush of blood creep up his neck to his cheeks. Certain subjects one did not discuss with women, particularly one's sister. But he needed to make her understand. "They were talking about my size. Um, that is, my size relative to the marriage bed."

"So what does it matter if your feet hang off the bed?—Oh!" Gwinnie blinked at her brother. "You mean how you'd fit together... *or not?*" she asked, incredulous. She started to laugh.

"It is not funny!" he ground out.

"Yes, it is," she said, nearly doubling over. "Oh, the naivety of a debutant!" she crowed.

"They were truly concerned," he protested, now angry with himself for admitting anything of that nature to his sister. The problem was they were twins and accustomed to being bluntly truthful with each other.

Lakehurst scowled at his sister as she tried to contain her laughter.

"I'm sure they were." She waved her hand airily in the air. "I can't see you with a simpering debutant, anyway. You, dear brother, are too worldly. You should seek out a bluestocking—they generally have a head on their shoulders—or look for a widow like Lady Darkford."

"No."

"Fustian," Gwinnie said dismissively. "And I have left her alone downstairs too long whilst I pry out your fears—ridiculous as they are. I'm going back downstairs to join her. You need to come, too."

"As soon as I brush my hair and clean the ink from my fingers."

"Good. I shall see you downstairs," she said, as she turned to open the door.

Oscar darted out past her into the old schoolroom and into the hallway beyond.

Gwinnie scowled after him. "You are not going to shed fur all over everyone, so don't even think of it. Wait for me by the terrace door and I'll let you out."

"Gwinnie! Oscar's a cat! He doesn't understand you," Lakehurst protested.

"*Hmph.* That's what you think. I think he's a little demon in disguise," she retorted as she swept out the door and followed the cat down the stairs.

～

WAITING for Lady Guinevere to return, Lady Cassandra Tidemark, the widowed Marchioness of Darkford, looked about the room. The only other time she'd been to Malmsby House had been the night of her brother's betrothal ball to Ann Hallowell, the Dowager Duchess of Malmsby's granddaughter, and she hadn't had reason that night to enter this room.

Lady Guinevere told her, as she escorted her into the room, that it was her grandmother's favorite space. With its pink, white, and gold ornamented walls and muraled ceiling, the shades of pink on the striped sofa, and the floral pink and green patterned upholstery on the chairs scattered about the room, the parlor had certainly been designed for a woman, Cassandra thought.

She knew she should have been annoyed at being left alone; however, she wasn't. Many in society would consider it the height of rudeness. She actually welcomed the opportunity to relax and prepare for the evening's social niceties. She hadn't been out in society often since her husband died almost eighteen months ago. Her brother's bringing her with him to this dinner was his way of encouraging her to be more relaxed in company once again now that her strict mourning period had ended.

She didn't know if anything would get her to relax anymore. Not truly. Too many memories. Too many nightmares.—And too much disbelief from others.

Cassandra picked up a book sitting on the table next to the sofa. A paper knife lay next to it, alluding to the book's new condition; however, Cassandra surmised someone must have already read it for all the page leaves had been cut.

The book *'The Mysterious Game'* by Anonymous listed 'Merriman' as the publisher at the base of the cover. The binding was a beautiful dark blue leather with a smooth, almost buttery feel, she thought as she ran her fingertips over the book. Gold-stamped lettering and gold-stamped leaves forming a frame on the front and spine of the book silently spoke of a high-priced book.

She had read little since Richard had died. Idly, she wondered why. She used to love reading.

As she flipped through a few of the pages, she noted dark and mysterious descriptions. The frontispiece engraving of a decrepit castle on a cliff reminded her of Baydon Castle, the Darkford ancestral home in the Mendip Hills.

A Gothic novel, she thought with a wry smile.

The door to the Lady Margaret parlor opened and Lady Guinevere returned.

"Sorry to be so long. I got into a conversation with my brother. Sometimes he can be so maddening!" she exclaimed, shaking her head. She crossed the room and casually flopped down into the chair across from Cassandra, although dressed elegantly for dinner.

Lady Guinevere did not display the formal behavior of a duke's daughter. She eschewed it, Cassandra decided, from the few times she'd been in company with her. The tall, flame-haired woman was built with Junoesque proportions. She was not fat. She was just... large statured. Cassandra had never met a woman of Lady Guinevere's formidable size. Perhaps that was why she adopted a hoydenish manner, to ease the effect of her size on others. It was most likely also why, though a wealthy duke's daughter, at eight-and-twenty, she remained unwed.

Cassandra laughed. "I know what you mean about

maddening brothers, as I have one of those, too. But I didn't mind being alone," she assured her. "I was looking at this book."

Lady Guinevere straightened. "Yes, it is the latest *Anonymous* book from the Merriman publisher."

"A Gothic novel?" Cassandra asked. "I've heard Gothics are all the rage."

Lady Guinevere nodded. "Quite exciting, full of evil and danger for the poor heroine," she said dramatically, then grinned and laughed. "I'll own I was up late last night to finish it. I could not put it down, and I know who the author is!"

Cassandra looked at her in surprise. She'd never known an author before. "Who is it?" she asked. "Someone in society?"

"I cannot tell you. I am sworn to secrecy. You should read it. You may borrow my copy," Lady Guinevere said, pointing to the book in Cassandra's hand.

"Perhaps," Cassandra said slowly. She paged idly through the book, reading a paragraph here and there. "The tone is definitely scary," she noted. And she did not like scary. She'd lived scary. She needed nothing to add to the nightmares she had experienced since the night her husband died. As it was, her husband's uncle and aunt said they feared for her sanity and the safety of her son.

She'd even heard their whispered talk of sending her to an asylum. That frightened her more than the nightmares. If she were locked away, they would be Alex's sole guardians and they could pillage the marquessate. The only reason they hadn't yet, was the support she received from her late husband's cousin, Raymond Stillworth, and their fear of her brother Miles, the Duke of Ellinbourne.

Maybe... Maybe... reading a book such as this

could be cathartic. A way to release the demon nightmares that endlessly gripped her.

She flipped to another page that opened easily to a
chapter fronted with another engraving, this one of a
woman tied to a table or altar. She bit her lip at the
picture. It represented too many nightmares. She
started reading.

"What?" she breathed in surprise at the words on
the page.

Lady Guinevere looked over at her.

Cassandra's brow furrowed as she read. She
quickly turned the page.

"No!" she cried, horrified. Her stomach churned
and pushed acid into her throat, burning.

The door to the parlor opened.

"*No!*" she said louder, surging to her feet, quivering
uncontrollably. She threw the book across the room.
Her slender chest rose and fell rapidly. She raised a
trembling hand to her lips.

"No!" she cried again, softer. She looked wide-eyed
at Lady Guinevere and then toward the door where
Lord Lakehurst stood. Her breathing ragged, she sank
down on the sofa, covering her face with her hands,
tears trailing down her cheeks.

Lady Guinevere rushed to her side and put an arm
around her.

"I'm sorry the book upset you," Lady Guinevere
said. She and her brother exchanged confused looks.

Cassandra shook her head, though she continued
to cover her face with her hands as she squeezed her
eyes tight against her tears.

"Shall I send for your brother?" Lady Guinevere
asked quietly.

"No, no, please. I'll be all right. Just give me a moment," she said, willing her tears to stop, for the lump

in her chest to shrink, for her pounding heart to lessen and her breathing to calm. She breathed in a deep, shuddering breath, letting it out in a whoosh as she dropped her hands from her face and raised her head. She swiped away the tears from her cheeks with her fingertips and looked up at the muraled ceiling squares to focus her mind away from the nightmares, nightmares that had plagued her for the last eighteen months. Would they ever cease?

No.

Not if there were continued reminders like that book. She stared at the blue book on the floor, an opened blot on the rose patterned rug, leaning against the leg of a chair by the fireplace.

Lord Lakehurst walked across the room to pick up the book.

"What was it that upset you in here?" he asked, his brows drawing together in a puzzled frown.

"Lakehurst," his sister cautioned, shaking her head.

"I don't know how the author knew what happened that night unless they were there," Cassandra said, brokenly, her voice husky.

Lord Lakehurst frowned. "There where? What do you mean?"

"Chapter seventeen," she whispered.

Lady Guinevere pulled back slightly.

"I know that chapter," Lakehurst told her, his brow furrowing.

"That is the night my husband died. That is precisely what happened in all its gory, horrifying detail," she said baldly, looking from one sibling to the other.

"Dear God!" Lady Guinevere said faintly.

"But this is a work of fiction," Lord Lakehurst protested as he sank into a chair at right angles to her.

He pulled his handkerchief from his pocket and handed it to her.

Cassandra thanked him mechanically as she accepted the folded cloth, then forcefully shook her head. "The author had to have been there. There is too much here that is true. *I must find out who this author is!*"

"Why?" he asked.

"To see that they arrest him for murder!"

"Whoa—" Lakehurst said, leaning back in his chair as he stared at her. Lady Guinevere laid a hand on her arm.

Cassandra shook her head. "I'm sorry, I'm sorry, I didn't mean that." Or perhaps she did. She didn't know anymore. She closed her eyes and compressed her lips together. Her emotions were raw and jumpy. She rocked back and forth.

"Lady Darkford?" Lady Guinevere said softly.

Cassandra let out her breath, her lips twisting. "Maybe my late husband's uncle and his wife are right. They think I need time in an asylum. For a complete rest. They fear I have Hysteria," she said ruefully.

"No!" Lord Lakehurst and Lady Guinevere said together.

"Talk to us, please." Lady Guinevere said. "What did you mean when you said this happened to your husband?"

She shook her head slightly, her brow furrowing at her memories. She did not want to remember. The nightmares were enough. She tilted her head up, opening her eyes to again stare unseeing at the muraled ceiling panels as she gathered her raw emotions, tucking them away.

Lord Lakehurst leaned forward to touch her forearm. "Would it help to know that the man stabbed at the beginning of chapter seventeen does not die?" he asked earnestly.

She looked at him. He was a big man, and his size should have frightened her as the man who killed her husband had been near his size, tall with broad shoulders. But Lord Lakehurst's eyes were a mottled brown, full of concern for her, his touch on her arm featherlight. The man from her nightmares had cold eyes as black as night, and the unwelcome memories of his touch made her skin crawl.

"He couldn't die," Lady Guinevere declared. "He's the hero!"

Cassandra saw Lakehurst look at his sister, his mouth twisting in a wry smile. "Just so," he said.

She looked between them. They seemed to have some unspoken communications that she couldn't fathom. The lives of twins, she supposed. That they were both familiar with the book took her by surprise. The book was new. That morning, she had read about the new Gothic book released by *Anonymous* in the day's paper. They had given more print space to supposition as to the identity of the author than a review of the book; however, it appeared the journalist had been dutifully impressed.

"Let me get you a glass of sherry," Lakehurst said, rising to his feet. He crossed to the beverage cart set against the wall and poured a generous portion of the light, reddish-brown liquid into three glasses. Cassandra watched him balance the delicate glasses in his large hand. He handed one glass to her, then his sister, before taking the last for himself.

He sat back down. "So tell us what happened," he said, his expression sympathetic, inviting her confidence.

Cassandra drew in a deep breath, letting it out

slowly. She didn't know why she felt comfortable with this gentleman. He was quite the tallest and largest man she'd ever seen. Larger than the smithy at Baydon Castle, and that man was big. She nodded mutely, looking forward to sharing her story with someone other than family. She wanted to hear their summation, if they thought the same as her late husband's uncle and his wife, that she was ill with Hysteria.

There suddenly were voices outside in the hall. She jerked her head up, looking fearfully from Lord Lakehurst to Lady Guinevere.

"Please do not say anything about my reaction to the book. Or that I ever looked at it." She patted her cheeks to bring color back to her face.

"Why?"

The voices were getting louder.

"Please?!" she repeated.

Lakehurst and his sister exchanged glances again, but when they looked back at her they nodded.

"We won't," Lord Lakehurst promised. "If you promise to tell us the tale later."

"And you call us Lakehurst and Gwinnie, not Lord Lakehurst and Lady Guinevere," Lady Guinevere added severely.

"I will try," she said hurriedly before schooling her features to a pleasant smile and looking toward the door of the parlor as it opened.

～

LAKEHURST and the two women stood up as his grandmother, the Dowager Duchess of Malmsby, and the others entered the parlor. His grandmother had her arm linked through his cousin Ann's arm, and the two women were giggling together like schoolgirls. Though her own red hair had gone white with age, her face revealed little of the evidence of her years. She bore just a few perpetual creases at the edge of her always-smiling eyes that reminded those who knew her how mischievous she could be.

"I gather all the pre-marital paperwork has been completed to everyone's satisfaction?" he said.

His father, the Duke of Malmsby, slapped the Duke of Ellinbourne on his back. "More than satisfactory," he said. "He insisted if anything should happen to him, Ann will have an ample income and will not be left dependent on an executor to control her money. Very enlightened thinking. I like that. I am glad to see this concluded before my journey to Northumberland tomorrow."

Miles shrugged slightly, discomfited by the Duke's praise. "I believe more men might stipulate such terms if they had to see what might happen to a widow when her well-being is not accounted for. My sister is totally at the mercy of what her uncle-by-marriage gives her as he controls the marquessate coffers."

Lakehurst turned to look at Lady Darkford. She had her lower lip caught between her teeth and was looking down at her clenched hands, a blush staining her cheeks.

"I'm sorry, Cassandra, to speak so openly," said her brother, "however, your situation greatly angers me. That you are entirely dependent on your uncle-in-law to buy so much as a ribbon is intolerable. I would happily fund a widow's jointure for you; however, the fact that you are forced to live with them or else they will take your son from you is not to be borne."

Lakehurst's eyes narrowed. "Live with them? On

what grounds?" he asked, his eyes shifting to Lady Darkford.

"That they cannot ensure I would be capable of giving him the proper education for a marquess as I am a clergyman's daughter without knowledge of the intricacies of the aristocracy," she offered softly.

"That is ridiculous!" the Duchess exclaimed. She shooed Gwinnie out of the way and sat down next to Cassandra. She covered Cassandra's clenched hands with her own. "We will have to do something about that!" she declared.

"Mother—" warned the Duke of Malmsby.

Lakehurst couldn't help but grin. He couldn't think how she—or anyone else in the family—might help Lady Darkford; however, he didn't doubt his grandmother would begin plotting.

"You're very kind, Your Grace; however, there is no way to circumvent the terms of Lord Darkford's will." Cassandra frowned. "I don't know why Darkford changed the terms at the time of Alex's third birthday, not six months before he died."

"Someone probably advised him to do so. Probably his cronies," the Duke of Malmsby said grimly. "Excuse me, Lady Darkford, for speaking plainly; however, my experience of Darkford in Parliament was he was a man too easily led by others."

"Gullible," Ellinbourne agreed, nodding.

Lakehurst sat down again as he observed Lady Darkford glower at her brother for his statement. Had she been deeply in love with the man? It appeared neither he nor his family had treated her well.

And what about her statement that her husband's death was like the events in his book? He'd used his grandmother's Versely Park estate, with its attached monastic ruin, as his inspiration for the story setting.

His heroine had been tied to a stone altar, the hero drugged and unable to help her. In rage and fear, his hero willed his mind to clear and his muscles to move in time to stop the demon-possessed man from burning the mark of Satan on the heroine's fair shoulder, which would bind her forever to the Prince of Hell.

His hero fought like a madman and sustained a deep knife wound, but managed to kill the man, forcing the demon to rise out of his host in a black, smoky miasma, and flee back down into the hellish bowels of the earth from whence he came.

With his last bit of strength, the hero cut the heroine's bonds before passing out.

What in that story scenario could possibly be like something that could occur in real life?

"Excuse me, Your Grace," Mr. Harold, the butler, said from the parlor door, "Dinner is served."

As the dinner numbers were uneven, Lakehurst offered his arms to his sister Gwinnie and Lady Darkford to escort them to the dining room. Lady Darkford handed his slightly damp handkerchief back to him, still neatly folded, and accepted his escort.

In the dining room, Lakehurst found himself seated between his cousin Ann and Lady Darkford. On the other side of the table sat Ellinbourne and Gwinnie. His Grandmother took the position at the end of the table opposite his father. He remembered his mother sitting there when she was alive. He still missed her, though it had been ten years since she passed.

Seated in the middle as he was, he felt left out from the conversations flowing around him for Ann was in a lively conversation at the head of the table with his father and Ellinbourne, while his grandmother conversed with Lady Darkford and Gwinnie. He found himself listening more to his grandmother's end of the table.

He couldn't conceive why he should suddenly feel drawn to Lady Darkford. He had met her at Ann and Ellinbourne's engagement ball. On that occasion, she had remained solemn, no matter how he had strived to draw her out. Not today. Perhaps it was because she threw his book across the room, high emotions flashing in her eyes, he mused. He didn't know anyone to have done that before!

He found himself smiling at that memory. He glanced over at her. His grandmother had asked about her son. Lady Darkford's withdrawn, waif-like countenance blossomed, a flower in the sunshine. Her dark eyes danced, and color returned to her pale face, along with a beautiful smile. She should smile more, he thought, for her smile transformed her.

He wanted to know why his book upset her so; but more, he wanted to know about her. He wanted to know about her circumstances and why her late husband's relations threatened her with asylum confinement. She did not appear to him as a woman ill with hysteria or other mental tribulations. Was this just his writer's itch, his curiosity to know more?

He looked over at his sister, laughing at something their grandmother had said. Perhaps he could recruit Gwinnie to help him learn more?—If he could tear his sister away from an afternoon's violin practice. Maybe a walk in Hyde Park, a trip to Gunter's Tea Shop, or perhaps a visit to a diorama with her son? Something unassailable for anyone to find fault with. The more he considered that option, the more he liked it.

CHAPTER 2

THE INVITATION

M r. Edmund Tidemark stared over the top of his wireframe glasses at Cassandra as he buttered a breakfast scone. "How was your dinner last night at Malmsby House?" he asked.

Cassandra inclined her head toward him. "Very nice, thank you," she said affably. She glanced down at her food, then raised her cup of hot chocolate to her lips. She did not want to engage her uncle-in-law in conversation about the previous evening.—Nor his wife, Vanessa, who was an avid gossip.

Cassandra had quite enjoyed herself—despite the issue with the novel. She found the entire Nowlton family to be friendly and caring. She could relax in their company and that felt satisfying.

"They are an odd family," Vanessa said. She took a bite of ham. "The Duke does not take part in society. Sends his son in his stead.—If he truly is his son," she finished speaking around a mouthful of food.

Cassandra compressed her lips. She set her fork down on the edge of her plate. "Why would you say that, Vanessa?" she demanded, feeling put out. Then she reprimanded herself for her hasty words. This was just Vanessa's way. She was a blowsy woman who wanted desperately to be in the throes of society. She thought marrying the brother of a marquess would give her the entrée she craved. That it hadn't given her that automatic entrée ate at her.

"He and that sister of his are so large..." Vanessa said coyly.

"I am not getting your inference," Cassandra returned.

"Well, no others in the family have that size," she said archly.

"Quite true, my love," said Edmund.

"...and the late duchess was from Scotland," his wife finished.

Cassandra saw his brows rise on his forehead as he considered his wife's words. He nodded slowly, as if he considered Vanessa's words to be of infinite, astonishing truth.

Cassandra frowned as she shook her head. Was Vanessa truly trying to infer Lord Lakehurst and Lady Guinevere were born on the wrong side of the blanket?

"I believe you might be forgetting the Malmsby red hair," she said, hoping to deflate this line of thinking. Once she had an opinion, Vanessa would spread it wide within her realm. Thankfully, she wasn't in the mainstream of society. Though Cassandra wondered if Vanessa's and Edmund's desire to wrest Alex away from her wasn't their contrivance—along with controlling his money—to get into society through their guardianship.

Vanessa frowned.

"A lucky happenstance?" suggested Edmund.

Vanessa perked up at his suggestion. Cassandra shook her head.

"I have met several members of the extended Nowlton family. There is a family resemblance that cannot be denied," Cassandra said.

Vanessa snorted but could not think of a response.

The butler appeared at the door with an envelope on a salver.

"Ah! Mail! Bring it here," Edmund instructed.

"Beg pardon, sir; this be for Lady Darkford," he said a little apologetically. He walked over to her. "A young person is awaiting your response."

Cassandra picked the envelope off the plate.

"Who would write to you?" Edmund demanded. "It probably should have been directed to me. Hand it here," he said, extending his hand.

Cassandra unfolded the letter and glanced quickly at the signature. "No, Edmund, this is meant for me. It is from Lady Guinevere Nowlton." She quickly scanned the letter.

"So what does she say? What does she want?" demanded Vanessa.

"She wants to meet Alex and suggests Alex and me accompany her on a walk through the park this afternoon with an ice at Gunter's afterward."

"No, absolutely not!" declared Vanessa.

"I beg your pardon," Cassandra said, lowering the letter to the table. "Alex and I walk in the park nearly every afternoon with his nursemaid. He has often asked for an ice, which I could not grant him as Edmund declines to give me pin money."

"Now see, here," Edmund began, red creeping up his neck.

"He should like this treat and I believe he deserves it," Cassandra finished. She looked up at the butler. "Inform the messenger we should be delighted to accompany Lady Guinevere."

The butler bowed his head. "Yes, my lady."

"I shall join you then," Vanessa declared.

Cassandra leveled her gaze at her. For the first time since Edmund and Vanessa Tidemark had moved into the Marquess of Darkford's London townhouse following her husband's death, she felt a spark of rebellion. "I'm afraid not, Vanessa. They did not invite you. It would be presumptuous of you to join us."

"But a chaperone! You need a chaperone!" protested Vanessa. "Tell her, Edmund!"

Cassandra shook her head. "I shall have Alex's nursemaid with me, and as Lady Guinevere mentions in her letter," she said, picking up the paper again, "her maid, Rose, will be with us as well." As would Lord Lakehurst, according to Lady Guinevere's note; however, Cassandra didn't see the need for them to know that.

She rose from her chair at the table.

"Where are you going?" Edmund asked.

Cassandra raised an eyebrow. "To the nursery to see my son and inform him of the outing."

"I'd like to read the letter from Lady Guinevere," he said, extending his hand.

"No," Cassandra said simply. She pulled the letter to her chest and walked out of the breakfast room.

A spurt of nervousness assailed her. She thought he might call her back or something; however, he did not. Cassandra climbed the stairs to the nursery on the second floor. Could dealing with Edmund and Vanessa really be this easy? She had been so weak-minded before. She felt more awake to life and suffused with a new courage she hadn't felt since Richard's death.

~

WHEN THE TIDEMARK butler closed the front door behind Cassandra, Alex, and his nursemaid that afternoon, Cassandra raised her face up to the sun, letting its warm rays touch her cheeks despite her deep-brimmed black bonnet. She loved the sunlight, something she'd only experienced on rare sunny London days, rare especially this year which had been inordinately cold and rainy. Vanessa insisted the drapes of the Darkford townhouse always be drawn in mourning, even now, eighteen months after Richard's death. And Baydon Castle, the Tidemark family's ancestral home, where they had been living when Richard died, had always been dark. Dark and foreboding. Just thinking of Baydon Castle in passing caused a shiver to race along her nerves.

Enough.

She was in London now, and she relished the days she and Alex went for walks in Hyde Park.

"Mama?" Alex said, tugging on her hand. "Are we going to go now?"

She looked down at her son and smiled. "Yes, of course. I was just taking a moment to enjoy the sunshine."

She descended the stone steps before the townhouse, holding Alex's small hand in her gloved one, the nursemaid following silently behind them.

She felt glorious this morning. Could that be because she'd finally said *no* to Edmund and Vanessa? Because of the weather? Or because they were to be meeting friends?

Cassandra surmised it might be a combination of the three, and that pleased her. She hadn't realized how lonely she'd been until the previous night's dinner party. She had actually laughed in company at some joke someone shared at the dinner table! She couldn't remember the last time she'd done that. How small her world had shrunk in the past six years since she married Richard!

As they walked the three blocks to the park, she remembered when she met the Marquess of Darkford during her first season. She'd been sponsored for her come-out year by her aunt, the 4th Duchess of Ellinbourne, alongside her cousin, Charlotte, the Duchess's eldest of five daughters. She'd been quite awed when the Marquess requested the honor of adding his name to her dance card. She'd stammered something, she didn't remember what, as this tall, blond-haired man with a rakish smile and clever blue eyes signed his name with a flourish. It was for the supper dance.

She'd thanked him as she'd curtsied. He'd touched a gloved finger to her chin, nodded, then turned to walk off.

As a country clergyman's daughter, she'd been surprised when the dashing Marquess's roving eye had settled on her. That began a formal courtship with an interestingly punctiliously correct amount of attention from the Marquess, no more.

Near the end of the season—after Charlotte had accepted a marriage offer from David Childe, the Earl of Coyle and there was much rejoicing in the Ellinbourne household—Darkford approached her for permission to address her father for her hand in marriage.

He told her bluntly he was not looking for love in a marriage. He looked for a reasonably educated woman not prone to the vapors. He desired a woman from a good family, who would provide him an heir. A marchioness to stand by his side; but—and he was clear about this—not get in the way of his enjoyments.

He admired Cassandra's quiet beauty, intelligence, and manner. She was everything he desired in a Marchioness—if she did not cut up over his personal activities, he finished with his rakish smile.

His matter-of-fact attitude stung Cassandra's young heart; however, she knew that as a clergyman's daughter with the little dowry she would bring to a marriage, her chances of marrying for love were slim. And she thought, perhaps, she was half in love with the dashing, handsome marquess. She made him the promises he desired, assuming his personal activities meant his mistresses as was the wont of so many gentlemen of the ton. And so she'd become the envied Marchioness of Darkford.

She did not realize, until several months after the marriage, that her husband's proclivities were not for a mistress. He had an unhealthy obsession with demons, devils, and the occult.

CHAPTER 3

THE OUTING

Lakehurst spotted Lady Darkford, her son, and his nursemaid as they negotiated their way through the noisy crowd of hawkers and the carriage and the horse traffic congestion on the street that ran before the park. At least it was early enough that "Rotten Row," the gravel road that ran east to west through Hyde Park to Kensington Gardens, was not likeways crowded with horseback riders and carriages. He compressed his lips. He should have thought of waiting for them across the street outside the park gates to escort them here. He touched Gwinnie's arm and pointed toward the street.

She turned from her quiet conversation with her maid, Rose, to see them. She waved at them and excitedly jumped up and down. Typical Gwinnie.

Gwinnie ran forward to greet them. She grabbed Lady Darkford's free hand, enthusiastically shaking it up and down as she looked at Alex.

Startled but pleased with the enthusiastic greeting, Lady Darkford blushed.

"You're tall!" Alex exclaimed, looking up at Gwinnie and over to Lakehurst.

Gwinnie giggled. "Yes, we are."

"Alex," his mother said, "this is Lady Guinevere and Lord Lakehurst. Make your bow, please."

He looked up at her, deep furrows between his brows and confusion in his dark brown eyes. "Uncle Edmund says I only bow to dukes and royalty 'cause I'm a marquess," he said.

"If you were an adult, that would be true," Lady Darkford gently agreed. "However, you are still a child and children bow and curtsy to adults they are introduced to. It is a show of respect," she told her son.

"Oh-h-h!" said Alex. "All right." His expression turned serious. He looked at Lady Guinevere and Lord Lakehurst and bowed deeply at the waist. "I am most pleased to meet you," he said solemnly.

"Oh, fustian," Gwinnie said. "We are going to have fun today!" She bent down to pick up Alex and settle him on her hip, scrunching up the fabric of her yellow-figured walking dress.

Lakehurst nearly laughed at the shocked expressions on Lady Darkford's and the nursemaid's faces at his sister's action and the frowns on the faces of strangers around them. That was Gwinnie. She didn't care a farthing for what anyone thought. She was her own unique person, and he loved his sister dearly.

"My brother found something in our old schoolroom he thought you might enjoy," Gwinnie told Alex, who could not help leaning back in her arms and staring at her in wonderment.

Lakehurst took his cue from his sister and opened the small canvas bag he carried. He pulled out a small wood sailboat attached to a coil of rope and handed it to Alex.

"A boat!" Alex exclaimed, bouncing on Gwinnie's hip.

"A boat!" protested Gwinnie, "I'll have you know that is one of his majesty's ships of the line, ready to sail on the Serpentine!"

Alex looked at his mother. "Can I, Mama?"

"May I," corrected Lady Darkford, then smiling, gave her consent.

Gwinnie set Alex down, then took his free hand. Swinging their hands between them, the two of them set off for the edge of the long, man-made lake commissioned by Queen Caroline in the last century. Created by damming the River Westbourne, it ran through Hyde Park and into the Kensington Gardens grounds.

Lakehurst offered Lady Darkford his arm as they followed, with the maids trailing after them.

"Your sister is a delight! Why is she not married with scores of children of her own?" Cassandra asked Lord Lakehurst.

"The simple answer would be to say she is too busy. Beyond that?" he shrugged. "A matter of circumstances, more than anything," he said.

Cassandra sighed. "I should give anything to be as carefree as she appears to be."

"She has many demands and stresses on herself. She uses days like today for respite."

Cassandra nodded slowly. "I think I understand that."

He led her to a bench in the shade of one of the elm trees Queen Caroline had planted near the lake. They sat down, silent, as they watched Alex and Gwinnie put the boat in the water. Alex fiercely held the long rope tethered to it in a small, clenched fist like he would hold a kite string he feared would escape him.

"Forgive me for saying so; however, I understand from what your brother said last night that you have not had an easy time of it with your son's guardian and executor," Lakehurst said.

Cassandra looked back at her son walking along the lakeshore, pulling the boat through the water. She smiled slightly, the curiosity was understandable given the events of the previous evening. "The fault is partly mine. I-I did not take my husband's death well."

"You loved him," he said gently.

She shook her head as she wryly smiled. "No, not at all, but I respected him as my husband. He was good to me and a good father," she told him crisply, not wanting to think of all else he had been. A man of a dual nature.

He nodded. Then his brow furrowed. "You said your husband's relations think you suffer from Hysteria?"

She laughed shortly, her eyes fixed on Alex and Gwinnie. "They do. I'll concede I mayhap have suffered so right after his death.—It was horrendous," she said heavily, remembering her wild hysterical attempts to get Edmund and Vanessa to believe her when she told them all that had occurred. And how angry she had been at their placation and whispered consultations with a doctor to drug her with laudanum. If it hadn't been for Richard's cousin, Raymond Stillworth, and her brother, the Duke of Ellinbourne, she might now reside in an asylum.

"They do not allow that I have changed in the last eighteen months. That is what has my brother so aggrieved, I feel."

He nodded.

Gwinnie had her skirts clasped in one hand and leaned slightly down to hold Alex's hand as they skipped together along the dirt bank, giggling. Cassandra smiled at the sound of Alex's laughter mixed with Gwinnie's. He had so few opportunities to merely play. A wave of guilt assailed her for not having provided Alex with more activities a child would enjoy.

She had been consumed with fear since her husband's death. She felt like the nightmare wasn't finished. The memories, the horrors and fears continued to plague her dreams... when she least expected them to, and without reason. Throughout her life, she'd considered herself a practical person, not given to flights of fancy. But the events of that night seared her soul, leaving scars greater than the one she bore above her left breast. There was more to come, she felt sure of it! Though in truth, she had no reason to feel so. It lay like a sleeping serpent coiled within her.

"I have a confession to make to you," Lakehurst said after a moment. "And an apology," he added.

She slowly turned from watching Gwinnie and Alex, pulling her thoughts back from the abyss they teetered upon to face Lord Lakehurst. "Yes?" she said, forcing a smile to her lips.

"That book you threw across the parlor..."

"Yes?" she said, again, her attention now entirely on the viscount, and with that attention came the heat of embarrassment rising up in her cheeks for the memory of throwing the book.

"I'm very familiar with every page of that book," Lord Lakehurst solemnly told her, looking down at his hands clasped between his legs.

She cocked her head to the side, now giving him her full attention. *What is he saying?*

"I know the book... I know that chapter..." he said

slowly. He looked up at her, "I know it because I wrote it."

Cassandra didn't know what she was expecting to hear; however, it wasn't a confession that he wrote that book!

"You wrote that!" she said, her voice cracking.

The memory of what she read and the memories of that night collided in her mind.

No! No!

He was one of them! He was there!

The thought made her heartsick. He had to have been there to write that chapter!

The serpent undulated within her.

How could he sit here and calmly admit he'd written for all to read that description of what happened to her, of how Richard died? What had been his role?

Murderer!?

Horror assailed her, rising up to swamp her senses and making her feel sick to her stomach. Her heart raced. She felt the color draining from her face. She gasped, wide-eyed, her hand rising to her lips.

No! No!

He reached out to her as she surged to her feet. "I —" he began.

She had to get away, to get away from him, to get away from the memories.

She ran toward the Serpentine where Alex and Gwinnie were guiding the boat through the water with their length of rope.

I have to get away! We have to get away!

"Alex! Alex!" she called, her voice shrill.

Alex's head whipped around at his name. "Come see, Mama!"

"No, we must leave immediately," she told him,

struggling to hide the fear and horror that filled her chest. She grabbed his arm and pulled him away from Lady Guinevere.

"Lady Darkford—Cassandra!" exclaimed Gwinnie. She reached out to her. "What has occurred?"

"I should have known when you said your brother was into demons and cults!" she spat out.

"Lady Darkford!" shouted Lord Lakehurst, running toward them.

"Keep away from me, *murderer*," Cassandra hissed, pulling Alex away.

"But, Mama!" Alex protested, still grasping his end of the rope attached to the little boat.

"*What?!*" exclaimed Gwinnie.

"Lady Darkford," Lakehurst began again, reaching her side, standing between her and the lake.

"No!" Cassandra yelled. She pushed him away from her.

Surprised at her action, she saw Lakehurst stumble backward in the slick mud at the water's edge, his boot heel tangling with the rope attached to the boat. He couldn't keep his footing. "Wha—?" he uttered as he lost his balance.

She watched in horror at what she'd done when he fell on his back in the shallow water at the lakeshore.

"Lakehurst!" screamed Gwinnie.

Cassandra swung her son up into her arms and hurried away. Alex's confused, wide-eyed nursemaid ran to catch up.

~

"*MAMA! BUT, MAMA!*"

Lakehurst heard Alex's high-pitched protest. His mother ignored him, intent as she was to put as much distance between them as rapidly as she could.

Around them, the park had gone strangely quiet. No voices, no carriage wheels turning or horses' hooves pounding.

"What did you say to her?" Gwinnie demanded as she pulled her brother to his feet. The hem of her gown wicked up the water, but she didn't seem to notice.

"I told her I wrote the novel," he said as he dripped water on the muddy shore as they climbed the bank to the gravel road. He ran one hand and then the other down his sleeves to encourage the soaked cloth to let go of the wet. He looked after Lady Darkford, hurrying down the path, her distraught child in her arms. "I gather that was a mistake," he said on a deep, blown out breath.

Gwinnie shook her head.

The excitement gone, voices rose around them, all eyes on the water dripping off him.

Lakehurst ignored the surrounding people. His attention remained on Lady Darkford. His brows drew together when he saw a man rise from a bench not far away and turn to follow Lady Darkford. He'd seen him sit down when he and Lady Darkford did. He'd noted him because he wore his hat pulled low over his eyes, and he wore a greatcoat, though the day was warm. Too odd, he'd thought then. Now that he knew she suspected her husband was murdered, he wondered if the man was following her. *Was she in danger?*

"Gwinnie," he said, not looking at her, "see the man behind Lady Darkford?"

"The one in the coat?"

"Yes."

"I think he is following her. We need to follow them."

She squinted in the direction he pointed. "Ah, yes! —Not us, though," she said, straightening, "even if we weren't wet, we'd be too conspicuous—*Rose!*" she called out.

"Yes, miss?" her maid said, turning from watching Lady Darkford, as all around them had been.

"Quick, look there!" she said, pointing. "A man is following Lady Darkford. Follow them to determine what occurs."

"And report back to us immediately afterward," Lakehurst added.

"Yes, miss, my lord!" Rose said excitedly. "And start screaming if he tries anything," Rose added with a grin, dipping a quick curtsy before hurrying after the man and Lady Darkford.

"Screaming?" Lakehurst asked his sister as her maid scurried down the road, dodging horses, carriages, and pedestrians as she tried to keep the man in sight.

"It is what we tell the women at the charity house to do if anyone bothers them. It draws attention and most of the men out to take something or do something they shouldn't don't want attention." She gathered the rope from the ground and pulled the boat to the shore. She picked it up and shook it to shed water, dumped it back in its canvas bag, then tucked it under one arm.

Lakehurst nodded. He took Gwinnie's other arm and started walking with her toward the park entrance, ignoring the curious glances and whispered asides from those around them.

"But what made you suspicious?" she asked as she walked beside him.

"Lady Darkford looked at me with such horror when I told her I wrote the book. All the color drained from her face and I thought she might cast up accounts. She couldn't get away from me fast enough."

"Hmmm... And she did make that comment about you being into demons and cults."

"But I'm not," he protested.

"No, you are not into them, per se, but you use them in your novels as plot devices to scare your readers."

Lakehurst acknowledged that was true, then, "Do we know how her husband, the Marquess, died? She said it was like my book, but I find that hard to believe."

"Why?" Gwinnie asked.

"Drugs and a Satanic ritual? I was attempting to make up something horrifying."

"And you did. But, if what Lady Darkford said is true, and you weren't original..."

He scowled. "Didn't Ellinbourne tell us once—before we met her—that her husband died eighteen months ago?"

"Yes."

"About the same time I was in Scotland visiting our mother's relations," he mused. "I don't think I ever heard how he died."

"Mr. Martin could probably find out," Gwinnie suggested.

"Mr. Martin?"

"You remember, Mr. Lewis Martin, the Bow Street Runner?"

"The friend of our Uncle Aidan," Lakehurst clarified. Then he laughed. "I remember that bone-shaker horse he rode when we realized you and the other ladies could be in trouble!"

"Yes," Gwinnie said.

Lakehurst looked at her and thought he detected a slight pink on her cheeks. Was that from the sun, or was she blushing at the mention of the Bow Street Runner? "You've been in the sun too long, Gwinnie, even with your bonnet. You're starting to burn," Lakehurst said, gruffly, dismissing the idea of Mr. Martin and his sister.

"We should hurry back to Malmsby House. I don't want to play at a concert with a bright red face. I would clash terribly with my hair," she quipped lightly.

"Do you have one tonight?"

"Yes. A musicale performance for Lord and Lady Dunwittie. Last of the season."

"Ugh. Dull set," he said.

"Yes, but we get to play anything we want. Some of the requests from the hosts of our other musicale performances are horrid." She scrunched her face in distaste. Lakehurst laughed.

"And my players could use the money to see them through a quiet summer," she added.

They turned the corner onto the street that ran before Malmsby House.

"I'm going to go in through the mews," Lakehurst said. "Don't want to have to answer any of Grandmother's questions, which she is bound to have."

"I agree. I'll go with you," Gwinnie said.

They stepped into the cool confines of the mews lane and made their way to the back entrance to Malmsby House.

"I feel like a naughty child sneaking into the house," Gwinnie said.

Lakehurst laughed. "But our intentions are good."

Gwinnie slid him a sideways glance. "Are they? Is purposefully avoiding Grandmother good?"

"Matter of interpretation, my dear sister. Simply a matter of interpretation."

CHAPTER 4
MORE QUESTIONS, FEW
ANSWERS

"**B**ut, Mama! Mama!" Alex wailed. He twisted within this mother's grasp. "Mama!" he yowled, tears streaming down his ruddy cheeks.

All around them, people stared at Cassandra and her son. Cassandra marched resolutely on, neither looking to the right, nor left, nor attempting to calm Alex. Her own mind was in a whirl of emotion. If she'd been six years old, she'd likely be howling as well, she thought.

But she wasn't. Her lips compressed in a thin line against her own tears. She hitched her son up in her arms higher, then reached up to pull the mourning veil she'd had gathered up on her bonnet brim back down over her face.

She could not believe Lord Lakehurst had written that book!

He had to have been there. He had to have been! Even if he didn't kill Richard himself, his participation in their sick rites made him culpable. Especially as the others who'd been there had disappeared like wraiths in the night when the monster, that spawn of Satan, stabbed Richard. Richard had died draped across her.

It seemed like hours before Carlyle, the oldest Darkford family retainer, found her, tied to the stone altar, in pain, covered in her husband's blood, and nearly hysterical with worry for her son whom, after he'd fallen asleep, she'd shut in the priest's hole in the upstairs sitting room for his protection.

Richard had ordered the staff away that night while he'd had his entertainment. Typically, she and Alex visited Baron and Lady Loftbridge on the nights of her husband's parties. She and Lady Loftbridge had become friends during their London season and had been delighted to discover their married homes would be nearby. She and Alex had planned to stay the night with the family in Wells until shortly before they were to leave, a message arrived to tell them not to come. There was an illness in the Loftbridge household.

Thinking she and Alex had nowhere to go, her husband had advised her to stay in her suite of rooms with the doors locked and to keep Alex with her. His friends could become rowdy, he'd explained apologetically, and in the throes of celebrations, were wont to lose the *veneer* of society they typically wore, he'd told her with his wry grin.

"My Lady," an out-of-breath Dulcie said as she ran to catch up with Cassandra. "Do you want me to take his little lordship?" she asked. "'Tis not seemly for you to be carrying the child."

Cassandra paused to look back at her. "That will not be necessary," she said crisply. She saw a man in a heavy greatcoat behind them. She frowned as she turned back and hurried on to the Darkford townhouse. Odd. She'd seen the same man sitting in the park. She noticed him because of his coat, an article of clothing surely too heavy for one of the first warm days they'd had this unusually cool and rainy June.

Alex's wails subsided into hiccupping sobs. He'd laid his head on her shoulder, sniffing. "I-I didn't get my ice," he complained pitifully.

Cassandra felt a wave of guilt assail her. She had promised him that treat. "I'll ask your Uncle Edmund for funds for tomorrow to get your treat. If he won't give us money, I'll send a note to your Uncle Miles," she promised. She hadn't wanted to take money from her brother Miles. Perhaps that had been just her pride, and she was being missish. She hadn't been able to convince Edmund to give her any money so far; why did she think he might change his mind now? Stubbornly, she hadn't wanted charity from her brother. As far as society knew, she was the wealthy Marchioness of Darkford!

They turned the corner into the street where they lived. Out of the corner of her eye, she saw the man turn as well. Cassandra picked up her pace, though Alex grew heavier and heavier in her arms. She only slowed once they reached the steps before the townhouse. It would be difficult to climb the steps carrying Alex. Reluctantly, she set him down and took his hand.

In the house she let Dulcie take Alex upstairs while she handed her bonnet, gloves, and reticule to a waiting footman. She crossed the hall to the visitor's parlor to the right of the door and looked out the window, careful to keep to the side of the heavy, swagged, brown velvet drapes. The gentleman who'd been behind them was across the street, talking to a street sweeper urchin, ten years of age, she guessed. The young lad claimed the right to clean up after horses on their street and earn the tips received for his efforts. The man pointed to her house as he handed the boy a coin, and then he walked down the street, turning once to look up at their house. She pulled away from the edge of the drape. She didn't want him to see her watching. The boy remained in front of the house, picking up rocks and skipping them down the street.

Cassandra frowned at the interchange between them. It did not appear the gentleman paid the boy for his street sweeping services. It was something else. Her brow furrowed deeper.

She started to turn away when she saw a woman walk up to the boy and engage him in conversation. *It was Rose!* Lady Guinevere's maid. What was she doing here?

It appeared she knew the boy, for they had an easy camaraderie, laughing together. She asked him some questions, then listened intently as he answered her, his arms flying about, wildly punctuating his words. She looked up the street, then back at the boy, nodding. Cassandra saw her take a coin from inside the palm of her glove and press it into the boy's palm as she talked earnestly to him. He nodded vigorously. Rose patted his shoulder and then walked hurriedly away.

The boy shadow-boxed his glee, reclaimed his tools, and jauntily walked up and down the street on the lookout for new horse droppings.

What was that all about? Cassandra wondered. She turned away from the window, her frown replaced by curiosity. She slowly walked out of the room, intending to go to her room to change clothes. She nodded to Edmund in passing as he came out of the library.

"A moment, Cassandra," Edmund said.

She turned toward him. "Yes?"

"While you were gone, we received notice that

Harrison Farrow is coming to visit on his way to Brighton for the summer."

Cassandra made a moue of distaste. Vanessa's younger brother, Harrison Farrow, was not a favored person. She found him ingratiating. And since Richard had died, he seemed to have acquired the notion she would welcome his suit.

"When?" she asked.

"He should arrive tomorrow. Said he would visit three to five days before journeying on to Brighton."

She nodded, wondering how difficult it would be to remain out of his range.

"Thank you for telling me," she said and turned to go up the stairs.

"You were not gone long today," Edmund observed.

She turned slowly back to look at him. "No, we were not," she agreed.

"Why?"

"I beg your pardon?" Cassandra asked, raising her chin as she looked at him.

"Why did you return so soon?"

She studied him a moment. There was no way she would tell him the truth of why they returned. He'd never believed the story of how Richard came to die as it were. And now there was a book that described it? No.

She frowned. "I suddenly did not feel well, so we returned home. Unfortunately, Alex did not get his ice. Tomorrow, may I prevail upon you to provide funds for an excursion to Gunter's for Alex? Should I feel well, of course."

Edmund frowned. "I don't—"

Cassandra interrupted him. "Edmund, now that I have returned to society—albeit in a limited fashion—

do you wish it bruited about the Ton that you withhold funds from me? That I cannot purchase even an ice for my son? Do you wish to be considered a nip farthing executor? How should that be received?"

"Now, Cassandra, you know you are not in a good state of mind…"

"Edmund, we can discuss this later," Cassandra said tiredly. "At the moment, as I told you, I do not feel well. I have a blazing headache and wish to lie down for a while." She turned away from him and continued up the stairs to her room, aware that Edmund stared after her.

In her chambers, she allowed Agnes, her maid, to help her out of her walking dress and short corset. She slipped on her dressing gown over her chemise.

"I'll get you some tea, ma'am," her maid said.

"Thank you," Cassandra said. She laid down on her bed and closed her eyes, thinking of the park events.

With her eyes closed, she could see in her mind Lord Lakehurst's face as he told her about the book. She compressed her lips together and sighed heavily. She'd been hasty.

She opened her eyes and stared up at the bed hangings.

Remembering, she realized his expression had not been cocky or otherwise ego filled, nor vicious and sinister. His words were, he prefaced, a confession and an apology. His manner appeared direct yet sincere, and she repaid his words with serpent venom. She had not stopped to listen. She often felt others did not listen to her and now, ironically, she found herself guilty of the same fault!

Even though that night was eighteen months past, the wounds left remained raw and festering, made worse as Edmund and his wife did not believe her retelling of the events of that night. After all, it had been old Carlyle who found her and freed her. As the groomsman was illiterate and deaf ever since he'd had the mumps as a young man, he could not verify her story in writing. And they refused to come to Baydon to hear him tell the tale—not that they would have listened to him if he had. His inability to hear had been why Richard allowed him to stay on the castle grounds when he had his fêtes. But he could see, and if someone was standing in front of him, he could read lips.

She lifted her right hand to run her fingertips over the scar above her left breast where the monster had begun carving the devil's sigil. He'd managed two curving strokes. A shiver ran through her as she traced the scar with her finger. In the chapter beginning, she'd read in the book the sigil was to be burned on the heroine's shoulder. Burned or carved, would the method matter? Would the devil have owned her soul?

She laughed to herself. She was being fanciful.— And besides, the sigil on her shoulder had not been finished.

Her maid knocked lightly on her door before entering, bearing the tea tray.

Cassandra sat up. "Thank you, Agnes. Place it here, please," she said, indicating the table next to the bed.

"Yes, ma'am. I took the liberty of bringing a couple of cook's scones as well, if that is all right."

Cassandra smiled slightly. "Perfect. You are extremely considerate of me and I appreciate it, Agnes."

"I try to be," Agnes replied with her slight curtsy. She backed out of the room and shut the door quietly afterward.

Cassandra leaned back against the headboard of the bed as she sipped her tea. She detected a bit of smokiness in its taste and smell. Richard had invested heavily in the possibility of a British tea trade in India as currently China ruled the market—and the prices. He, and his cousin Raymond Stillworth, had procured all manner of teas and tea cuttings from China as they strove to learn as much as possible about tea from the secretive Chinese.

For the first time since Richard died, she wondered about the warehouse full of barrels, crates, and bales of tea he had brought to England. What had Edmund done with all that? Did he know the value of the goods? He, she knew, was not a tea drinker. Odd that she should think of that tea now. Was she finally waking up from the miasma of guilt and regret she'd lived in for the last eighteen months?

Raymond had invested with Richard in the tea venture, and though Richard held the majority percentage of the investment, Raymond had done much of the research and made a trip to India and China three years ago. She supposed she should learn more about the fledgling tea business, as now Alex was the majority owner.

She nibbled on the cinnamon and apple scone.

She needed to mentally and emotionally wake up. She needed to take back her life for the sake of Alex as well as herself.

She wished she had borrowed the novel from Lady Guinevere. Mayhap if she had read it first...

Lord Lakehurst drifted into her mind again. She smiled as she thought of the big man. He really was an awkward gentle giant. She should write an apology to him—and to Lady Guinevere. Then, too, there existed her curiosity concerning the activities and intention of

Lady Guinevere's lady's maid, Rose. Should she mention seeing Rose in her notes to them?

She sipped her tea. She still had much to think about and sort out in her mind and heart.

LAKEHURST STARED out the dormer window of his writing retreat which years before had been their governess's room off the schoolroom. His desk filled the dormer window embrasure, the window looking out the back of the house to the terrace and garden below. It was a quiet room, being away from the main part of the house, which suited his creative writing pursuit.

He'd been staring out the window for a good part of the last hour, his thoughts far away from his current work in progress.

Lady Darkford fascinated him. She drew him to her, unlike he'd ever been drawn to another woman. Her light brown eyes, a mélange of autumn color with patches of brown, green, and gold—held a waif-like quality as she looked out at the world; however, in contrast, her slight figure radiated determination. Her hair looked black unless seen in glittering candlelight, as he'd seen it yesterday at dinner, when it reflected the dark browns of the peat bogs of Scotland. She wore it pinned in a simple chignon.

She stood taller than most women—though not as tall as Gwinnie—with a long graceful neck and long arms. Her slender form—unhealthily slender, he thought—accentuated her height. He thought her an interesting combination of timidity and quiet strength. A woman with strengths and weaknesses he'd like to know better.

He hadn't heard from Rose yet, and he couldn't

stop seeing Lady Darkford's expression when he said he wrote the book. There had been anger there, yes, but terror as well. Was terror too strong a word? He let it rest in his thoughts, remembering. No, it was not too strong. There had been terror in her eyes.

Was she terrified of him?

He grimaced. She'd called him a murderer. She had to be terrified of him, her fears so different from the London debutants. That terror shook him to his core, his stomach churning with discomfort.

He slammed his fist into his other palm.

What happened that night? He must know!

Sharp rapping on his door pulled him out of his painful thoughts.

"Come in," he called out. He shoved his chair back as the door opened to the butler in the doorway.

"Excuse me, sir, the Dowager Duchess requests you join her in the Lady Margaret parlor for tea."

"Now?"

"Yes, sir."

Lakehurst drew in a deep breath. "All right." He ran his hand through his hair. "I'll be down shortly." He should have realized his grandmother would question them on their excursion with Lady Darkford. The Dowager Duchess of Malmsby would know something had gone wrong. He'd rather handle the situation with Lady Darkford himself; however, knowing his grandmother, she'd march into the situation whether he said yea or nay. Now he'd most likely be faced with collateral damage.

The Dowager Duchess of Malmsby rhythmically tapped a spoon against the edge of the tea tray set before her. She was not happy.

She raised an eyebrow as she frowned at her granddaughter. Gwinnie sat in a chair at right angles to her, back straight, feet flat on the floor, a wholly unusual posture for her. Her clasped hands were in her lap, her eyes downcast, though surreptitiously, she repeatedly slid her eyes in her direction.

The Duchess knew it was grieving Gwinnie not to say anything, to wait until her brother arrived. She saw her clamp her lips tighter against speaking when her patience thinned. It would do her good, the Duchess complacently decided.

When the white parlor doors opened to admit her grandson, she merely looked up at him and waved her hand to indicate the chair he should sit in.

She saw Lakehurst hesitate a moment before crossing to the chair. She hid a smile. It amused her to see her two grandchildren on tenterhooks at their age. Reminded her of their ten-year-old selves.

Silently she handed each of them a cup of tea, then picked up her own.

"When I visited Cook in the kitchen to discuss a menu change, she told me how you two had returned today through the staff entrance with wet clothing, particularly you, Lakehurst. You each grabbed a biscuit she'd just removed from the oven before continuing up the back stairs. Then, as I was turning to leave, Rose came in. She would have hurried up the backstairs as well; however, I persuaded her to tell me what was going on," the Duchess said in a conversational tone.

Gwinnie and Lakehurst exchanged glances.

She sipped her tea, then set her cup down. "So

who wants to tell me your side of this afternoon's events?" she asked, folding her hands in her lap.

"We wanted to get to know Lady Darkford better," Gwinnie burst out, no longer able to contain herself. "We hit upon the notion of inviting her and her son to go to Hyde Park with us and then afterward to Gunter's Tea Shop for an ice."

The Duchess nodded. "Admirable," she said. "Now, tell me why and how—according to Rose—Lady Darkford came to push Lakehurst so hard he fell into the Serpentine, and why you then asked your maid to trail a man whom you suspected might be trailing Lady Darkford?" she asked pointedly.

Lakehurst sighed heavily. He leaned forward, resting his forearms on his thighs. "It started last night when Lady Darkford threw my book across the parlor," he said.

Gwinnie nodded.

"What?" the Duchess said, staring at Lakehurst, a frown pulling her brows together.

"No, wait..." The Duchess held up one of her be-ringed hands. "Judging by how you say that, I believe I will need another fortifying cup of tea," she said.

She obviously had not expected his response. To catch the Duchess unawares was a feat all her grandchildren tried to do growing up and seldom succeeded. He didn't feel comfortable with his success today.

The Duchess refilled their teacups, passed the plate of cakes Cook had provided, pulled her feet up on the sofa, tossed a shawl across her legs, nestled back into the corner of the sofa, picked up her teacup again and looked at Lakehurst. "Now, I am ready. You may proceed."

Despite how low he felt at the moment, Lakehurst

had to smile at his grandmother. She'd settled herself into a position conducive to listening, determined to pay close attention to what he said. He appreciated that.

"I think we all knew from Ellinbourne that she'd been widowed eighteen months ago. I never heard how he died nor thought to ask. Do you know?" he asked his grandmother.

"I knew he died of stab wounds," she acknowledged, "and that his wife was quite distraught."

"Did you ever ask how the stab wounds occurred?" he asked.

She shook her head. "I assumed footpads or highwaymen," she said, frowning. "Do you know it to be something else?"

He shook his head. "I don't *know*, anything," he said, straightening up. "However, after she read the beginning of chapter seventeen, she threw the book across the room. She said it described how her husband was killed. She said the author had to have been there and she would see that they were arrested for murder. Then she burst into tears."

"Your book describes his death?" the Duchess asked. She stared at him a moment. "How can that be?"

He lifted his shoulders and shook his head. He didn't know. "I was in Scotland when Lord Darkford was killed," he reminded her.

She nodded. "Yes. I remember.—Did someone relate a similar tale to you that you used in your book?"

"No! This came out of my imagination entirely. And I did tell her, after she threw the book across the room, that the hero in the book lived, that he wasn't killed."

"Lakehurst—" Gwinnie interrupted. "If she thought it was a description of the events of his death," she said slowly, "does that mean she was there as well, and was the woman tied to an altar?" she asked hesitantly.

"*Dear God,*" the Duchess whispered. "That poor child. I hope that is not the case, but I fear you may be right, Gwinnie."

Lakehurst stared at his sister, a sick feeling churning his stomach. He had not thought that through well enough. "I would pray not," he said softly. He paused. "However, that could account for the terror I saw in her eyes. How could it not?"

"Terror?" the Duchess repeated. "This is not good."

Lakehurst ran a hand through his hair. "After last night, I had some misguided thought that if she knew who the author was, it would give her peace of mind, she'd know the book wasn't about her and the Marquess of Darkford."

"And I agreed with him," Gwinnie admitted. "Her husband's relatives think she ought to go into an asylum for a complete rest."

"An asylum! *Bah!*" The Duchess snorted inelegantly. "And most likely, they would not allow her ever to come out again. They'd bribe the doctor director of any asylum they'd take her to to say she is too ill for society. At least that is what Ellinbourne said is his concern. The only thing that keeps them from doing that is her relationship to him. I can understand how telling her you were the author, rather than giving her peace, upset her further. Your intentions were good; however, she does not know you well enough to take your identity as the author as a positive statement."

"Obviously, it wouldn't be—not if that is what she truly lived through," he said, disgusted with himself. "That was an arrogance I didn't know I had."

His grandmother chuckled at that. "Yes, I can see

that would cut you down. Our position in society can insidiously cause us to lose track of our humility. But how did that slip of a woman manage to land you in the water?"

"Slick mud," he said.

Gwinnie nodded. "We brought an old toy boat from the schoolroom with us for Alex to play with on the Serpentine. It had a long rope attached to it. When Lakehurst stepped backward after she pushed him, his heel got caught in the rope which initially set him off balance and the slippery mud at the edge of the water did the rest," she explained.

The Duchess shook her head at the mishap. "So the young Marquess did not get his Gunter's ice.—Did you at least give him the boat?"

Gwinnie shook her head. "There was no time. Everything happened so fast. She picked up her son and marched away with him in her arms."

The Duchess's eyes opened wide. "She carried him?"

"Yes, and the nursemaid had to run to catch up with her."

The Duchess smiled. "I say '*Bravo.*' There aren't many in society who would carry a child in public."

Lakehurst snorted in disagreement. "Except for our Gwinnie, here."

"What?" Gwinnie said defensively.

"Today, you picked up Lady Darkford's son and had him riding on your hip as you discussed the sailing ship with him and where to launch it from."

Gwinnie made a moue and gave her brother a dark look.

He and the Duchess laughed.

"Lady Darkford did receive a fair share of observation from those around," Lakehurst said when they'd stopped laughing.

The Duchess nodded, then frowned. "So tell me about the man who followed her as she carried the boy out of the park in front of everyone."

"We don't know for sure if he was following, or if it was coincidence," Lakehurst said.

"Go on."

"There was a man on another bench watching us."

"Everyone was watching us," Gwinnie protested drily.

"Yes, but on one of the few beautiful days we've had this summer, he wore a greatcoat and had his hat pulled low over his eyes.—I know, nothing noteworthy to that, just another London eccentric. However, his head tracked her progress down the path and after she'd passed him, he got up and followed her," Lakehurst said.

"So you, Gwinnie, seeing this as well, asked Rose to follow him for you," the Duchess said.

"Yes. From the work Rose and I do with the charity houses, with the Earl of Soothcoor, and with the resources he has put at our disposal, we have learned a great deal about crime and safety in our city. It was concerning."

Gwinnie's words surprised him. He knew of her involvement with Soothcoor's charities. He hadn't realized how involved she'd become. He thought her main interest was her violin.

He'd become too wrapped up in his writing. He'd lost the close connection he and his sister had long held. That inexplicably saddened him. Drifting apart as they grew older was bound to happen; however, he'd missed out, much like his father admitted he'd missed out when he allowed his brother, Aidan, to run their everyday lives.

Like father, like son, Lakehurst supposed.

His writing was important to him; however, it shouldn't rule his life to the exclusion of others. How could he even think of marrying if he didn't know how to share himself?

"Obviously, you waylaid Rose and have spoken to her since she has returned. I have not," Lakehurst said to his grandmother. He set his teacup back on the tray. "What did she discover in following the man? Anything? Or was I mistaken?"

Lady Malmsby took her last sip of tea before setting her cup down beside Lakehurst's. She looked at him and shook her head. "Oh, you were not mistaken," she said.

"I knew it!" Lakehurst exclaimed, slapping his knee. He straightened. "What did she discover?"

"After Lady Darkford entered her house, the man approached a young street sweeper, a young lad that Rose said she knew from your charity work, Gwinnie," their grandmother explained, turning toward Gwinnie.

"That is fortuitous," said Lakehurst.

Gwinnie nodded. "We know many of the young children that work for pennies in the streets. If they are orphans, we try to get them into schools. If they support others in their family—which many do—we encourage them to take a nighttime class to learn to read and do sums."

"From what Rose told me, this young boy does avail himself of some of the resources the Earl of Soothcoor offers."

"I wonder who it is," Gwinnie said. "Did she say his name?"

Lady Malmsby shook her head. "But she approached him after the man left. He told her the man paid him coins to search him out at The Wild Boar Tavern to report any visitors who came to Darkford House. She said she paid him for the information and for him to report to her, or a woman named Sarah Knolls, anything else the man may say or request of him."

The Duchess turned toward Gwinnie. "Who is Sarah Knolls?" she asked.

"I am," Gwinnie confessed. She shrugged. "Mrs. Southerlands said the women at the charity would not talk easily to a duke's daughter. So, I created a persona to make the women feel more comfortable."

The Duchess frowned. "What else don't I know?"

Gwinnie grinned at her. "I don't know. What do you know? You can't think to know everything."

"As matriarch of this family, why not?"

Gwinnie and Lakehurst laughed. "Probably because there are too many of us! And with Uncle Aidan now married and not living in our pockets, you'll probably know even less!" Lakehurst said.

The Duchess nodded slowly. "I see I have to broaden my sources."

Lakehurst exchanged dismayed looks with his sister.

Then the Duchess perked up. "But first I need to do something about this mess you have made, Lakehurst."

"Grandmother, I—" began Lakehurst.

She held up her hand. "Do not interrupt. We will have Stephen go to Gunter's to order ices to be delivered to the Marquess of Darkford with the compliments of the Dowager Duchess of Malmsby. Then he will take the boat the young Marquess enjoyed—we certainly don't have any use for it seeing as neither of you has seen fit to marry and provide me with great-grandchildren," she said pointedly, "to the Darkford townhouse, with a note from you, Gwinnie, saying you want him to have the boat and hopefully you can sail it with him in the future."

"What about me?" Lakehurst asked.

The Duchess looked down her nose at her grandson. "You will discover from Ellinbourne what happened the night Lady Darkford's husband died while I see what damage control I can do.—And take the measure of Mr. and Mrs. Tidemark. I will visit Lady Darkford tomorrow.—Hopefully, she will talk to me."

"I'm sure she will. I don't think she would hold you responsible for anything she perceived I may have done," Lakehurst said grouchily.

"Perhaps we should ask Mr. Martin to discover who the man is who followed Lady Darkford and why," Gwinnie suggested.

"An excellent idea," the Duchess said. "I shall send him a note at the Bow Street office."

"You should have been a General in Wellington's army," Lakehurst quipped.

"I know, I know," his grandmother said, nodding.

They all laughed, and for the first time since the incident with Lady Darkford, Lakehurst felt himself relax.

CHAPTER 5

MR. AND MRS. TIDEMARK

With trepidation, Cassandra joined Edmund and Vanessa Tidemark at breakfast the next morning. She did not want to answer questions from Vanessa about yesterday afternoon, and she knew Vanessa would be full of them. She had avoided her at dinner by the simple of expedient of a dinner tray in her room, claiming the continued headache as her reason. She could not avoid her indefinitely. It was best to get past the barrage she knew would be forthcoming.

She'd hardly seated herself and accepted the cup of tea from the footman when the butler appeared with another letter for her.

Edmund Tidemark frowned heavily. "Who is this message from? That Lady Guinevere again?" he asked.

"I trust not," Vanessa declared. She reached for the jam pot. "She might be a duke's daughter, but did you know she plays music for money? I was quite shocked when Mrs. Waghorn told me that bit of information," she said as she spread a large dollop of jam on her toast. "Quite shocked, I tell you."

"Did she also tell you that any payment Lady

Guinevere receives is donated to Mrs. Southerlands' House for Unfortunate Women?" Cassandra asked, exasperated. "—And no, the letter is not from Lady Guinevere. It is from the Dowager Duchess of Malmsby. She says she will pay a morning call on us today at eleven o'clock."

"It is the height of rudeness for her to only acknowledge one person on a visit," Vanessa exclaimed, quite irritated.

"Wait a minute, pet," her husband said, reaching over to lay his fingertips on her pudgy hand. He looked at Cassandra. "Did she say 'us?'"

Cassandra nodded solemnly. "Yes, in the paragraph right after she asked how Alex liked his ice that she had sent to him yesterday afternoon, she mentions you." Cassandra looked up at the Tidemarks. "Alex did not receive an ice yesterday afternoon that I am aware of," she said pointedly.

Vanessa blushed.

"Vanessa! Don't say you withheld it from the boy!" Edmund exclaimed.

"Now, Edmund," Vanessa began. "I only meant to have a taste."

"You ate it all?" Cassandra asked, staring at Vanessa. Of all the things Vanessa could do, or had done in the last eighteen months, this was by far the worst. Stealing a child's treat.

Vanessa's face crumbled. "I only meant to take a taste, but it was so good!" she wailed.

"Vanessa!" Cassandra cried out.

"I'll see that Alex gets an ice," Edmund said tiredly. "What flavor was it?" he asked his wife.

"Orange," she said in a feeble voice. She dabbed at her eyes with a handkerchief. "I really didn't intend to eat it all," she repeated.

"I know," Edmund said in a long-suffering tone.

"When you do, can I have another, too?" Vanessa asked.

Cassandra frowned at her audacity. Her husband did not. Though she'd lived with them for eighteen months, she still learned how insular they were, so caught up in themselves.

"Yes, yes. I'll send the footman out after breakfast." He turned to Cassandra. "I suggest we not say anything about this unfortunate occurrence to the Duchess."

Cassandra stared at him a moment before she nodded her head in reluctant agreement. She knew Vanessa liked sweets. She had no idea she would steal a child's gift of a sweet! It was kind of the Duchess to make up for the unfortunate circumstances of yesterday. And she thought it fitting that Edmund would finally be forced to provide for the ice he had seemed so reluctant to pay for yesterday afternoon.

"And regarding the Duchess, we shall await notification she is here in the library."

"Oh, I can wait out here for her," Vanessa said.

"No, Vanessa," Cassandra said. "As she sent the note to me, I would prefer to be the person to greet her, as you still require introductions."

"But I know who she is," Vanessa protested.

"Yes," Cassandra said, "However, she as yet does not know you. In society, this requires a proper introduction. I will present you to her first, then I shall introduce you to her. That is how things are done. Now, if you will excuse me, I must tell nurse to have Alex ready to come downstairs during the Duchess's visit as she wishes to meet him as well."

A footman rushed forward to pull out her chair for her. She smiled pleasantly at him and left the room.

~

"Mr. Harold, please have a carriage brought around, the light, town carriage with the ducal arms on the door," the Duchess instructed the butler as she descended the stairs dressed in her most formidable visiting attire. "And please request Mrs. Morrison to meet me in the Lady Margaret parlor."

"Immediately, madam."

As the Duchess walked down the hall toward her favorite room, she heard Gwinnie playing her violin in the music room. Vivaldi, she thought. She smiled. The footman hurried before her to open the parlor doors for her to enter.

"Thank you, Stephen," she murmured.

She sat down on her pink-striped sofa and stared out through the glass-fronted double doors to the terrace. Oscar lay outside in the sun. She idly wondered what Lakehurst was doing, for if her grandson was in his writing lair, Oscar stayed with him. That Oscar lay outside indicated Lakehurst was not writing. She wondered if this situation with Lady Darkford was affecting his creative endeavors. She hoped not; however, she could conceive how it would.

Well, she would do what she could to help Lady Darkford. It would be an entertaining enterprise. And besides, she quite liked the woman. Though timid appearing in company, the Duchess felt there were depths to the woman that deserved to be brought forth. And the overbearance of her relatives was not acceptable. Though Lady Darkford's uncle-in-law was born the brother of a marquess, from what she had heard, he had the manners of a cit—or a greedy moneylender.

The widow might make the ideal match for Lakehurst. She certainly seemed to interest him, and he did not seem to intimidate her, either intentionally or unintentionally. That was a good sign.

She could not believe the rumors she heard coming from the debutants of London! At least this was the end of the season, and most would forget their gossip over the summer. They could return for the little season without such missish nonsense bandied about. Too big a man. Bah!

Her grandson was a quiet man by nature, quite unlike his boisterous sister. But his emotions ran deep. She thought that was why he was able to write the books he did, books that plumbed the depths of people's emotions.

The parlor doors opened to admit Mrs. Morrison.

"We are to go visiting today?" she asked.

"Just to one place. We go to the Darkford town-house. As you have no doubt heard by now, Lakehurst and Gwinnie did not have a good outing with Lady Darkford and her son yesterday."

"Yes. Though more whispers concern your future actions, Your Grace," Mrs. Morrison said wryly as she crossed the room to sit near the Duchess.

The Duchess grinned. "I can well imagine. Most of the staff have known me for many years.—They don't bandy such talk to their peers in London."

"No, Your Grace. They know that could spoil the fun of seeing what is to occur."

The Duchess's eyes danced. "Precisely. Though today, I must say I shall be more duchess in manner."

"How do you mean?"

"From my understanding of things Ellinbourne and Lady Darkford have said, the Tidemarks have been quite repressive. They are interested, I believe, in keeping her under their control. This will not do at all.

I think some embarrassment for their behavior might be in order. But we shall see how it plays out."

Her companion nodded. "I can see I may regret leaving you for the summer to visit my sister. I shall miss the fun."

The Duchess laughed.

~

"Your Grace," Cassandra said from the doorway to the Darkford House visitor's parlor. She'd seen the Duchess arrive through the street-facing windows as her carriage drew up before her home. She'd been apprehensive about the Duchess's visit ever since she'd received the note that she would visit that day, but one look at the warm smile on the Duchess's face, and the twinkle in her eyes did much to relax Cassandra. She hurried toward the woman, extending her hands.

The Duchess grasped her hands in hers, squeezing her fingertips briefly. "Well, I am delighted to see there are no lingering effects from yesterday," she said as she released Cassandra's hands and took a step back.

Cassandra blushed slightly and looked down as she ruefully smiled. "No, I am much better today. I sent 'round a missive to Lord Lakehurst to apologize for my behavior yesterday."

"You have nothing to apologize for," the Duchess assured her. "But I think we should have a talk. And, I'd like to meet your son and your son's guardian and his wife if they are here today?"

"Yes, yes they are," Cassandra said, curious as to why the Duchess should wish to meet them, and a bit concerned about how the Duchess would take Vanessa, who could be quite the toadeater.

"Excellent," the Duchess said. She turned toward

the woman, who stood primly behind her. "This is Mrs. Morrison, my companion."

"Mrs. Morrison," Cassandra nodded to the slight, darker-skinned woman who stood behind the Duchess. Romany, perhaps? The woman curtsied. "Welcome," Cassandra said.

"Mr. Drummond, please invite Mr. and Mrs. Tidemark to join us in the parlor and request the cook to prepare tea and cakes for all."

"Yes, ma'am," the butler said, bowing before turning in a stately manner toward the stairs to give the Tidemarks the message.

Cassandra threaded her arm through the Duchess's. "I was so pleased to get your note this morning saying you would call. I worried that the tale of my behavior yesterday should give you a dislike of me."

The Duchess laughed. "Hardly!" she said as they walked into the brown and gold parlor.

Cassandra led her to a gold brocade sofa and sat down beside her. Mrs. Morrison took a chair off to the side, nearer the windows, where the light shined brighter for her needlework.

The Duchess patted Cassandra's hand. "Now, tell me, my dear, what happened yesterday?"

Cassandra tensed. "I accused Lord Lakehurst of killing my husband," she said, looking straight ahead. "And then I pushed him into the lake," she said with bravura, turning to look at the Duchess for her reaction to her words.

The Duchess looked at her blandly. "And?"

Cassandra blinked. "My behavior does not horrify you?"

The Duchess laughed. "Not in the slightest! From what Lakehurst has told me it sounds as if he behaved decidedly ham-handed in how he relayed to you his authorship, especially since he knew your reaction to the book from the day before! He should have learned more about why you reacted as you did before he simply blurted out he wrote the book.—And I should tell you—to ease your mind—Lakehurst was in Scotland eighteen months ago visiting his mother's family when the events that took your husband's life occurred. He wrote the book while he was there."

"But those few pages I read they were so close to what transpired!"

"Can you tell me about that time?" the Duchess asked.

"Yes, but another time, please," she said as she heard the click of the parlor door opening. She looked up to see her uncle-in-law and his wife enter. She would have liked to ask the Duchess about Rose and the street sweeper. That would have to keep for now.

"Your Grace, I'd like you to meet Mr. and Mrs. Tidemark. Mr. Tidemark is my late husband's uncle," she said.

The Duchess inclined her head.

Cassandra turned toward her relations. "Vanessa and Edmund, I'd like you to meet the Dowager Duchess of Malmsby."

Vanessa curtsied deeply, then struggled to stand upright. Her husband put a hand under her elbow to assist her. When she stood steady again, she eagerly approached the Duchess. "It is so wonderful to have you visit our home!" she enthused.

Edmund bowed, then steered his wife to a large chair near the Duchess. "I echo my wife's words," he told the Duchess. "Welcome to our home."

The Duchess frowned, a confused look in her eyes. "I thought this was Lady Darkford's house, as Lord

Darkford's widow. Is it not in the entail, with her right of residency until her son comes of age?"

Vanessa's eyes widened and a dark flush creeped up Edmund's neck. Cassandra kept her lips still against a smile.

"It is not part of the entail, but well, yes, of course she has right of residency. However, under the circumstances, we live here as well."

"Oh!" said the Duchess. She leaned back on the sofa. She nodded. "Circumstances drive much in our lives, don't they?" she said, her tone all understanding.

Edmund smiled at her. "Yes, they do."

Vanessa nodded.

"And what circumstances are those that have you living here?" the Duchess asked.

Cassandra thought the Duchess looked like a harmless, inquisitive little bird. If she hadn't heard from her brother about the Duchess's sneaky nature, her words would have relaxed her as they did Edmund.

Edmund rubbed his hands together in front of his chest. "You see, Your Grace, our niece by marriage has not been well. The—ah—events surrounding my nephew's death were quite tragic and disturbing to Lady Darkford."

"Well," said the Duchess, "I should think any man's murder should be tragic and disturbing for their wife. How is this an issue?"

A discreet knock at the door prevented Edmund from answering. It was the maid with the tea trolley and cakes.

"I haven't ordered any tea yet," Vanessa blurted out, obviously affronted.

"I did," said Cassandra. "As soon as the Duchess

arrived, I invited you to join us and requested refreshments."

"Oh! Oh, yes... well, that does make sense," Vanessa said, frowning slightly.

Cassandra motioned to the maid to wheel the tea cart to her. "Tea, Your Grace? I can tell by the aroma this is one of my late husband's favorite teas. There is a hint of smokiness to it. He invested in the tea trade. He was one of those interested to see if they could grow tea in India since China can be difficult to trade with."

"That is fascinating. I believe I should like to try this tea without anything in it to get a true idea of its taste."

"A good idea; that is the best way to judge a tea. I will say you may want a drop or two of cream," Cassandra said as she handed the Duchess a teacup.

"I had no idea, Cassandra, that you were that knowing when it came Richard's interest in tea," Edmund said, slight confusion in his eyes.

Cassandra smiled as she prepared a cup of tea for Vanessa with plenty of cream and sugar, as she knew she preferred. "Richard often had me sample different teas and asked for my description. He liked the words I chose to describe their flavors," she said placidly. There was a great deal neither he nor Vanessa knew about her for the simple reason they did not engage her in conversation.

"This is a rich, full-bodied tea," the Duchess said. "And I can see what you mean about the smokiness. I think I will take a small splash of cream to even that out."

Cassandra nodded as she picked up the cream pot and added a dash to the Duchess's cup before preparing the teacups for Edmund, Mrs. Morrison, and herself.

"I find it a bit harsh," Vanessa said. "Not to my taste at all unless I add sugar and cream. I don't think it would be a popular tea."

"I don't know that I would agree with that," said the Duchess. She held the cup to her nose as she smelled the steam rising. "I know plenty of my peers who would appreciate this tea's finer qualities."

"Oh, well, I suppose—maybe..." Vanessa said hurriedly.

Cassandra knew she was embarrassed to be contradicted by the Duchess.

"But to return to our conversation before the tea appeared, how is Lady Darkford's reaction to her husband's death deemed unhealthy? She has forsaken deep mourning, as she should—though frankly I think she could return to colors—and she told me at dinner the other night that she takes her son to the park every day. She is not confined to her room. Perhaps the house is kept too dark, as I noticed when I stood out front that all the drapes remain closed."

"Hmmm, well, perhaps—" Edmund faltered.

Cassandra took pity on him. "I was quite despondent following his death. I believe they haven't noticed the change."

Edmund brightened. "Yes, that is it precisely. My apologies, my dear niece, Cassandra. We've been quite blind."

"So now seeing I am better, you will give me pin money and allow me the freedom to spend it as I see appropriate?" Cassandra asked.

"They have withheld funds?" the Duchess asked. She turned toward Edmund. "Mr. Tidemark, was this advice given to you by your solicitor or spelled out in your nephew's will?"

Edmund glared at Cassandra. She stared back at

him. As she had decided the day before, she would no longer allow them to rule her for their own personal and social aggrandizement.

The Duchess kept her expression one of simple curiosity.

"It was while she was so ill we thought that the best course, but of course now that we clearly see how recovered she is..." he trailed off.

Cassandra noticed he did not give any commitment. She looked at the Duchess who had raised an eyebrow at his weaseling answer.

"Well," the Duchess said, "one of my purposes today is to invite you to dinner tomorrow night."

Vanessa sat straighter. "At Malmsby House?" she asked brightly, clasping her hands together.

"Of course, at Malmsby House," the Duchess confirmed.

"Vanessa, hold a moment. Didn't you tell me just this morning that your brother would be arriving tomorrow morning?" Edmund asked. "We couldn't leave him here while we went out to dinner."

Cassandra considered Edmund's ploy to be a master stroke to get out of spending more time with the Duchess and others who might have more questions about his treatment of her. It had become obvious to her in the last few months that Edmund enjoyed his ability to control her. Perhaps because he'd never been able to control his nephew.

Vanessa's face fell. "Yes, I quite forgot," she said weakly.

The Duchess and Cassandra exchanged glances.

"Why don't you bring your brother with you?" the Duchess offered. "And that other gentleman, too, that you mentioned the other night, Lady Darkford, your husband's cousin, I believe?"

Vanessa looked ecstatic while her husband looked like he'd tasted a bitter fruit.

"Raymond Stillworth," supplied Cassandra. "I don't know if he is in town, but if he is, I am sure he would welcome the invite. And I think you should like Raymond, Your Grace. He is almost the image of my late husband but with a more open and sociable manner about him. At least Richard and I always found him good company. I can give you his direction."

Edmund nodded. "Good man, Stillworth. He is the son of my late sister Bernice and her husband, David Stillworth."

"Mrs. Tidemark, what is your brother's name? I'll have an invitation sent here for him."

Vanessa beamed. "Harrison Farrow, Your Grace. And thank you, Your Grace, thank you."

The Duchess waved her hand negligently. "Well, now that we have had our tea and our comfortable coze, where is the young man I came to meet?"

"Waiting to meet you, Your Grace," said Cassandra, smiling. She rang the bell. When the butler answered the bell, she requested Alex to come downstairs with his nursemaid.

"Immediately, my lady," the butler said with an answering smile.

Within moments they heard a clatter down the stairs and loud whispers of "*Wait, my lord! Wait!*" before the double doors opened and Alex entered.

His appearance drew a tear to Cassandra's proud mama's eyes. He stood very straight and tall and moved slowly into the room. He looked around at everyone, his eyes darting to the Duchess, but he stopped by his mother. "You wished to see me?" he asked formally. He was dressed like a little gentleman and his dark wavy locks combed and pomaded into obedience.

"Yes," she said. She turned him toward the Duchess. "Your Grace, allow me to present my son, the Marquess of Darkford, Alexander Samuel Raymond Tidemark. Alex, this is Her Grace, the Dowager Duchess of Malmsby."

Alex executed a formal bow toward the Duchess.

The Duchess chuckled. "Well, now that the formal introduction is done, come over here and talk to me. I understand you met my grandchildren yesterday."

"Grandchildren?" Alex parroted, confused, as he crossed over to where the Duchess sat.

"Yes, Lady Guinevere and Viscount Lakehurst."

Alex brightened. "Lady Guinevere is fun! I like her!" he said enthusiastically.

"I like her, too," the Duchess told him as she pulled him onto her lap. "Did you know she plays the violin?"

"She does?"

"Yes, and very well, too. Do you play an instrument?"

"No, at least not yet. I'm only just turned six," he seriously explained to her.

"Well, I'm sure sometime this year, you will start to learn all manner of things."

"I already know my numbers and my letters... well, mostly. Mama teaches me," he confided to the Duchess.

"Excellent!" the Duchess said. "And I'm sure your mother has done a wonderful job."

"I have made the request to Edmund in the past to see about a governess or tutor for Alex. He says it is too soon," Cassandra said. Out of the corner of her eye, she saw Edmund shift in his chair.

The Duchess raised an eyebrow in the direction of Edmund. "I am sure he will. Most likely, he didn't *notice* how ready the young Marquess is for his lessons," she said.

Cassandra clamped down against an incipient smile.

"After the summer," Edmund said loftily.

"Do you have country plans this summer for our little Marquess?" the Duchess asked.

"No, we are staying in the city," Edmund said in quite a heavy manner.

"Oh, children need to spend time outside! I shall see what I can do to assist in that endeavor."

"Your Grace, I hardly think—"

"So tell me, how did you like your ice yesterday?" the Duchess asked Alex, ignoring Edmund.

He shook his head. "I didn't get an ice yesterday. I got one this morning."

"This morning!" the Duchess exclaimed, looking about the room.

Cassandra saw Vanessa blush, her face crumbling.

"There was an unfortunate occurrence yesterday," Edmund hastily explained. "There was a communication mix-up as to whom the ice was for. By the time I learned of the issue, the ice was gone. I ordered a replacement for Alex this morning," he explained brusquely.

The Duchess blinked as she took in his explanation, her eyes sliding to Vanessa's discomfort, then back to Edmund. "Morning is an odd time to have an ice, but I am pleased to hear he got it." She looked down at Alex. "Did you enjoy it?"

"It was smashing!" he enthused.

"Alex, I think it is time you returned to the nursery," Cassandra said kindly.

"Yes, Mama." He slid off the Duchess's lap and turned to bow to her.

She laughed and pulled him toward her to kiss his cheek, then let him go. "I'll see you again soon," she said with a wink.

Alex scampered to the door.

"And we should go as well. Mrs. Morrison?"

"Yes, Your Grace." Her companion rose and joined her.

Everyone rose as the Duchess did. "I look forward again to seeing you all tomorrow night at Malmsby House."

WHEN SHE RETURNED from her visit with Lady Darkford and the Tidemarks, the Duchess insisted her grandson leave his writing and her granddaughter leave her violin practice to join her for a cold collation in the dining room.

"Gwinnie, that little boy is enchanting!" the Duchess said as Gwinnie entered the room.

"He is a darling," Gwinnie agreed.

"You know I should so love a great-grandchild to pamper," the Duchess said casually.

"Tell that to Ann and Helena as they are soon to be married.—And what about a grandchild from Uncle Aidan? He has some catching up to do, I'd say, and he and Bella are on a prolonged honeymoon. Don't give me that sad, wistful expression. It's too late for me. Pester Lakehurst if you must pester anyone."

"Nonsense, it is not too late for you. You, my granddaughter, could have been married years ago. You are entirely too caught up in your hobbies. Sarah Knolls, indeed. I was not pleased to learn that your father was already familiar with that aspect of your life and I was not." The Duchess pouted.

Gwinnie shrugged, refusing to defend herself to her grandmother. She knew her grandmother wished she could affect some control over her life. She was wise to her grandmother's machinations. *Hmmm.* Over the years, she'd learned a lot from her grandmother. Now might be the time to put what she had learned into action.

Lakehurst walked into the room and took a seat at the table.

Gwinnie shook out her serviette and placed it in her lap. "Actually," she said as casually as if she were discussing the weather, "I am considering adopting an orphan, as Mr. Martin and the Earl of Soothcoor have done."

Her brother's eyes widened.

The Duchess tilted her head as she considered her statement. "One of those children like that boy Rose said she talked with yesterday?"

"Yes," she nodded. "However, I would be more inclined to adopt a girl. Or perhaps a young brother and sister?"

"I think I missed something in this conversation," Lakehurst said, his brow furrowing.

Gwinnie laughed. "Not much. Grandmother was merely attempting one of her guilt ploys for great-grandchildren."

"*Ahh!* Then that was a splendid chess move, Gwinnie! Your turn, Grandmother." He turned an earnest expression toward the Duchess.

"*Bah*," their grandmother said, waving her hand dismissively. "You two are no fun."

Gwinnie and Lakehurst laughed.

"You taught us well!" Gwinnie said, her eyes twinkling. "Now tell us how it went this morning. I assume that is the reason for your summons."

"Yes. It is obvious Mrs. Tidemark married above her state. And for reasons I could not fathom, her husband—the son of a marquess, mind you—caters to her."

"Perhaps it was a love match. Those occur you know, as you have seen within our family," Gwinnie countered, "and sometimes without reason as well, if one considers Aunt Catherine and Lord Candelstone's marriage."

Grandmother tilted her head consideringly. "True."

Lakehurst snorted with aborted laughter. Grandmother glared at him.

"The worst about that woman was she ate the ice we sent to Alex yesterday."

"She what?" Lakehurst exclaimed, jolted out of his teasing attitude.

"*Ate Alex's ice!* However, from my understanding, Mr. Tidemark arranged to get a replacement ice for Alex this morning."

"An ice in the morning? Who has an ice in the morning?" Lakehurst grumbled.

She shrugged. "I assume it was to ensure he had his treat *before* I arrived," she explained.

She waved her hand impatiently. "That is irrelevant at the moment. Do either of you know a Raymond Stillworth or a Harrison Farrow?" the Duchess asked them.

"I don't know the Farrow fellow; however, I have run into Stillworth a time or two at evening entertainments. Likeable gentleman. I gather he has a modest income, and he is not part of the gambling set. Pretty much invited everywhere. Hostesses use him to make up their numbers. A low-key type of person compared to his cousin, the late Marquess of Darkford," Lakehurst said.

"Evidently, this Mr. Farrow is Mrs. Tidemark's brother," their grandmother explained.

"So why are you asking about them?" Gwinnie asked.

"Because I invited them to accompany the Marchioness and the Tidemarks to dinner here tomorrow night. We'll have Ellinbourne and Ann as well."

"Why?" Gwinnie asked.

"To see that you all go to Baydon Castle for a house party while I take Alex to Versely Park."

"What? Why?" Lakehurst demanded. "*No!* I can't leave London now. I have a book to finish, you know."

"Take your papers with you. I'm sure there will be much inspiration for you in that area, being in the Mendip Hills," the Duchess tossed out.

Gwinnie compressed her lips and shook her head. "But why? We know you, Grandmother. What is your thinking?"

"Several things. First, Lady Darkford remains terrified of that place. It is her son's patrimony, so she needs to get over that for his sake. Second, the Tidemarks don't believe her explanation of events. They did not go to Baydon after the Marquess died, insisting the Marchioness and her son come to them. It was Ellinbourne who went to get them and escorted them to London. I'm certain the Darkford townhouse staff will hear about the stories of that night through the staff at Baydon, and through them, the Tidemarks will learn what they haven't bothered to listen to from Lady Darkford or anyone else. And lastly, and most importantly, I want you to find out what really happened that night.—By the way, I was quite put out.

The Tidemarks insisted on referring to the Darkford London townhouse as '*theirs*' and I had to call them on their statements on several occasions. Please ensure they do not do that at the castle as well."

"How can you be so sure they will agree to this venture?" Lakehurst asked.

Gwinnie laughed. "And how can you doubt it? This is Grandmother! We may have developed some armor against her machinations, but I assure you the Tidemarks will have none."

Her grandmother smiled at her. "Thank you, my dear." She turned to Lakehurst. "Have you had an opportunity to speak to Ellinbourne yet?"

"We are meeting in an hour at Dysard's Coffee House."

"Good, good. Also ask him about this Farrow gentleman, Mrs. Tidemark's brother. I sensed Lady Darkford did not care for him."

"You think they are both suitors for the widow?" Gwinnie asked.

"I wouldn't be surprised," she said, nodding. "Oh, and Mr. Martin will be here at five today."

"Mr. Martin?" Gwinnie repeated.

"Yes. I sent a note round to him and he said he could be here at that time. I don't know how much information he can get for me before the dinner party tomorrow night, but it is worth asking."

CHAPTER 6

ELLINBOURNE'S TALE

It was early in the afternoon for Dysard's Coffee House regulars to gather. Lakehurst suggested the location to Ellinbourne for that reason.

Private clubs had supplanted the coffee houses as social gathering locations for men. Dysard's was one of the few remaining, and one of the few that still catered to men from all social strata. That was why Lakehurst favored the establishment. But its unique existence wouldn't last much longer. He'd heard the owner intended to turn Dysard's Coffee House into Dysard's Chop House. Lakehurst wished him luck, but doubted he would frequent the converted establishment.

When he walked into the shadowed coffee house, there was a scattering of men sitting around the scarred, heavy wood tables that filled the large room. The large room smelled of coffee and tobacco, and a haze from pipe smoke hung in the air.

Ellinbourne wasn't present yet. Lakehurst chose a booth against a back wall, away from the windows. Window tables were prime locations for the coffee drinkers. From there they could see and be seen and have light for reading the papers Dysard provided. Seeing and being seen wasn't Lakehurst's intention. He desired a quiet conversation, one that wouldn't be heard and bruited about the ton.

He'd ordered his coffee before he saw Ellinbourne enter. He stood up to wave him in his direction.

"Thank you for agreeing to meet with me to discuss the Marquess of Darkford's death," he said as Ellinbourne set his ever-present sketchbook on the table and then sat on the bench across the table from him.

"I could scarcely do otherwise when you sent me your novel and bade me read chapter seventeen!" Ellinbourne said. He removed the book from his pocket and put it on top of his sketchbook on the table between them.

"By your reaction, I assume the description in my book is close to what happened to the Marquess?"

"Damned close. Oh, not exact, from what I know of events; however, one would think you'd been there. In your note, you said you wrote this eighteen months ago when you were in Scotland, at the same time as Richard's death."

"Yes. The book greatly upset your sister when she read parts of it the other evening and yesterday, when I told her I wrote the book, she assumed I'd been there. She called me a murderer."

Ellinbourne straightened. "I could see where she might," he acknowledged. He pursed his lips.

"Could you tell me how he died?" Lakehurst asked. "I understand that the Tidemarks do not believe her explanation of the events."

"I think it is more *convenient* for them not to believe her than them actually not believing her," Ellinbourne said archly.

"More convenient? Interesting."

"Edmund Tidemark has long turned a blind eye to his nephew's interests," Ellinbourne said.

"What were Darkford's interests?"

"The supernatural combined, I'd say, with the traditions of Dashwood's Hellfire Club in the last century."

"I am familiar with the stories of the Hellfire Club and their activities in the caves at West Wycombe Hills."

"The Marquess had caves on his property in the Mendip Hills and decided to use those as Dashwood did. He even had Dashwood's club motto carved in the stone at the entrance: *Do What Thou Wilt.*"

"That comes from Rabelais," Lakehurst said.

"Yes. But beyond the hedonistic aspect of Dashwood's *'Order of the Friars of St. Francis'* with worship to Bacchus and Venus, the Marquess had a fascination for demons, devil rituals and the veneration of Satan."

"Dashwood's group never went that far."

"No. Dashwood and his cronies were against popery, and were all for having drunken orgies in priests' vestments, but not into devil worship, despite the group's nickname. Our father, before he died, often said he regretted he'd allowed one of his daughters to marry Darkford. Not knowing he was a man with those proclivities."

"As a clergyman, I imagine he would be. So, what happened? How did he end up dead in one of his rituals?"

"From what Cassie observed—"

"Cassie?" Lakehurst asked, pouncing on the name. He liked it.

Ellinbourne smiled. "Sorry, that is her family's pet name for her. From what Cassandra observed that night, her husband was not the leader—at least not that night. Another man was, a tall man—"

Lakehurst groaned. "Like me," he said flatly.

Ellinbourne shrugged. "I don't know. Remember, Darkford was tall as well. She said he wore a dark red cape with a hood that shadowed his face and wore a black mask. They all did. She said this leader had a deep, husky voice, and he was the only one that seemed... normal."

"Normal?" Lakehurst asked.

"Yes. Not drunk or drugged. The others appeared to be under the influence of something else. She didn't think it was either alcohol or laudanum. Something else."

"Like Mesmer's animal magnetism? I could see that being one of Darkford's interests."

Ellinbourne shrugged. "I don't know. More like the Abbé Faria's theories and practices. All I know is what Cassandra told me. They seemed to be under the command of this one man, however that was done, and they moved as if they were sleepwalking."

"How many were there?"

"Cassandra said she only saw four, which was surprising, as she knew his *meetings* normally had at least twenty members plus assorted *angels.*'"

"Prostitutes."

Ellinbourne nodded. "That night, Darkford told her to lock herself in her suite of rooms and to keep Alex with her."

Startled, Lakehurst looked up from the coffee he'd been about to finish. "Darkford feared for her?"

Ellinbourne spread his hands out. "That would be my guess," he said grimly.

Lakehurst set his cup down. His brow furrowed as he studied Ellinbourne. "What happened?" he asked harshly. This went beyond what he could have imagined. Knowing what was in his book, he dreaded listening, but listen, he must.

"They came for her," Ellinbourne said. "Possibly for Alex as well; however, she'd made him take some laudanum and hid him in the priest hole that was in the corner of her sitting room behind a cabinet."

Lakehurst shook his head and breathed in deeply. He tried to imagine her fear. The kind of fear he wrote about; but he wondered if his words could ever do justice to the terror she must have felt that night.

"Cassandra tried to fake an escape through the hidden passage that led from Darkford's bedroom to the outside and instead hid under his bed, but somehow, she didn't fool the leader. He dragged her out from under the bed and had two of the other men hold her while he forced her to drink some nasty potion. The next thing she remembered is being in a large cavern lit with torches along the walls. It was where Darkford and his friends conducted their meeting rituals."

"Why didn't she run through the passage to escape?"

"She didn't want to leave Alex behind."

Lakehurst nodded.

"When I learned of Darkford's death, I journeyed to Baydon to get her and Alex and bring them to London. I visited the cave. Darkford had had the caves decorated years before, when he started his club, to resemble a cross between a ruined church, a gentlemen's club, and a brothel. There was a stone altar with metal rings pounded into it at the ends, which is where they laid her down and tied her in place."

Lakehurst grabbed his head between his hands. "Bloody hell," he swore. "Like my novel." His stomach churned against the coffee he'd drunk, acid rising in his throat.

Ellinbourne nodded. "Y-yes," he said slowly. "Very close. But where you had a demon-possessed man with a branding iron for the devil's mark, this man, who had her tied to the altar, had a knife to carve the sigil on her left shoulder above her breast," Ellinbourne said grimly.

Lakehurst raised his head. "What!" he exclaimed. His loud exclamation drew heads turning in their direction. "Please tell me he was not successful."

Ellinbourne's lips compressed in a tight line. "He did not complete the design. He carved only two lines. Like this." He opened his sketchbook and withdrew a pencil from his pocket. Quickly, he drew the two lines slightly curved at the bottom that formed a stylized X shape. "Cassandra screamed, pleading with Darkford to make him stop. Her screaming must have broken through whatever had kept Darkford under that man's control. Cassandra said her husband grabbed the man's hand, and they fought over the knife. The leader managed to stab Darkford in their struggle. He fell across Cassandra."

"Dear God," Lakehurst murmured. He could almost see the scene in his mind. Perversely, a curse of his writing talent.

"The men ran from the cave to the stable to get their horses. The only staff Darkford let stay on the estate during his meetings was Carlyle, a deaf stable groom. He saw them leave, and when Darkford didn't appear, Carlyle went into the caves and found Cassandra and Darkford."

"Darkford was dead?"

Ellinbourne nodded. "He'd bled out while laying across her," he said baldly.

Lakehurst felt sick to his stomach. "Thank you for telling me. The events sound unnervingly like my novel. I can understand why she reacted the way she did."

"When I took her away from Baydon, I wasn't comfortable leaving her with the Tidemarks; unfortunately, just two months earlier our uncle, the 5th Duke of Ellinbourne, had died and I had inherited the title. The obligations I had to learn and sort out overwhelmed me. I regret I allowed the Tidemarks to remove her as one of my obligations. That was a mistake I regret every day."

"How can I... How can I—I don't know..." Lakehurst shook his head, confounded by the confidences Ellinbourne had shared. "Earn her trust?" he finally said.

"Why?"

"Why?"

"Yes. Why do you wish to earn her trust?" Ellinbourne asked. "To appease any feelings of guilt you might have for even devising a story that could be eerily real?"

"No! Though I suppose there is a bit of that. But, no." He looked off across the room for a moment, thinking through the feelings that roiled inside him. He felt drawn to her, that he knew. The rest of what lay inside him existed as a confusing mélange of emotions.

He looked back to Ellinbourne, who sat across from him, studying him with a stern mien. "I don't know what I feel," he admitted to him, "however, I do know I want the opportunity to get to know her better. Though I denied it to my sister and grandmother, she has intrigued me since I met her at your betrothal ball."

Ellinbourne nodded, then slowly smiled. "I think you just might be good for each other."

"You misunderstand," Lakehurst said hastily. "My interest is the curse of a writer's curiosity, that is all."

But even as he protested, he knew he lied.

CARRYING HIS NOVEL WITH HIM, Lakehurst came clattering down the central staircase at the same time the footman, Stephen, opened the front door to Mr. Lewis Martin, the Bow Street senior agent who'd helped the family on other occasions. Neatly dressed, Mr. Martin could have passed for one of the London clerks who hurried about the Fleet Street part of the city.

Whenever he saw him, Lakehurst couldn't help wondering about his family. Where did he come from? Well-spoken and obviously well-educated, he stood out among his peers. Lakehurst greeted him and told Stephen he'd conduct him to the Duchess in the Lady Margaret parlor.

"Thank you for coming on such short notice," Lakehurst said.

Mr. Martin smiled and shrugged. "I like the Duchess," he said.

"Where is your shadow?" Lakehurst asked, referring to the orphan boy the Bow Street agent had adopted.

"At the Graeme Home for Boys. Just for the summer. His request."

"Isn't that the Earl of Soothcoor's orphanage?"

"One of them. Named after the earl's maternal grandfather, he says."

"Why would the boy ask to go there?"

"In the summer, the boys don't have academic classes. Aside from trade classes—which go year 'round—they are learning to hunt with a bow and arrow and, would you believe, fly-fishing."

Lakehurst laughed. "Things a city boy wouldn't learn in the city. What tradework is he pursuing? I thought he wanted to be a runner like you."

"He says he still does, though I try to dissuade him. He likes woodworking."

Lakehurst started to open the door to the Lady Margaret parlor when he noticed Mr. Martin's attention shift elsewhere. A slow smile spread over the man's face. From the room across the hall came the sound of a violin.

"Lady Guinevere?" Mr. Martin asked.

"Yes," Lakehurst said.

"She's very good," Mr. Martin said, turning back toward Lakehurst.

Lakehurst nodded as he opened the parlor door. His sister loved her music, but he could tell by her music choice this day that her violin was her therapy. The events surrounding Lady Darkford disturbed her.

"Mr. Martin!" said the Duchess from her seat on the long sofa. "Come in, come in." She waved him to the chair at a right angle to her position.

"Your Grace," Mr. Martin said, bowing before taking the seat she'd indicated.

Lakehurst sat on the other end of the sofa.

"Thank you for coming, Mr. Martin," the Duchess said.

"My pleasure," he returned. "I understand from your rather cryptic note that you wished to speak to me about the death of Lord Darkford eighteen months ago?"

"Yes."

"As it did not occur in the city, you probably know as much or more than I do," he said.

"I understand that," she said, "however, events related to his death have occurred that require investigation."

Lakehurst shifted on the sofa. "May I explain, Grandmother?" he asked, staring at her. He knew his grandmother's preference for control, but he felt vested in the mystery.

He saw one of her mobile eyebrows rise, but she inclined her head.

"Thank you." He handed his novel to Mr. Martin. "Please read the beginning of chapter seventeen. I have marked the spot."

Mr. Martin looked at him quizzically but did as he requested. When he looked up from reading, Lakehurst continued. "I have come to learn that the events described in that chapter are eerily close to what happened to Lord Darkford—and Lady Darkford."

Mr. Martin frowned, confused. "Are you saying this author has first-hand knowledge of Lord Darkford's death?" he asked, handing the book back to Lakehurst.

Lakehurst shook his head as he accepted it. "No. I wrote that. While I was in Scotland eighteen months ago."

"Then how do you know your story—" he said, pointing to the book, "is what happened?"

"From Lady Darkford and her brother—who you know—the Duke of Ellinbourne," he said on a long sigh.

Mr. Martin acknowledged knowing the Duke of Ellinbourne. Lakehurst knew they'd met at the Duchess's house party at Versely Park two months prior when Mr. Martin worked undercover as the head footman during the party.

"Ellinbourne said Darkford liked devils and demons and was fascinated with the stories about Francis Dashwood's Hellfire social club in the last century. He combined aspects of both into a club that met in the caves below Baydon Castle in the Mendip Hills. Like the legendary Hellfire Club, the meetings were parodies of religious rituals with debauchery but with more of an emphasis on Satan."

"But Darkford wasn't circumspect about his invitation list. He invited openly. Before we left Dysard's, Ellinbourne wrote down a few names he said Cassandra knew had attended at least one meeting. Stillworth and Farrow—who you said were coming to dinner tomorrow night, Grandmother—were on that list," Lakehurst said, turning to her.

"That's not really surprising," she said, "since Stillworth was his cousin and Farrow was his uncle's brother-in-law."

"Mr. Fortesque, the vicar from Baydonton, the village closest to Baydon Castle, tucked in one of the Mendip Hills valleys, attended at least once that was known by Lady Darkford. Ellinbourne said even he had been invited on one occasion. He declined, he said. I don't know who else; however, I would assume others in society were. Closer questioning of Lady Darkford could reveal more—though I should have a care to question her."

"Certainly not at my dinner party!" the Duchess exclaimed.

"Exactly."

"If your intention for this party is to ask questions," Mr. Martin said, "be careful questioning Mr. Stillworth and Mr. Farrow, Your Grace," Mr. Martin said. "At least until I have an opportunity to ask questions of my sources about these gentlemen and others who were in Darkford's circle."

"Can you find out who was in Darkford's circle?" the Duchess asked.

"That is not difficult. Porters at clubs are always open to a coin crossing their palms."

"Please send a bill for what you expend for your sources."

"But why this intense interest now?" Mr. Martin asked.

"Lady Darkford has just begun to socialize again, and is speaking to people," the Duchess said.

"Worse," Lakehurst cut in. "She is being followed."

"Followed?" Mr. Martin's brow furrowed. He leaned forward.

Lakehurst nodded. "Yesterday, at Hyde Park, a man followed her to her townhouse. Afterward, he talked to a street sweeper boy and bribed him to let him know at the Wild Boar Tavern who visited and when she left the house."

"How did you come by this information?" Mr. Martin asked sharply.

"Rose, Gwinnie's maid, followed the man and spoke to the boy afterward."

Mr. Martin nodded. "I know Rose from the time she spends at Mrs. Southerlands' with Lady Guinevere."

"I just learned the other day that Gwinnie goes in disguise as someone named Sarah?" the Duchess said repressively.

"Miss Sarah Knolls," Mr. Martin supplied.

She raised a singular brow again. Lakehurst remembered being intimidated as a child by that raised eyebrow. No one could do it quite like his grandmother, though others might try. He used to practice the action standing in front of a mirror—to no avail. His eyebrows just wouldn't work that way.

"Your Grace, I could wish you were not having this dinner party," Mr. Martin said.

"Why? I think it could be quite amusing."

He shook his head. "Your Grace, this is a serious matter. Serious events have occurred. From what Lord Lakehurst has said he learned from the Duke, I would surmise Lady Darkford, and potentially her son as well, might be in danger."

"Danger. Why do you say that?"

"I can speak to that," Lakehurst said. "According to what Ellinbourne told me, that last meeting was an unusually small gathering. Not one of his normal parties. No other women were present. With a man now following her as she starts to show herself again, she might well be targeted."

"Why?"

Mr. Martin shook his head. "Perhaps Lady Darkford knows something she doesn't realize she knows. But does evil ever make sense, Your Grace?"

She slumped back against the cushions of her sofa.

Lakehurst nodded. "It makes me wonder if your idea of having us go to Baydon is wise. The villains could still be in that area and we would bring her directly back to them."

"It could be a two-edged sword, my lord," Mr. Martin said.

"How so?"

"It is difficult to protect a person in London. Strangers are all about. Life is cheap and murderers, thieves, and kidnappers—they are all for hire here. In the country, at one estate, everyone knows the people there. It is a closed environment. Take servants with you that you can trust and have them also provide security."

"I wish Malmsby were not off in Northumberland nor Aidan on his honeymoon," said the Duchess testily. "They could accompany you." She took a deep breath. "I am almost inclined to not promote the trip, but I fear Lady Darkford needs it to banish her ghosts. And the dynamics with the Tidemarks do concern me. Can you not go as well, Mr. Martin?"

"No, Your Grace. Not for at least a week. I am stuck in town to appear as a witness for the prosecution in a couple of scheduled trials."

"When do you expect this trip to take place?" Lakehurst asked his mother.

"As soon as possible, before anyone has had a chance to think it through, and perhaps the people who are following Lady Darkford to understand what is happening."

"I would say that is wise," Mr. Martin said, nodding. "There is a thief-taker who works in that area that I know. I'll send word to him to see if he might be of assistance. Mr. Liddle. Mr. Harry Liddle. He will have heard any unsavory rumors floating in the area. He may look a little uncouth and sound it as well; however, you can trust him."

"Thank you, Mr. Martin," Lakehurst said.

The double doors to the parlor opened with a whoosh, in typical Gwinnie fashion.

Lakehurst noted that Mr. Martin and Gwinnie saw each other immediately and smiled.

Mr. Martin rose to his feet to bow. Gwinnie waved her hand carelessly, indicating he should sit again.

"I lost track of time. Have I missed the discussion?" she asked as she strode forward toward the sofa.

"Move over, brother of mine," she said, putting herself between the Duchess and her brother.

"Yes, I'm afraid you have," her grandmother said, smiling.

"Bother," Gwinnie said. "So, Mr. Martin, are you all in the know now? What do you think of this plan to go to Baydon Castle?—Never mind. No need to rehash it now. I shall pester Lakehurst later."

"Probably when I'm trying to write," Lakehurst told Mr. Martin.

Mr. Martin laughed.

"Probably," Gwinnie agreed. "I had a thought," she said, bouncing to face her grandmother. "We should include Ursula."

"Why?"

"Safety in numbers. Women banded together."

"Like a herd of cows," her brother said sarcastically.

"Laugh if you will, but there is a lot to be said for that. Hard to cut one from the herd for mischief. I've seen it stand to good advantage in my work with the women at Mrs. Southerlands'."

Lakehurst tried not to laugh, but suddenly the vision of the women as a herd had him snorting with laughter. Soon, Mr. Martin and the Duchess joined in.

Gwinnie just smiled.

CHAPTER 7
GATHERING

V iscount Lakehurst came downstairs to the gold parlor fifteen minutes before any guests were scheduled to arrive. Since his grandmother had chosen the more formal gold parlor as the gathering location over her Lady Margaret parlor, Lakehurst knew she intended to intimidate the Tidemarks into doing whatever she suggested. He almost felt sorry for them. While his grandmother was a prankster, she wasn't a mean person by nature. They must have excessively riled her when she met them yesterday.

Before him were his cousin, Ann Hallowell, in a subdued pale blue gown, contrasted to her stepmother Ursula Hallowell's pink gown festooned with ruffles and tucks. Ann's fiancé, the Duke of Ellinbourne stood between them, his ever-present sketchbook under his arm.

Lakehurst hadn't seen his cousin and her stepmother since the betrothal ball, so made his way directly to greet them. His little cousin had blossomed since her engagement. Gone was the retiring, quiet woman replaced by a pleasant, smiling woman—still quiet—however, with that retiring manner replaced with a quiet confidence. She glowed with happiness.

Mrs. Hallowell seemed to have regained some of the bubbly effervescence that she'd lost when she discovered her promising relationship with Colonel Brantley had been contrived to get access to the Malmsby family. Personally, he couldn't see what the lively woman had seen in Colonel Brantley—a corpulent older man—even if she did prefer older gentlemen, as Ann assured him.

"How are plans progressing for the wedding?" he asked Ann. "Have you set a date yet?"

"The plans are going well; how could they not with Grandmother involved?" Ann said with a warm laugh. "The when remains uncertain. Miles wishes for his sister Margaret to attend. He sent word to her. We are awaiting her reply. Hopefully, in person."

"She is in Massachusetts, correct?"

"Yes, she is a governess in Boston."

He nodded. "I remember hearing that at one time; however, I don't always listen as closely as I should," he acknowledged.

"Particularly if your mind is on one of your stories," his cousin said archly, then laughed.

"Guilty," he admitted.

The parlor door opened to admit Lady Darkford and others he assumed to be her relations.

"Excuse me," he murmured to Ann and Mrs. Hallowell. He made his way over to Lady Darkford.

"I trust you are better today? That my grandmother explained about the book?" he asked softly as he took her hand and drew it to his lips to kiss the knuckles.

"Yes, but it is for me to beg your pardon," she said.

"Nonsense—"

"And so I told her!" said a woman who bustled up beside her, dressed in dark blue and all soft and pillowy looking. He guessed her to be in her fourth decade.

"Vanessa! Please allow me to introduce you before you take liberties to address Lord Lakehurst," Lady Darkford admonished with a gentle laugh.

The woman blinked, then went wide-eyed. "Oh! Oh, yes... Well do go on..."

When the formal introductions were done, the woman went on. "You are quite tall, aren't you? Taller than Mr. Stillworth, I believe," she said, waving toward a gentleman who had entered with them.

"I know of Mr. Stillworth; however, I have never had the pleasure of meeting him. Would you do me the honors?" he asked the woman.

"Me?—Yes, of course. Immediately," she said happily, slipping her arm in his and leading him over to where Mr. Stillworth stood. "Mr. Stillworth is my nephew, you know, through my husband, of course," she said. "Raymond dear, here is Viscount Lakehurst to meet you," she said as they reached Mr. Stillworth.

Inwardly, Lakehurst chuckled. The woman had no notion of social niceties. Most of the time he didn't either, so the fact she introduced him to Mr. Stillworth instead of the other way around amused him.

It surprised him to note that, though slender, Mr. Stillworth stood nearly as tall as he did. His was a long, almost rectangular face with regular features and light brown hair.

After an exchange of pleasantries, Mr. Stillworth encouraged Mrs. Tidemark to return to Lady Darkford's side. "So she might introduce you to others," he said smoothly.

She agreed happily and hurried away. "My apologies for my uncle's wife. She has great enthusiasm but intemperate manners," he said with quiet dryness. "But my uncle has ever supported her," he said as he watched her corner the Duke of Ellinbourne in a discussion.

"But can you tell me why I am here?" he asked Lakehurst.

"My grandmother said your name was mentioned by Lady Darkford."

"It was? I am most certainly gratified; however, I am surprised."

"Why so?"

"My uncle told me I look too much like my cousin Richard for her comfort. For that reason, he doesn't like me coming around the townhouse to visit."

Lakehurst furrowed his brow. "I was not an intimate of the Marquess; however, I would concede you have something of his look."

"When we were children, we were sometimes confused as one for the other. That did make for some fun moments," he said complacently. "But growing up, I grew taller and my hair darker."

"From some things Lady Darkford has said in passing, I gather the Tidemarks have assigned emotions to Lady Darkford that are not true."

"That is distressing to hear; however, I cannot help but hope that is true. But you said Lady Darkford suggested my name?"

Lakehurst nodded. "After Mrs. Tidemark asked for her brother to attend."

"Ah. Now I understand. Mrs. Tidemark adores her brother."

"And you don't?"

"No, but more to the point, Lady Darkford doesn't.

Around her, he can be a toad, but neither Tidemark nor his wife see it."

Lakehurst snorted.

The parlor door opened again. It was the Duchess on one arm of Mr. Martin and his sister Gwinnie on his other arm. Beside him, Lakehurst was aware of Mr. Stillworth straightening. He saw him look from Gwinnie to him.

"Is that glorious creature your sister?" he asked, his expression brightening.

Lakehurst nodded. "It is."

"I think I should enjoy this evening after all," Stillworth said, walking toward the threesome.

Lakehurst laughed.

THIS IS A MISTAKE. *I should have dissuaded the Duchess,* Cassandra inwardly moaned. She looked about the opulent parlor with its real gold inlays on columns, frames, cornices, and mantle pieces and the glittering crystal chandeliers and candle branches. Everything sparkled, coruscating with rainbow prism light from blazing candlesticks. She didn't know the last time she had been anywhere so bright it nearly made her eyes hurt. She closed her eyes against the glittering brightness of the chandelier, but still saw sparkles through her closed eyelids. She looked down, then opened her eyes again.

Harrison Farrow and Edmund Tidemark stood on either side of her. Unwanted bodyguards. What were they guarding her from? She wondered if Mr. Farrow would ever leave her side. Since he'd arrived at the Darkford house at midday, he'd been an obsequious leech—if he ever could be convinced to leave her side 'twould be a miracle. Though perhaps it would be interesting to see what the Duchess thought of Mr. Farrow.

Not that he was a bad person, she reasoned. In his mid-thirties, he was of medium height and build, with the nascent evidence of encroaching corpulence in his later years wrapped about his person. His rather round face appeared pleasant enough beneath medium brown hair that receded to the crown of his head. In dress, he preferred dandy attire with high stocks, bright waistcoats, and yellow pantaloons. This evening, paired with his yellow pantaloons, he wore a cerulean blue jacket over a striped waistcoat of blue, red, and gold.

She looked across the room to where Viscount Lakehurst stood laughing at something Mr. Stillworth said when the Duchess entered. She hoped he'd come back to her side and lead Mr. Farrow away as he had Vanessa, though she acknowledged that had likely not been his intent. She now believed she would always safe next to him, even if she'd flown up into the boughs in anger and fear at the knowledge he was the author of the book. In a small part of herself, she knew she'd never feared him, despite his large size. Guiltily, she admitted to herself, she rather liked his size.

She decided to cross to the Duchess's side.

"Where are you going?" her uncle asked.

She looked at him and frowned. "To pay my respects to the Duchess, of course," she said.

"Oh, yes. Rightly so. I shall accompany you. Harrison, come along to meet our hostess," Edmund said, to Cassandra's dismay. They followed behind her as she crossed the room to the Duchess. She spared a curious glance to the gentleman who escorted the Duchess and Gwinnie. He had bright blue eyes in a well-tanned face beneath wavy blond hair. He smiled congenially back at her.

Gwinnie dropped his arm to embrace Cassandra gleefully. "You are looking wonderful, isn't she, Grandmother?" Gwinnie enthused. She tucked her arm into Cassandra's. "I'm so happy to see you!"

"And I you," Cassandra said, overwhelmed by Gwinnie's enthusiasm.

"Mr. Tidemark," said the Duchess. "I'm glad to see you here this evening."

"Thank you for inviting us and including my wife's younger brother, Harrison Farrow."

"At your service," Mr. Farrow said, bowing low over the Duchess's hand.

"It is nice to meet you, Mr. Farrow. You must tell me all about yourself. However, first, may I make you known to Mr. Martin, who has been a particular friend to the family?"

The gentlemen all perfunctorily bowed to one another as Mr. Stillworth came up.

"Lady Darkford, might I prevail upon you..."

Cassandra recognized he, too, wished for formal introductions. "My Lady Malmsby, this is Mr. Raymond Stillworth, my late husband's cousin and business partner in his tea ventures. Lady Guinevere, Mr. Martin, please meet Mr. Stillworth," she said, finishing the round of introductions and witnessing the round of courtesies that followed.

Tiresome, she thought, but she smiled at all. She felt dismayed that Mr. Stillworth appeared to desire further acquaintance with Gwinnie. She didn't blame him, though she'd hoped he would help keep Mr. Farrow at bay.

She turned to leave the group to converse. Mr. Farrow turned to follow her.

"Mr. Farrow!" she heard the Duchess say. "Don't leave, I wish to become better acquainted," said the Duchess.

Cassandra glanced back to the Duchess.

"You, too, Mr. Tidemark, stay. We can have a comfortable coze before dinner," the Duchess said, indicating with a sweep of her hand a sofa and chair grouping where they could sit.

Cassandra knew neither Mr. Farrow nor Edmund could refuse her request. She continued to where her brother and his fiancée sat with Mrs. Hallowell.

"I was considering how to pull the leeches from you," her preternaturally calm brother whispered. "Are they always intent on staying by your side?"

She laughed. "Yes, but Edmund's attachment is because of Mr. Farrow. For all Edmund is sincerely attached to his wife, he does not trust Mr. Farrow. I believe he fears if he doesn't stay close by, Mr. Farrow will attempt something ungentlemanly toward me. But neither does he rescue me from Mr. Farrow. I'm not sure I understand the difference for Edmund—allowing the verbal liberties Mr. Farrow takes while safeguarding against the physical liberties—but so it is."

"Verbal liberties?" Lord Lakehurst asked, joining them.

"Yes, I would like to know more about those, too," her brother said, frowning as he crossed his arms across his chest.

Cassandra wished she hadn't said anything—especially anything Lord Lakehurst could overhear. "It is nothing, really."

"Cassie," Ann said with the familiarity of family,

"you know you are not going to get away with that," she admonished.

Cassandra sat down. "Mr. Farrow is of the mind that it is only a matter of time before I accept his suit."

"He wishes to marry you?" Lord Lakehurst asked.

She nodded ruefully. "And because he has the intention, he makes remarks about the marriage bed," she admitted.

"No!" exclaimed her brother, Ann, and Mrs. Hallowell while Lord Lakehurst swore, "Bloody hell!"

All eyes in the room turned in their direction. Cassandra saw a dark blush rush up into Lakehurst's face.

"I beg your pardon, ladies," he said tightly, bowing his head slightly. "Ellinbourne!" he then said, turning to the Duke.

"I know. I need to disabuse him of his pretensions —and speak to Tidemark for not doing so!"

"I should be doing that," Cassandra said. "But until this past week, I have been much too complacent with the Tidemarks."

"What changed?" Ann asked gently, drawing her down to sit on the sofa next to her. The others took chairs nearby.

Cassandra smiled, for the knowledge had just come to her and filled her soul with a new peace— and, curiously, questions. "Your company, your interest in me," she said, "and honestly, Lord Lakehurst's book."

"My book!" Lakehurst said. "But it frightened you. I don't understand."

"Yes, it did frighten me because it brought with it a flood of memories that I had been repressing in daylight but relived almost nightly in my dreams."

"Your nightmares," her brother said. "Tidemark told me you suffered nightmares."

"You poor dear," Mrs. Hallowell said, reaching over to gently squeeze her hand.

Cassandra smiled back at her. "It's all right," she said softly. She looked over at the others. "It was strangely cathartic," she admitted with a confused frown. "I haven't had a nightmare since I read those pages. But I do have thoughts and questions I didn't have before."

"Like what?" her brother asked.

"What is most concerning to me—as I think on it —is neither Alex nor I were supposed to be there. We were to be visiting friends. But someone went to the trouble of assuring we were in residence that night."

Her brother frowned, as did Lord Lakehurst.

"What do you mean?" her brother asked.

Lord Lakehurst leaned forward in his chair, his elbows resting on his knees as he stared intently at her.

"When Richard had his meetings, we had long established neither Alex nor I would be in residence. Neither would most of the staff. They were regularly given the night off, except he let old Carlyle stay as he saw to the horses and he is deaf."

"But you were there this time," Lakehurst said.

She nodded. "That day, we were to leave to visit with friends in Wells for a week, Baron and Lady Loftbridge. They have two children near Alex's age, so it is a treat for Alex. But before we left, I received a letter— ostensibly from the baron—asking us not to come. They had an outbreak of the pox on their estate and in town. He did not want to risk our health. Richard was not happy with that news. He made me promise I would keep Alex with me and keep the doors to my rooms locked. He said his guests could get rowdy, and he didn't want any unintentional drunken mistakes made by the guests that could be prevented."

"That was thoughtful," Ann observed.

Her brother nodded slightly, confusion still clinging to his face.

"The letter was a forgery," Lakehurst said.

"Yes, though I did not discover that until afterward."

"Someone wanted to do mischief that night," Mrs. Hallowell said.

"More than mischief, I'd say," Lakehurst said, straightening.

The butler appeared at the doorway, announcing dinner was served.

The Viscount rose and offered an arm to Cassandra and Mrs. Hallowell. "Ladies, shall we?" he asked, smiling from one to the other.

Mr. Farrow came hurrying toward them. Cassandra stiffened. She did not wish to go into dinner on Mr. Farrow's arm and she knew that was his intention.

The viscount must have felt her reaction for he glanced down at her, then looked toward Mr. Farrow. "Ah, Mr. Farrow! Good man. You've come to offer your arm to Mrs. Hallowell. Splendid. Though I should wish the company of two beautiful ladies, sometimes it is dashed awkward to walk three abreast past furniture," he said heartily.

Mr. Farrow paused, and looked as if he would say something, but instead compressed his lips together.

Lakehurst gently released Mrs. Hallowell from his arm. That lady saw nothing amiss with his actions and took Mr. Farrow's arm with alacrity.

"Thank you," Cassandra said softly.

Lord Lakehurst reached over to pat her arm with his other hand. "My pleasure," he murmured.

～

WITH THE DUKE OF MALMSBY journeying to Northumberland, Lakehurst sat at the head of the table, with the Duchess at the other end. To his right sat Lady Darkford, and on his left sat Mr. Stillworth.

They had shortened the dining table as much as it could be while still remaining comfortable for the diners. There was no epergne in the center of the table to obstruct vision or conversation. The dining room walls were covered with green silk, the drapes were made of velvet in a darker shade and swagged with tartan material. Most of the paintings hung on the wall were Scottish landscapes. If the Lady Margaret parlor was his grandmother's favorite room, this room had been of his mother's design in homage to her homeland and her favorite room. He'd always thought the room to be too dark; however, he wouldn't change a bit of it until the drapes rotted and the silk walls shredded. It represented his mother and all that she loved of Scotland.

Lady Darkford talked with Mr. Martin. Lakehurst turned to Mr. Stillworth.

"Stillworth, I'd like to learn more about this tea business you and the late Marquess were involved with."

"Baydon Imports?"

"Is that the name of the company?" Lakehurst asked.

Stillworth nodded. "Richard wanted to name it Darkford Imports. I objected, as that might make it seem as if he owned the company himself. As we are co-founders, I didn't like that idea. We considered Tidemark but settled on Baydon Imports since Baydon Castle is our shared ancestral heritage."

Lakehurst nodded in understanding. "Do you just import tea?"

"No, the core import has been coffee. What we wanted to do is successfully grow the *camellia sinensis* plant—the tea plant—in a country other than China! We are—I suppose I should say we *were*—experimenting in different climate zones in India."

"Were?"

"With Richard's death, my Uncle Edmund has not been willing to continue the tea experiment," Stillworth said, glancing down the table at his uncle, disgust clear in his voice. "We had a few good harvests and produced some excellent teas, but he'd prefer to stick with coffee. Safer investment, he says."

Lakehurst looked down the table to where Edmund Tidemark was talking to his grandmother.

"Conservative?"

"Extremely."

Lakehurst glanced at Lady Darkford and saw she was in a conversation with Mr. Martin. "I understand he and his wife consider Lady Darkford to be mentally unstable."

Mr. Stillworth snorted. "Yes." He shook his head. "They never approved of Richard's choice for a wife. I, for one, thought she was good for him. Even too good!"

"What do you mean?"

Mr. Stillworth raised his chin in her direction. "She didn't fuss about his meetings at Baydon. Always tried to be away."

"Were you an attendee?"

He laughed. "I was out of the country for most of his 'meetings' as he called them. On my return, I attended occasionally."

"What went on at these meetings?"

Mr. Stillworth tilted his head to the side, his eyes

narrowing. "I don't believe, my lord, that is a fit discussion for the dinner party."

"Oh," Lakehurst said archly. He raised his wineglass in salute to Mr. Stillworth. "Another time, then."

Mr. Stillworth lifted his wineglass and bowed his head in agreement. "Another time."

"*Go to Baydon!*" they heard loudly from the other end of the table. It was Mr. Tidemark in response to something said by the Duchess.

Everyone looked in their direction.

The Duchess saw she had everyone's attention due to Mr. Tidemark's outburst. "I was just telling Mr. Tidemark that after discussion with His Grace, the Duke of Ellinbourne, I recommend a Baydon Castle house party."

"What! *No!*" Lady Darkford exclaimed.

Lakehurst reached over to touch her hand. They should have warned her. "Sh-sh. Just listen," he said softly.

She looked at him, confused, but nodded shortly and looked back at the Duchess.

His grandmother smiled benignly. Lakehurst repressed a laugh.

"Yes! A trip of discovery, to dispel ghosts, and for Lady Darkford to feel good about being in company again."

"Your Grace—" Mr. Tidemark started to protest.

"I know, it is a brilliant idea, isn't it?" she enthused. "And I have the guest list all thought out for you. You and Mrs. Tidemark, Lady Darkford, her brother the Duke," she said, nodding in Ellinbourne's direction. "His fiancée, Ann, and her stepmother, Mrs. Hallowell, my grandson Viscount Lakehurst, my granddaughter Lady Guinevere, Mr. Stillworth, and now that I met him, I think we should extend an invitation to Mr. Farrow as well."

"Oh, no, no, no!" said Mr. Tidemark.

"You don't think we should include Mr. Farrow?" she asked quite innocently.

Lakehurst rolled his eyes. His sister raised her serviette to her lips to hide a laugh.

"That is not what I meant, Your Grace. I—"

"I know you are thinking about young Alex. I haven't forgotten about him. I am planning a treat for him. I will take him with me to Versely Park for the summer. As we discussed just yesterday morning, London in the summer is not good for children. They need fresh air and to be able to explore nature. And companionship. It just so happens that this summer the vicar and his wife are taking in his older brother's son while they travel on diplomatic business. Our vicar is the third son of the Earl of Wheaton," she rambled on. "The middle brother—Charles—is with the foreign office. Poor man was born with a twisted foot so he could not join the military, but has done well for himself in the foreign office. He married Edyth Mann, you know, Baron Mann's daughter. Two boys are of an age and will have a splendid time of it together."

"No-o-o," protested Mrs. Tidemark, her eyes wide. She shook her head so vigorously one of her hairpins flew out of her hair and landed on Mr. Farrow's plate.

"No? No to what?" asked the Duchess, leaning forward.

Mr. Farrow carefully extracted the hairpin and set it by his sister's plate.

"Alex must stay with us. Here, in London. We must stay here."

"Why?" Lady Darkford suddenly demanded. "Do you not trust the Duchess?"

Lakehurst smiled.

"But, but…"

"But what? I think that is a splendid idea for Alex." She looked at the Duchess. "He will go with you. Thank you, Your Grace," she said formally.

"Surely you cannot wish to return to Baydon Castle," Mr. Farrow said.

"No, I do not. I have had nightmares of the night Richard died. However, that is my son's property and I need to set aside my feelings for the sake of his future." She inclined her head. "And perhaps facing my fears will help stop the nightmares."

The Duchess smiled and nodded at her. "Precisely my thoughts, my dear."

Mr. Tidemark looked from his niece to the Duchess, twin furrows between his brows. "I suppose it would be all right for you to go," he said slowly. "I can perceive the benefit; however, Mrs. Tidemark and I do not need to go," he stated. He pushed his wire-frame glasses up his nose.

"Oh, but I insist," the Duchess said sweetly. "Surely you understand the importance of family to support a person who has gone through the trauma Lady Darkford has experienced."

"I just realized there will not be staff available to handle a house party," Mr. Tidemark said.

"And why is that?" the Duchess inquired wide-eyed.

He sniffed, his nose wrinkling. "I let most of them go, of course, after my nephew died."

"Did you, now. *Hmmm.* Lady Darkford, were you aware he had released the staff from service?" the Duchess asked, turning to her.

Mr. Tidemark's face showed signs of heightened color.

"No, I wasn't. Edmund, some of those people had been with the family a long time."

"Yes, well, it wasn't all of them, I misspoke in haste. The Gallaghers, that Irish couple are there as caretakers, and Carlyle remains as well. He tends to the few animals, hens, goats, etc. But there is no staff to cater for ten people!" he protested with a slight whine in his tone.

"Oh! Is that all?" scoffed the Duchess. "Not a worry. As no one will be here at Malmsby House I will send staff from here. Don't you think that is a good idea, Gwinnie? Lakehurst?" She turned toward Mr. Tidemark. "That will keep them out of mischief while we are away," she confided.

From a corner of the room, Lakehurst heard an aborted laugh. He looked over to see the footman, Stephen, struggling to keep a straight face. He winked at him.

"So, it is settled," the Duchess decreed. "There will be a house party at Baydon Castle as soon as it can be arranged. I will depart for Versely Park the day after tomorrow. Lady Darkford, will that be enough time to get our young Marquess and his nursemaid ready?"

"I believe so, Your Grace."

"I require a minimum of three days to prepare for the journey," Ellinbourne said. "I need to spend a couple of days at the Royal Art Academy to discuss the disposition of my painting at the close of the spring show. I don't know if Aiden will have returned by the time the show ends. I'll need to assign someone to take possession of my painting."

The Duchess waved her hand airily. "Aidan hired the solicitors Hargate and Hargate to handle the artwork destined for his gallery. I suggest you talk to them."

"Thank you, I will."

The Duchess looked around. "It is what, a two-and-a-half-day journey to Baydon, isn't it? Simple."

"Simple?" echoed back Mrs. Tidemark in a whisper. Her eyes were wide and she'd lost all color in her face. She turned her head and looked at Lady Darkford.

To Lakehurst she looked frightened. He wondered why.

AFTER THE TIDEMARKS, Lady Darkford, Mr. Farrow, Mr. Stillworth, and Mr. Martin left for the evening, the family and Ellinbourne gathered in the Lady Margaret parlor. Lakehurst was pouring after-dinner drinks for all when Mr. Martin returned.

"Welcome back, Mr. Martin," Lakehurst said as he held out a glass of brandy to him.

"Thank you, my lord."

"We haven't had the opportunity to discover if you have learned anything about the Marquess's death or the people who might be involved," the Duchess said.

"It has been too short of time to discover much, however, I have sent out queries and alerted my friend Mr. Liddle to be expecting the house party."

"Are we to hire him to be a footman at Baydon as we hired you at Versely Park two months ago?" asked the Duchess.

He smiled. "No. He is too well known in the area. He often works with the local magistrate so it would not be unusual for you to wish to speak with him to learn more about the events surrounding the Marquess's death. Subterfuge is not required," as he sat down in a chair near the fireplace.

"I have learned a few things. Mr. Stillworth is a man of adequate, but modest means. His properties are small but profitable as such. He has them leased out. He is heavily invested in Baydon Imports with personal funds and with the time he spent in India."

"At dinner he told me Mr. Tidemark has not been willing to move ahead with the plans he and the Marquess had made for the business."

Mr. Martin nodded. "And that has put him in a bit of a bind financially. He is not ruined; however, his economies must be dear and his outlook for wealth considerably dimmed."

He took a sip of his brandy and frowned thoughtfully. "But there is something else, something I can't identify as yet. He and Mr. Tidemark have another *'irritation'* between them that has nothing to do with the business. That requires separate investigation and thought."

"It should be interesting to see them thrown together for a house party."

Mr. Martin nodded. "I would agree. Keep a watchful eye on their interactions."

"Does he have aspirations for Lady Darkford?" Lakehurst asked.

"Yes, I believe he does; however, he is coy at this time because of what is between him and Mr. Tidemark."

"I believe my sister likes him well enough as a friend. I don't know if she would favor him as a suitor. You know, don't you, that he looks very like the late Marquess?"

"You mentioned something to that effect the other day to me but the others don't know."

Ellinbourne nodded. He looked around at the rest of the company. "Mr. Stillworth looks like he could be a twin to the late Marquess, though they are only cousins. His hair is darker and he is maybe an inch taller, but otherwise they are nearly identical. For that reason, I do not believe Cassie would favor his suit."

"How near are they in age?" Mr. Martin asked.

Ellinbourne shook his head, his brows drawing together as he considered the question. "I don't know. From something my sister said, I gathered they were very close in age, maybe a month apart at most?"

"And he's the son of Mr. Tidemark's sister?"

"Yes, that is correct."

"Have you learned anything of Mr. Farrow? Something about that always smiling face strikes me as devious," Lakehurst said.

Mr. Martin laughed. "He is on the far, far outer fringes of the princes' set."

"Really? I wouldn't have thought him to come up to even that level."

"He and his associates ape the royal hangers-on. They attend the same entertainments where they might catch a glimpse of the prince and his cronies so they might say *'when I attended the races with Prinny yesterday'*..." he said in a voice mimicking Mr. Farrow.

Everyone laughed.

"But that takes funds. Is he wealthy?"

"I'm told his grandfather made a fortune as a cotton mill owner who branched into coal hauling."

"Odd combination."

"It was to move coal to his factories before canals were built in Lancashire. He was later one of the early investors in the canal business in Lancashire."

"Smart man."

"One may not say as much for his prodigy," said the Duchess.

"Actually, Mrs. Tidemark appears to be the least of the family. Rupert Farrow, Mrs. Tidemark's eldest brother, keeps the business interests going and is wealthy and respected in Lancashire. As the youngest, Mr. Harrison Farrow was coddled by his mother. My source who has knowledge of the family says so long as Harrison Farrow does not get in debt, his brother continues to allow him a rich allowance to keep him out of the way."

"How did you learn all this?" Lakehurst asked. As an author he had a natural curiosity for information. The knowledge Mr. Martin had, though he was a Bow Street agent, seemed out of the realm of his purview as a London centered officer of the law.

He grinned. "The Gentlemen's Trade Club."

"Of course!" the Duchess said.

"You've heard of this club?" Lakehurst asked. "I've never heard of it."

She nodded. "It was started by your Aunt Elizabeth's friend, Lady Norwalk."

"Yes! Helena wrote to me about her!" Ann said excitedly.

Gwinnie nodded. "She wrote to me as well."

Lakehurst scratched his head, frowning. Ellinbourne looked interested, but otherwise was as clueless as he was.

The Duchess nodded. "Lady Norwalk has built a fortune investing in new technology she believes will be profitable," his grandmother explained. "Several years ago, she discovered younger sons of peers who were curious about the potential for these inventions. They did not have the funds to invest; however, they did have the energy and drive to make the new technology successful."

"And they had the idle time," Ann said.

"Lady Norwalk trains them in evaluating new inventions for her, for which she pays them. If the discovery is profitable, they get a share of the profits that she encourages them to invest back into the technology. She also pairs these young men into trades that could use their intelligence, drive, and connections," the Duchess continued.

"Breaking the barriers between the classes," Gwinnie said, "which I heartily approve."

Lakehurst grinned at his twin. "Do you even know what a class is?" he teased.

She considered that. "Not really," she said, her lips compressing into a tight line as she shook her head.

Mr. Martin laughed.

The Duchess took a sip of her brandy. "Since she rarely comes to London, she has made the ground floor of her London townhouse into a club where these young men can meet, dine, and exchange information."

"I have found the club to be a fount of intelligence for how our economy really runs, and who are the true power brokers." Mr. Martin said.

"And it is not the aristocracy," the Duke of Ellinbourne concluded.

Mr. Martin smiled slightly.

CHAPTER 8

LONDON MAYHEM

A light tapping on her bedroom door roused Cassandra from sleep. She stretched one arm above her head as she looked about her. She realized she'd not closed the bed curtains the night before. In the faint morning light coming from around the edges of the bedroom drapes, she saw the bedroom door opened silently.

"Excuse me, my lady," Agnes whispered. "Are you awake?"

"Yes, come in." Cassandra pushed herself to a sitting position. "What time is it?" she asked, yawning.

"Just going on six, m'lady. This come fer ya. Lad said it were important." She held out a folded letter in her hand as she crossed to the canopied bed.

Cassandra threw her covers off and slid out of her bed, grabbing her wrapper draped over the end of the bed. She quickly slipped on the pale green slubbed fabric garment over her white cotton and lace night rail. She took the letter from Agnes.

"I'll get you a light," Agnes said, turning to a table at the side of the bed for a tinderbox. She got a flame going and lit a candle, then walked around the bed to open the drapes to let in a little more light.

"Thank you, Agnes," Cassandra said absently as she broke the seal on the letter and opened it.

Satan's Bride,
It does not matter where you are or who you are with.
My lord and master will complete his mark and claim you.
Nothing and no one can protect you.
Satan hungers for you.

CASSANDRA GASPED. Her right hand touched the scar on her left shoulder, the beginning of the devil's sigil that would call him forth, she'd been told.

"Is everythin' all right, my lady?" Agnes asked.

Cassandra crushed the letter in her hand. "Someone is trying frighten me."

"Frighten ya, my lady?" Agnes repeated.

"Yes... Frighten me and I refuse to be frightened. I have friends, now."

Friends.

The word had come unbidden into her thoughts and her heart felt lighter for it. The image of Viscount Lakehurst surfaced with his large, comforting size. He would protect her, she was certain.

"Fetch me my aubergine day dress, please. I'd like a tray in my room, and tell Dulcie I'd like Alex and her to be ready to go on an outing in an hour—No, two hours. I'd like you to accompany us as well. Can you do that?" she asked decisively.

"Yes, m'lady," Agnes said, dipping a curtsy.

Cassandra sat down at her vanity. She would *not* be frightened, she reiterated. She would discover what was going on. She smoothed out the wrinkles she'd made in the letter as Agnes scurried about the room getting her clothes and putting the room to rights, and read the note again.

"*Why now?*" Cassandra asked herself as Agnes left the room. "*Eighteen months of silence. Why now?*" She repeated to herself.

She raised her head, her gaze unfocused, her mind confused.

Slowly she perceived she was looking in the mirror and for the first time since that awful night, she saw herself. Really saw herself.

There were hollows in her cheeks she hadn't remembered and circles beneath her eyes. Her gaze continued down her face to her slim neck with a hollow at the base that extended into hollows above her collarbones. She'd lost weight. She'd known that, could tell by the fit of her clothing; however, she hadn't realized how much she'd lost.

She moved her hand from the scar to skim the hollows on her shoulders until resting at the base of her neck. Her pale skin looked almost translucent. She moved her hand up over her cheek and across her lips. Her eyes had a haunted look.

"*What have I been doing?*" she asked her mirrored image, her voice a whisper in her thoughts.

"*Nothing*" echoed down corridors of her mind. Then the word "*existing*'" came forward. "*Merely existing*". She inhaled deeply.

"This will not do," she said aloud. She placed her palms down on the vanity table and pushed herself up. In the mirror she saw her body was too thin. It was no wonder the Tidemarks continued to think her ill. While she might have cast aside the emotional fog from Richard's death, she hadn't woken to life yet. She turned to look out the window at the perennially gray London sky. London had been a dismal place all year. Colder and rainier than normal. She'd allowed the weather to echo her feelings. Her son deserved better.

She didn't know how she felt about being separated from Alex for a few weeks as he went to Versely Park and she to Baydon. She might have protested if Vanessa hadn't protested first, but she did, and that was enough to keep her quiet. She wouldn't want to agree with Vanessa on anything regarding Alex. And he'd spent too much time in the nursery since they'd come to London. A daily hour walk in the park was not enough exercise for a young child.

What did the Tidemarks know of children? Nothing. But she did. And she should have known better. She'd been living too long in her nightmares.

"Enough," she said to her image.

~

"LAKEHURST! LAKEHURST! WAKE UP!"

His sister thrust his bed curtains open.

Lakehurst groaned and rolled over. "Go away."

"You need to wake up."

"No, I don't. What time is it, anyway?"

"Just past seven."

"I definitely don't," he said, pulling the covers over his head.

The covers jerked down. "Yes, you do."

Lakehurst made a grab for his covers.

"It is about Lady Darkford," Gwinnie said.

"What?" he said. He halted his angry cover recovery and opened his eyes to look at his sister. She was still in her nightclothes, a dark green wool shawl thrown around her shoulders. He struggled to sit up.

He saw Gwinnie's maid, Rose, standing by his open bedroom door, worrying her hands together. That was unusual for Gwinnie's maid. He ran a hand down his face, his mind still in a fog. He'd been up until early in the morning writing.—Or trying to. Lady Darkford had been much in his thoughts.

"All right. I'm awake. What is this about Lady Darkford that has you bursting into my room?"

"Something has happened."

He swung his legs over the side of the bed. "Hand me my banyan," he said, waving toward a chair behind Gwinnie.

She turned around to grab it. "Remember the street sweeper who was approached by that man who followed Lady Darkford home from the park?" she asked hurriedly as she handed the garment to him.

"Yes," he said irritably as he shrugged on his banyan.

"That man came up to him early this morning, soon after he'd come to her street."

"This early?"

"Probably an hour ago, now. The boys get to their favored streets early to stake their claim for the day if it is typically a profitable street for them," she explained.

"All right, all right. So this man approached the street sweeper," he said, tying the banyan shut. He pushed past her to ring for his valet.

"He gave the boy a note to take to Lady Darkford. Told him to take it around back where the servants were sure to be up and answer his knock."

"What was in the note?"

"I don't know, and neither did the boy. He said it was sealed with a wax wafer."

"You suspect something threatening for Lady Darkford?"

"Yes. We need to go see her. Who knows what that man wrote that had to be delivered so early, but it can't be good."

"Davy said as how the man insisted it be done immediately," Rose said from her position by the door.

Lakehurst looked up at her, his brow furrowing.

The door from his dressing room opened. "You rang, my lord?" said his valet.

He turned toward his man. "Yes, can you get me a pot of coffee? Strong coffee?" he asked.

"Immediately."

Lakehurst looked at his sister. "What are you doing still standing here? I'm up. I need to get dressed." He looked her over. "You should, too. We'll go to Darkford House together."

She nodded, and left his room with her maid.

Lakehurst went into his dressing room. He typically rose before seven so there was already fresh water in the wash basin, though it had grown cold. He removed his banyan and nightshirt and scooped up a handful to splash his face, then used a wet cloth to wipe down his neck, chest, and arms. He lathered his face and leaned close to the mirror to shave. He preferred to shave himself. Something about another man with a blade near his throat had always disturbed him, even if the man doing the shaving had been a longtime retainer.

Satisfied with his results, he wiped the lather from his face and picked up a comb. He ran the comb through his hair. In the mirror, he saw a big, tall man with large hands. Across his broad chest spread a sprinkling of red hair darker than the hair on his head. He finished combing his hair, set the comb down, then stared at the palms of his hands.

In his youth at boarding school, he grew big and tall much sooner than his schoolmates. By the time he was twelve, they called him *Farmer Nowlton* due to his large size and large hands. At that age, he was also clumsy and became the butt of jokes. He kept much to himself preferring to read rather than learning any of the gentlemanly sports such as boxing or fencing since no one wanted to spar with him due to his size and long reach.

University had been somewhat better, as many had at least grown to his height if not to his build. But by then, he'd formed his habit of reading and began writing to while away his time. He wrote stories that made him smile, if no one else. He had a few friends, other men who were not of the Corinthian set, but they were now all married, tending to their new families. They'd tried to see him married as well, but none of their introductions worked. As his friend Jasper Hendrick admitted to him, his wife said women feared a man of his size.

Lakehurst had taken to talking quietly and moving slower so as not to startle women when he came upon them. He had not realized until he overheard Mary Sudbury and her friends that the women feared his size in more ways than his height. That had been an embarrassing revelation. He'd felt the heat rise in his face, so he bid a hasty goodbye to his host and hostess and fled the ball. He'd walked aimlessly that night, consumed by what he'd heard. He'd had a mistress or two since he'd been on the town, and they never complained, but a virgin? Would he hurt them too badly?

Perhaps Gwinnie was correct. He should set his sights on a widow.

A widow like Lady Darkford.

The thought of her roused him. He inhaled deeply, at first surprised, and then not. He liked the woman and felt drawn to protect her.

—If she'd let him.

His valet returned with his much-needed coffee.

"Mama, you're walking too fast!" complained Alex.

Cassandra closed her eyes briefly as she slowed her pace. She looked down at Alex. "I'm sorry, my darling." She smiled down apologetically at her son, chagrined at the pace she'd set. He was huffing a little. "I'll slow down. We are almost there," she said.

She looked back at Agnes and Dulcie. Both women were breathing heavily. Her eyes widened. Half-way down the block was the same man who followed them from the park. Fear flooded her.

"We must hurry!" she told the women. She swooped down to pick up Alex and increased her pace again, nearly running. Being so early in the day, the streets were light of all traffic, making it easy to go faster—and easier to be followed.

She turned the corner. Ahead lay Malmsby House, a white stone mansion that shone in the morning sunlight, their goal, their sanctuary.

At the top step, she put Alex down and rang the bell, then pounded on the door. She almost fell into the house when the door suddenly opened. Coming down the grand staircase was Lady Guinevere, dressed to go outside. And then, there in the entrance hall stood her protection. She ran toward him.

Lakehurst scarcely had time to register who was at the door before Lady Darkford ran to him. He reflexively closed his arms around her as she landed against his chest. She smelled of lilies.

"That man. He followed us," she gasped out.

Lakehurst immediately set her aside and ran past the two maids entering and down the steps. He ran down the block toward the way Lady Darkford must have come. He turned the corner. In the distance, he spied the man they had seen in Hyde Park, but he was too far away to catch. He walked back to the house. Inside, Gwinnie had her arm around Lady Darkford who had dissolved into tears.

"Mama, Mama, don't cry," said Alex, pulling at his mother's skirts. The nursemaid ran forward to pick up the child.

"Sh-sh, it's all right, my little lord," she cooed at him. "Your Mama will be fine in a moment," she said.

Rose pulled a small vial of camphor from her reticule. "This should help, my lady," she said, waving it under her nose.

Gwinnie jerked her head away. "Oh, that is strong!" she declared.

Cassandra waved her hand toward Rose. "That's enough, thank you. I am all right now. Just give me a moment."

Lakehurst frowned. Every servant on the ground floor seemed to have gathered in the hall. He picked up Alex. "Come, let's go into the Lady Margaret parlor," he said.

One of the footmen leaped forward to get ahead of him to throw open the door.

Lakehurst set Alex down near the terrace doors while Gwinnie steered Lady Darkford to the couch and sat down with her. He walked over to them.

"Cat! Cat!" Alex excitedly called out. Alex tried to open the terrace door, but he couldn't get it open.

Lakehurst looked out onto the terrace. Oscar lay out on the warm terrace stones sunning himself.

"Can I see the cat?" Alex asked.

"Is the cat friendly," the nursemaid asked. "It won't bite or scratch him, will it?"

"No. Oscar is very friendly," Lakehurst said.

"Oscar, his name is Oscar?" Alex repeated.

"Yes. I'll let you out with him if you promise not to chase him and your nursemaid promises to go with you."

"I'll go with him," Dulcie said.

Lakehurst helped to get the door open to let them out. He watched Alex for a moment. The boy crouched down next to the cat and tentatively held his hand out. Oscar lifted his head and bunted his hand. Lakehurst smiled. They'd be all right. He turned back toward Lady Darkford.

He sat down in the chair at angled to the couch. "We understand you got a letter today," he said, gently.

She looked at him, her expression eloquent of confusion. "How did you know?"

"Rose requested the street sweeper to come tell her if anything happened. After he delivered the letter to you, he came here."

She looked at Rose and slightly smiled. "I did see you passing him a coin the other day."

"Yes, my lady," Rose said. "We wanted him to tell us about that man. He came here straight here this morning from the Darkford townhouse."

"May we see the note?" Lakehurst asked.

She nodded and pulled her reticule onto her lap, then pulled out the crumbled note and handed it to him.

"Rose," Gwinnie said. "Please take Lady Darkford's maid to the servant's hall and see that she gets refreshments, and that refreshments are offered to the nursemaid and the young Marquess as well."

"Yes, my lady," Rose said, dipping a curtsy.

"Good suggestion," Lakehurst quietly told his sister as he passed her the letter to read.

"The cheek! The arrogance!" Gwinnie declared. "This—this *servant of Satan*, whoever he is, doesn't know who he is dealing with!"

A small laugh escaped Lady Darkford at Gwinnie's pronouncement. Lakehurst wanted to hug his sister right then for breaking through the miasma of fear that must consume the marchioness.

"What does he mean by *complete his mark*?" Gwinnie asked.

Lakehurst saw Lady Darkford bite her lower lip. It was no doubt hard for her to speak of it. "You remember in my novel where my heroine would be branded with the Devil's mark?"

"Yes."

"In Lady Darkford's experience, they tried to carve the mark on her with a knife, is that not right, Lady Darkford? That is what your brother told me."

She raised a hand to her shoulder and nodded.

Gwinnie compressed her lips as she frowned. Then she brightened again. "I know, you should get one of those ink things that some of the young bucks are sporting. What are they called?"

"Tattoos," Lakehurst supplied.

"Yes, tattoos, thank you. Mayhap a butterfly or a flower right where they would think to put that horrid mark," Gwinnie said.

Lakehurst nodded slowly. Trust his sister to get to the heart of the matter. Lady Darkford did not need to be condemned always to see that scar and what it represented. "Cast evil aside, turn it into one of God's beautiful creations," he mused.

"Yes."

Lady Darkford looked at Gwinnie with wide eyes. Lakehurst knew that even if she never got a tattoo, the idea that she *could* do something if the scars continued to haunt her had to be reassuring.

"Oh, I don't think I could, could I?" Lady Darkford asked.

Gwinnie grinned. "If you do, I'll get one, too," she brightly offered.

Lakehurst closed his eyes and shook his head.

The double parlor doors burst open.

"And why do I need to learn from a housemaid that Lady Darkford is here?" his grandmother said from the doorway. "Oh? What is the matter?" she asked as she quickly crossed the room.

A footman pulled the doors closed after her.

"Lady Darkford has received a threat," Gwinnie said.

"A threat?"

Gwinnie passed the letter to her grandmother.

His grandmother snorted after reading the letter and dropped it on a side table. "Rubbish," she said. She sat down on the other side of Lady Darkford. "No originality, no plans, just threats. Trite. So trite, unimaginative," she said as she took Lady Darkford's hands in hers. "Do not let it worry you for a moment."

"But—"

His grandmother shook her head. "There is no 'but.' You have friends and allies. Know this," she emphasized, squeezing Lady Darkford's hands between hers. "Mr. Martin said you would be safer in the country, that it will be easier to protect you there.

London is too full of rascals who will commit crimes for pennies. We are sending members of our staff with you."

His grandmother looked up at him. "Lakehurst, we need you, Gwinnie, and Lady Darkford to leave as soon as it might be arranged. Today, if possible, with as little fuss as possible."

"I have no luggage," protested Lady Darkford.

"We will send the maids back to the Darkford townhouse to pack. I'll send a note to the Tidemarks advising them you will be staying with us until it is time to leave. Which will be the truth, I just won't tell them when that time will be."

Lady Darkford laughed a little, her eyes glistening. "Then if we are all to travel together, I insist you call me Cassie, as my family does."

"Yes!" enthused Gwinnie.

"Capital idea!" said the Duchess. "You will be much more comfortable traveling together without the weight of a formal title on your tongue all the time. And you will be family when Ann and Ellinbourne wed."

Lakehurst smiled and nodded. "I suggest we send the traveling chaise ahead today; if anyone asks, the stable hands can say it went out for minor repairs before the journey."

"And it will be interesting to see if anyone does ask," said the Duchess drily.

"Indeed. The ladies can go for a drive in Gwinnie's curricle and I will go for a ride separately. We will meet at the Piebald Stallion coaching inn and they can transfer to the chaise there."

"Clever," the Duchess said, nodding.

"It's like something out of one of his novels!" Gwinnie suggested, bouncing with excitement.

"I don't know! This is all happening so fast!" Cassandra protested.

"This will be fun!" enthused the Duchess. "You will see. I do miss Aidan though, he is so good at arranging things quickly."

"We depended on him for far too long," Lakehurst reminded her.

"Yes, I think we were missing out," the Duchess said. She smiled brightly. "I do so love a good prank, and my dear Lady Darkford, we will be pranking your villains in a most satisfying way."

Lakehurst and Gwinnie laughed at their grandmother's statement.

"When the maids have packed the luggage at the Darkford townhouse, we will have a coach collect them and meet you at the Piebald Stallion."

"What about Dulcie and Alex's things?"

"We will send the footman, Stephen, with the maids. I know he can drive a carriage. He will bring the curricle back with the nursemaid, her bags, and Alex's luggage."

"He might actually enjoy the opportunity," Lakehurst observed. He'd seen the footman giving the nursemaid a few extra glances when they arrived.

"Lady Darkford and I will go talk to the maids discretely, for they will need to pack as well."

"I'll speak to those in the stable. There are a couple of men there I know we can trust."

The Duchess laughed. "Those that always helped me with my pranks in the past," she said ruefully. "I shall meet with the butler and the housekeeper. They will know how to handle the rest of the staff."

The Duchess clapped her hands together, pleased with the planning. She turned to Lady Darkford. "You are in excellent hands with the Nowlton family. Never you worry.—Now, everyone, let's go to our assigned tasks," the Duchess said, rising to her feet. "This is the most fun I've had since the house party at Versely Park."

"Fun!" protested Lakehurst. "You had a murder there!"

She waved her hand dismissively as she walked toward the door. "That was not as interesting as getting Ann and Ellinbourne together. That was a coup," she declared as she left the parlor.

Lakehurst had to agree.

CHAPTER 9

BAYDON CASTLE

Apprehension wound insidious thin ghostly fingers around Cassie as the carriage began the climb that would take them up to Baydon Castle. They'd stopped briefly in Baydonton, the village in the valley below the castle, to change horses. The road up to the castle was steep, rutted, and rock-strewn. Not a road for tired horseflesh.

Late afternoon shadows lay deep across their way, gifts from the steep cliff faces that bordered the road. The road clearly suffered from the eighteen months of neglect. Twice the coachman stopped the carriage to allow outriders to remove limestone boulders from their path that had tumbled down from the cliffs.

Inside the carriage, she, Gwinnie, and their maids sat quietly, each now lost in their own thoughts whilst for much of the journey, they'd talked easily amongst each other, servants and mistresses. And she delighted in being addressed as Cassie by Gwinnie and Lakehurst. She found comfort in her childhood name, and a genuine sense of friendship she hadn't realized she craved.

Her late husband had not liked her nickname, insisting on addressing her as Cassandra, and so she had been for over six years. She found she liked being Cassie again.

The only sound from inside the carriage came from the endless click-clicking of Rose's knitting needles knitting mufflers and shawls for the occupants of Mrs. Southerlands' Charity House.

Cassie had talked the most, telling them about Baydon Castle. None of the others had ever been there as Agnes, her maid, had only come into her service in the past year.

Cassie did not want to be in the carriage. Could she now, so close, tap on the carriage roof and request the coachman to stop and let her out? The closer they got, the heavier the emotional weight of the past became. It was Cassandra who'd lived at Baydon Castle, not Cassie, who she relished being again.

She had not wanted to return to Baydon Castle. She'd be happiest if she never saw it again, yet here she was.

The coach rocked into and out of a deep rut. She grabbed the leather strap by her head and swayed with the motion. She and Gwinnie slid into each other, then apart again, each murmuring apologies.

No, no going back. No stopping this journey with its attendant nightmarish memories.

Up the next small rise and a small turn to the right, one would be able to see Baydon. She clenched her gloved hands into fists.

There.

A rambling castle of gray limestone, almost black against a gray afternoon sky. She shivered. The wind swept across the nearly bare plateau; trees leaned before the steady wind. The horses whinnied, and the carriage rocked. She smelled the wildflower grasses on the wind. She'd forgotten how she'd loved them.

Only half a mile more.

Gwinnie reached out to lay her hand on her arm. Cassie turned her head and weakly smiled at her in thanks for her comforting touch. Gwinnie sensed what emotions roiled within her; Cassie was certain of that. Gwinnie, for all her careless manners, possessed a kind, empathetic heart.

When the carriage rolled to a stop before the castle's great oak and iron door, Cassie felt she was an actor in a theater production for which the curtain rose. She laughed at herself for that strange and unusual feeling.

As she descended from the carriage, Mr. and Mrs. Gallagher came out of the castle to greet them like they owned the place. She'd never felt entirely comfortable with the couple; however, at least they were familiar faces. Though well into their fourth decade, they did not bear the careworn appearance typically seen among staff of their age. Mrs. Gallagher was a tall, spare woman with a handsome, long, angular face. Her luxurious bounty of dark brown hair only showed streaks of gray at her temples in a striking manner. Mr. Gallagher's hair had gone grayer in the eighteen months since she'd last seen him. He wore it a trifle longer and swept back off his face. He now wore a neat beard and mustache, both nearly white. They radiated a manner of superiority quite above their positions.

When Richard had been alive, they always second-guessed her requests to them by going to him for verification before they did as she asked. That habit irritated Cassie, even if she somewhat understood it, as it was an old habit to take direction from the marquess.

Worse, when Richard had been killed, they were certain she had somehow been responsible, even if they could not conceive how that might be. As a result, they'd been slow to follow any direction she gave.

It appeared nothing had changed in eighteen months. They stood on the doorstep, frowning at her.

"The castle's not ready fer guests. We had no word yous were coming. What do ya expect us to do?"

The housekeeper's rough country speech was at odds with the gentry image she displayed. Cassie had forgotten that dichotomy.

"Did you not receive my note this morning?" Cassie asked.

"Well, aye. 'Afore noon, but what did ya expect us to do with that news?" she demanded, arms akimbo.

"Ready the castle for our arrival?"

"Ain't no staff. Mr. Tidemark said as to turn 'em off. Just the two of us for this big property."

"Isn't Carlyle still here?" Cassie persisted.

"In the stable. Useless old man. Don't ken why Mr. Tidemark said not ta turn him out, too. Somethin' about the marquess's will." She snorted. "And I'm expected ta feed him, too. I ain't no cook, ya know. I cain't be cookin' fer ya. I'm the housekeeper. Cooking's fer cooks."

Cassie felt any confidence she'd gathered about her slipping away. All she had was bravado, and she'd never been good with that.

"I can cook," said Gwinnie from beside her.

Mrs. Gallagher sneered as she looked up at Gwinnie. "And who might yous be?" she snarled. "Sum farmer's chit dressed all fancy like ya be, I'm judgin'."

Cassie gasped at the insult.

"Milly!" protested Mr. Gallagher.

Gwinnie howled with laughter, nearly doubling

over. Cassie looked at her in surprise but felt some of the helpless tension forming in her slip away. Her laughter brought Viscount Lakehurst from the other side of the carriage where he'd been conferring with their coachman, John Norton.

Mr. Gallagher's jaw dropped, and he instinctively stepped backward at seeing Viscount Lakehurst, and dragged his wife with him.

"What's going on? What's the joke?" Lakehurst demanded. "And why are you still standing out here in the cold wind?"

"She called me a fancy dressed farmer's daughter," Gwinnie said between laughs, gasping for air to get the words out.

Cassie found herself fighting against a laugh, too. Behind her, she heard the maids giggling.

Lakehurst shrugged out a short, acknowledging laugh. "I've been called a farmer a time or two," he said. He looked at Mr. Gallagher, his eyes narrowing. "You," he said, his voice dropping into displeasure. "You will escort Lady Darkford and my sister, *Lady* Guinevere Nowlton, into the castle immediately and see to their every comfort. I am going to the stable to check on the accommodations for the horses. When I return, I expect to see the ladies—and their maids— well attended to."

"Yes, sir," Mr. Gallagher said, bowing.

"My lord," corrected Cassie.

She saw Lakehurst turn to her and wink. She smiled back at him.

"My lord," ground out Mr. Gallagher, bowing again and pulling at his wife's arm to curtsy. The woman curtsied with ill grace.

"This way, my ladies," Mr. Gallagher said to Cassie and Gwinnie, gesturing to the door. He hurried to open it before them. "If you will hand me your wraps, there is a fire in the parlor where you may rest. Milly will bring you tea, then we'll see to your bed chambers," he said, bowing again.

"And bring brandy, as well," Cassie instructed. "We could all use the restorative."

She saw the Gallaghers exchange glances and wondered if the wine cellar had experienced decimation in the last eighteen months. A question for another day.

"Yes, my lady, we will," assured Mr. Gallagher.

She nodded and led Gwinnie, Rose, and Agnes to the parlor.

"If we might know where the linens are kept, Agnes and I can see to your bed chambers," Rose said.

"Thank you for the offer, Rose. But you and Agnes need to have a few moments of rest—and a sip of brandy—as well as Lady Guinevere and I.—Plus, I want the Gallaghers to scurry a bit."

Devoid of holland covers that would typically be placed on furniture in unused rooms, most of the comfortable pieces of furniture were drawn up near the fireplace where a nice fire did blaze.

"I guess we can see where your caretakers spend most of their time," Gwinnie drily observed.

"Acting as lord and lady of the castle," Rose sniffed disapprovingly.

"Yes, I'm afraid so," said Cassie. She sat down at one end of the long sofa. Gwinnie sat on the other end.

Agnes found a tinderbox on the fireplace mantle and lit candles for more light.

"Thank you, Agnes. Now you rest, too."

"Oh, miss, if ya don't mind, I should like to stand and walk a bit. Been sittin' too long."

"I understand. Of course." Cassie considered

walking a good idea. "After our tea and restorative, I shall take everyone on a small tour of the castle—the first of several tours, most likely. The castle is a warren. Agnes, do not think to wander about yet."

"No, miss. I won't."

Mr. Gallagher followed Lord Lakehurst into the room and brought a bottle of brandy.

"Mrs. Gallagher will be along directly with your tea, my lady," he said as he set the bottle on a table at her elbow.

"Agnes, in that cupboard to the right of you are the brandy glasses. Can you bring enough for all here?"

"There are only four here," she said, pulling the glasses out of the cupboard and setting them on its top.

Cassie frowned. "There should be eight in the cupboard. Mr. Gallagher, where are the rest of the brandy glasses?"

"Oh, ah, most likely in the butler's pantry. I'll fetch them directly," he said hurriedly.

Lakehurst laughed as he sat down in a chair by the fireplace.

"Yes, you may laugh. The thought already occurred to me that they have made free with the castle to their benefit," Cassie said wryly.

He shrugged. "Understandable. Not, perhaps, what we would like; however, understandable."

"What is the state of the stable?"

"Much better than I expected. That deaf man Ellinbourne told me about has things well in hand. Seemed to understand what needed to be done and got to it quick enough. I have no worries for our livestock."

"Good. That is a relief. Carlyle is a good retainer and has been with the Tidemark family for a long time. He sat Richard on his first horse. Richard made sure to include him in his will to ensure his future."

Mrs. Gallagher brought in the missing brandy glasses with the tea cart.

"Thank you, Mrs. Gallagher," Cassie said stiffly, not comfortable with the woman.

"We brought food provisions from the village," Lakehurst said. "I set the basket inside the front door. There is still luggage to unload from the carriage; but that can wait until all have had something to eat and drink."

"Very good, my lord," said a much more subdued Mrs. Gallagher. "I'll see to the rooms now," she softly told Cassie.

Cassie nodded. "The rose bedroom for Lady Guinevere, I think, and the brown and burgundy room for Lord Lakehurst. There will be more servants coming in the next two days and then we can expect seven additional guests to join us, including Mr. and Mrs. Tidemark."

"Mr. and Mrs. Tidemark?" the housekeeper repeated, her eyes wide.

Cassie thought she looked a little flustered.

"Yes, along with Richard's cousin, Mr. Stillworth and others."

"Mr. Tidemark ain't been here since he married," she said.

"I know. However, as guardian of my son's interests, I have told him he needs to take a more active role in managing the estate. We probably won't see much of him while he is here, as I expect he will need to examine the estate books."

"Yes, ma'am," she responded hurriedly. "I'd best get to the rooms now."

"Yes. But don't forget to take the foodstuffs to the kitchen first."

"Right away." She curtsied again and left, nearly running from the room.

"That was rather a change of manners," Gwinnie observed.

"A guilty change of manners," said Lakehurst.

Cassie nodded.

~

LAKEHURST PROWLED behind the ladies as Cassie took them on a brief tour of the castle.

Cassie.

He enjoyed thinking of her as Cassie. It came naturally, so naturally it easily supplanted her Lady Darkford title in his mind. And he liked the easy camaraderie they'd developed during their journey. Of course, how could they not have all been at ease with Gwinnie around! His sister made any day sunny.

Overall, the castle rooms were spare in adornment, as one might see on an estate where money remained tight. In London, they believed the Tidemarks were wealthy; the source of their wealth the quarries in the Mendip Hills. He would have to ask Cassie. The library was the only room they'd entered that had more in the way of statues and paintings. And in there, satyrs were the subject matter. The bed chambers had elegant, expensive bed hangings, drapes, and rugs, but the walls were simply painted and devoid of paintings. An interesting contrast.

They ended their tour in an empty, cold kitchen. Lakehurst had never known a kitchen to be cold. They were the warmest room in a building. The massive fireplace with its ovens and spit were cold and swept.

Only a small coal stove to the side radiated heat, residual from heating the tea kettle, he presumed, and now the fire had been allowed to die. He and Gwinnie exchanged glances, each frowning.

"This kitchen used to be one of my favorite places to visit," Cassie said as she looked around. "It was always lively. The cook was a jovial man who made the most delicious cakes. Not a crumb ever grew stale or saw the bins," she said with a smile. "Unlike some of the others, I'm sure he found a new position. I do worry for some of the others," she said with a frown. "Well, that is for another day's concern," she said firmly. "Now we all need food."

"Where would Mrs. Gallagher have put the provisions we brought?" Gwinnie asked. "We should get them out while Mrs. Gallagher prepares the rooms."

"Yes, no sense in bothering her with our meal, as she so plainly stated she is not a cook," Cassie said. "They should be over here in the pantry." She pulled the door open, holding a lantern high to see inside.

"Oh, no!" she cried out in dismay. Lakehurst immediately came up behind her.

Thick dust and spider webs covered the crocks and glass jars stored on the long shelves along the side and back of the pantry. Contents of grain sacks stacked on the shelves and on the floor spilled out from rat gnawed holes. Black rat and bug droppings speckled what remained of the sacks' contents. The smell of damp, mold, and feces wafted outward.

Gwinnie looked inside. "No, I don't think she stored them in here," she said drily.

"One should hope not," stated Rose, coming up beside her.

Cassie saw movement in a corner. She swiftly

closed the door. "I wonder what happened to the cats?"

She looked around. "So, if food is not stored in a food pantry, where would it be?" She looked around the large kitchen.

"A mystery, and the hunt is on!" declared Gwinnie with a twirl and grin, causing them all to laugh.

She started pulling open cupboard doors and opening drawers. Rose found the hall to the servants' wing. Agnes went to the butler's pantry. Cassie joined Gwinnie in searching the kitchen. Lakehurst opened a door that revealed stairs going down. He grabbed a lantern and ventured that way.

"*Found it, my lady!*" came Agnes's voice from a distance.

Lakehurst came back up the stairs carrying a bottle of wine.

Rose came back into the kitchen.

When Agnes returned through the butler's pantry into the kitchen she said, "The basket's on the dining room table."

"Good," Cassie sighed in relief.

Lakehurst held out the wine bottle he'd found. "Your wine cellar is not in the same sad neglected state as your food pantry; however, the contents appear lighter than I assume they would be given the late Marquess's entertainment habits," he said.

Cassie frowned, then shrugged. "I was afraid of that," she admitted. She turned toward Agnes. "Are the plates and cutlery clean in the butler's pantry?"

Agnes nodded and said she would set the table for them.

"For all of us," Cassie said. "You and Rose are to eat with us. Afterward, you may take food to the men in the stable."

Lakehurst followed the women into the dining room. He noted how Cassie appeared more confident now. Was it from being back in her old home? Or the taking charge of affairs? Regardless of the cause, she no longer wore the mantle of a shy, retiring widow. He was happy for that; however, he was dismayed at the state of the castle. He didn't understand how it could have come to be so neglected while the stable was cared for. It didn't make any sense to him.

Mr. and Mrs. Gallagher baffled him as well. They appeared to be in their mid-forties. They were nicely dressed. He'd go so far as to say they dressed above the positions they held. If they were rightly above the position—which he doubted due to their coarse speech—why were they here?

~

AFTER THEIR MEAL, Lakehurst told the ladies he would take the food out to the men in the stable. He wanted to talk to them, and also see if he could discover how to communicate with the deaf man. He'd already learned the man could talk, though his words were sometimes indistinct; but he could neither hear, nor read or write.

Grabbing another bottle of wine, he headed out to the stable as the twilight horizon streaked dark red against the deep blue of the coming night. The wind had slowed, though it still carried a bite. Tomorrow he'd send to the village for a couple of hogsheads of ale. Tonight he'd share the castle's wine. He took the food and wine into the tack room where there were long benches used for cleaning and maintaining the leather reins, harnesses, bridles, and saddles. The amount of tack in the room, all polished and supple, ready for use, surprised him. The smell of good leather pervaded the room.

He called the men to the tack room, and they sat and sipped some wine as they ate the food he'd brought. He particularly watched the old man who couldn't hear. Ellinbourne said his name was 'Carlyle.'

"How are you finding things here?" he asked John Norton, the coachman, and Henry, the young groomsman he'd brought from London to ride ahead to secure lodgings and food for them for each stop. He'd been the man sent to deliver the message to the Gallaghers that they were coming.

"Good, my lord," said Norton. "Sleepin' quarters are fine 'cept there's no coal for the little stoves, nor much in the way of wood to burn neither. We'll likely be sleepin' 'neath horse blankets this night with that nip in the air."

"Wouldn't know it's late June by the weather all over England this year," Lakehurst said.

"Aye, and that's a fact," nodded the coachman.

"Tomorrow, I'll see if I can find some coal."

"Carlyle here says there's plenty at the castle," waving his hand at the old stable hand, "but the caretakers don't let him have any."

Lakehurst looked over at the man. "You'll get coal," he said as he looked at him and noticed how threadbare his clothes were. His vest looked like it had been hand-stitched from an old horse blanket.

"Thank you, my lord," the man responded.

Lakehurst frowned. "I thought you can't hear."

"Cain't." He tapped his lips. "I ken read lips purty well if'n the person be lookin' at me and they don't talk too fast."

"Excellent! We'll talk more tomorrow. Can you show us where the coal is kept?"

"Aye, but the Gallaghers, theys keep the door locked."

"Gather some buckets," he told the men, "and go with Carlyle to where the coal is kept. I'll get the key from Mr. Gallagher."

"Thank you, my lord, thank you," the old man said, bowing profusely.

Lakehurst found Mr. Gallagher talking with Cassie in the front hall. "The key to the coal cellar, please," he said, his hand out.

"Coal cellar? Why do you need the key to that? I just brought coal up to all the bedchambers."

"It is not for you to question me," Lakehurst said, staring down at Mr. Gallagher.

The man took a slight step backward.

"The key!" Lakehurst demanded.

"Yes, Mr. Gallagher, give Lord Lakehurst the key," Cassie said.

Gallagher scowled at her, then struggled to remove the single key from his chain.

"Just give me the lot," Lakehurst said impatiently.

Reluctantly, Gallagher handed them to Lakehurst.

Lakehurst tossed the keys up in the air, caught them, then turned to go.

Gallagher turned to follow him.

Lakehurst glared at him. "I don't need you right now. Continue your discussion with Lady Darkford. It sounded like she had other tasks for you this evening."

"But—" Mr. Gallagher started to protest.

Lakehurst ignored him and went out, decisively closing the door behind him.

CHAPTER 10

THE GALLAGHERS

"Mr. Gallagher, is Mr. Browning still the estate agent?" Cassie asked, pulling Mr. Gallagher's attention away from the front door Lakehurst closed behind him.

"Yes, and no, my lady."

"Yes, and no is hardly an answer, Mr. Gallagher. Explain please," she said. "Come, let's sit in the study."

"No!"

Cassie frowned at him. "What do you mean, no?"

"It's just that is such an uncomfortable room and hasn't been warmed in eighteen months. It would not be comfortable, my lady."

"I assume you would say the same about the library?" she asked, suspicious.

"Yes, my lady."

Her lips pursed as she considered his manner. "Please see that those faults are rectified throughout the castle. We will have a houseful of people in a couple of days, and the condition of the house is not conducive to guests." She walked toward the parlor, Mr. Gallagher following her.

"A houseful?" he asked.

"Yes, I am expecting my brother, his fiancée Ann Hallowell and her stepmother, Mrs. Hallowell, Mr. Stillworth, who you well know, Mr. and Mrs. Tidemark, and Mrs. Tidemark's brother, Harrison Farrow. Far fewer people than Richard entertained; however, it is more than this castle is currently ready to entertain. Am I not right, Mr. Gallagher?"

"You said Mr. and Mrs. Tidemark are coming?"

"Yes."

"But they haven't been here since they married," he protested.

She tilted her head to the side as she regarded him. "I am aware of that," she said slowly. "As I told your wife, he needs to take a greater interest in the estate for my son's benefit. Mr. Tidemark's father is long dead, and any dissatisfaction he felt with Mr. Tidemark's choice of bride is moot, would you not say?"

"Yes, yes. Of a certainty, my lady," he hastily agreed, his face taking on a pinched expression.

"Good. Then we understand each other. If Lord Lakehurst or Lady Guinevere request you to do something, you can consider it a request from me. Is that understood?"

"Yes, my lady."

"Good, you may go now."

"Excuse me, my lady; may I be so bold as to say you are different than you were eighteen months ago."

"Eighteen months ago, I had a living husband," she responded. She stared at him until he grew fidgety and left.

She took a deep inhale of breath when the parlor door closed behind him.

"You know you will have to get rid of him and that

wife of his," Gwinnie's voice said from the other side of the couch.

Cassie started. "Oh, I didn't know you were here!" she said.

"You didn't see my feet hanging over the end of the couch?" Gwinnie said, peddling her feet up and down.

"No, I did not."

"First time in my life I've been invisible!" Gwinnie said as she sat up and swung her legs to the floor. She turned and leaned over the back of the couch, resting her chin on her arm.

Cassie laughed. "I dare swear, Gwinnie, that no matter your height, your personality would keep you visible."

"Am I that bad?" Gwinnie said, pouting playfully.

"No, you are that good, and I love you for it. You have done wonders for me, you know. Your wealth of confidence has spilled over to me."

"Glad it can be of use to someone," Gwinnie said, getting up and walking around the couch. "Most of the time it just gets me in trouble," she admitted.

"I haven't seen that," Cassie said. "But you are right about the Gallaghers. My conversation started in the hall with me asking if Mr. Browning remains as the estate agent. His response was *yes and no* but he evaded further discussion. He seemed quite rattled, however, with the idea of a house party."

"He did at that. I could clearly hear that in his voice."

"I have never liked them, nor they me, so I hope the thoughts scurrying about in my head are not my bias."

"You think they have been tampering with the estate invoices and receipts to better line their own pockets?"

"Yes, I do."

"So do I. That dress Mrs. Gallagher wore was silk, and housekeepers I know don't have that amount of lace trimming on their everyday gowns," Gwinnie said.

"I am tempted to ask for her chatelaine."

Gwinnie's lips quirked up to the side as she nodded. "If you do, I'd ask for his keys as well."

Cassie looked at her. "And lock them out of the library and the study, as those are the rooms he steered me away from, claiming there are too cold and uncomfortable."

Gwinnie grinned. "I was ghastly tired when I laid down on the couch for a few moments; however, now I feel startlingly refreshed."

The parlor door opened. It was Lakehurst. He jiggled Mr. Gallagher's keys in his hand.

"Do you know where Mr. Gallagher is? I need to return his keys to him."

"No, you don't," Cassie contradicted. "Gwinnie and I were just talking about how I should take charge of all the keys. There is something odd about how they ran—or didn't run—the castle property."

"I would agree on not running the castle right. They never paid that man Carlyle, nor gave him coal. From something Mr. Carlyle said as I helped get the coal, the will said Mr. Carlyle would have room and board for life, but there was nothing about being paid, so they didn't. They gave him nothing but food, as they were obligated for that."

"Unfortunately, I don't believe I can turn them off without Edmund agreeing," Cassie said.

"I don't think you will have trouble getting Mr. Tidemark to agree," he said drily.

"I'd best find Mrs. Gallagher and see if I can wrest her chatelaine."

"I'll go with you and help wrest it from her if she doesn't give it up willingly," Gwinnie said with gleeful anticipation.

Cassie laughed. "I don't think any physical wrestling will be necessary; however, I would appreciate the opportunity to continue to soak in any of your confidence that continues to slop over your filled cup."

Gwinnie laughed.

"If you don't mind, Cassie, I will see if I can find paper and pencil in the study. I'd like to start a list of what I think we must purchase in the village tomorrow," Lakehurst said.

"That would be most welcome. And be sure to lock that room and the library behind you, as those two rooms were the ones Mr. Gallagher specifically steered me away from."

Lakehurst's brows rose. "I will do so," he promised.

~

CASSIE AND GWINNIE found Mrs. Gallagher facing off against Rose in the blue room. To Cassie, it seemed Mrs. Gallagher was attempting to tell Rose she could not use the linens she had discovered in the linen press on Lady Guinevere's bed. Agnes stood to the side, her eyes wide as she stared from one combatant to the other.

"What is your issue with Rose using these linens on Lady Guinevere's bed?" Cassie asked, waving at the folded linens Rose held.

"Them's meant for another room," she said.

"What does it matter?"

"That is what I said, my lady," Rose said. "The ones she gave me for this room were ripped in the corner and stained. Someone doesn't know their job," Rose said loftily.

Mrs. Gallagher bristled. "I knows my job, it's yous as don't know yours."

"My job is to care for Lady Guinevere, and that's what I'm doing."

"Enough!" Cassie said. "Mrs. Gallagher, do we have a shortage of linens? I'd best know that now, as we are expecting more guests soon."

"I can't—"

"We also have servants coming. Please give me your chatelaine."

"What? No!"

"I do not have one right now, so as mistress of the castle, I need yours for the nonce."

Mrs. Gallagher clapped her hand around the clip that held the chatelaine to her gown.

"Mrs. Gallagher, it is only until I can get one of my own." She held out her hand.

Mrs. Gallagher slowly unhooked the chatelaine and gave it to Cassie.

"I thank you for your service. Our maids will finish up our rooms. You are free to go for the evening. I know this has been a tumultuous day for you. What I need from you in the morning is a list of the supplies the castle will need to support a house party. I'm sure you had to support the house parties my late husband had so are accustomed to thinking in terms of parties," Cassie said sweetly.

Mrs. Gallagher left. Cassie watched after her for a moment.

"You know," Gwinnie said conversationally, "too much sugar always gives me a stomachache."

"Don't worry, I don't think the sarcasm was lost on her," Cassie said tiredly.

~

EARLY THE NEXT MORNING, Lakehurst found Cassie in the kitchen. She was crouched before the coal stove feeding it fresh coal.

"Here, let me do that for you," he said.

She turned around to look at him and laughed slightly. "I am certain, my lord, I have more experience doing this than you do. Remember, I am a clergyman's daughter. Not only did I do chores like this at the vicarage but also in the homes of the pensioners and others in need," she said, closing the cast iron door and standing up. She took the teakettle to the stone sink and pumped water into it.

Lakehurst watched her. "Cisterns?" he asked.

She nodded. "There is also a spring nearby that flows almost year-round. Very good tasting water it is, too. Tea or hot chocolate? We didn't bring any coffee with us, I'm sorry to say."

"You like coffee?" he asked.

"Sometimes. Edmund does not drink tea, so I want to get coffee for him while he's here."

"I included coffee on the list I wrote last night."

"Good. Have you seen Mr. or Mrs. Gallagher around this morning?" she asked.

His lips twisted. "I haven't; however, I have it on good authority that they are no longer here."

"No longer here? What do you mean?"

"Before first light, Mr. Gallagher had Carlyle hitch up the carriage they used to go into the village. When the groomsman Henry woke and asked what was going on, he said he was going into the village to buy provisions. But when he drove off, he drove the carriage to the far side of the castle first. Henry spied on him and said he picked up luggage and Mrs. Gallagher before driving off."

"They went out through the hidden passage! That's interesting."

"Hidden passage?"

"Yes, the castle has several, though most have been blocked."

"Sounds like Versely Park, my grandmother's home. I used the hidden passages in Versely Park in my novel."

She laughed. "Another reason I thought you were here was the hidden passages!"

He cocked his head as he regarded her. "I'm glad to see you can laugh about the similarities."

"I as well. I wonder why the Gallaghers ran?" she mused as she put the full kettle on the stove. "I suspected they might be reporting more expenses than actually occurred. Well, I am not of a mind to chase after them. I'm glad they are gone."

"We should be sure to tell Mr. Liddle about them when he appears as he's a thief taker."

"Not worth his time to chase after them unless we can uncover proof."

He nodded.

"At the moment, where they are is unimportant," Cassie said. "Getting the castle supplied is more important, along with getting it staffed. There is not much left for breaking our fast. I don't know where the Gallaghers kept their food supplies unless it was in their chambers, and I'm sure they took those with them."

"Even if they did, and we found them, I wouldn't

trust they wouldn't have poisoned them first," Lakehurst said.

Cassie laughed. "Thus says the writer of gothic romances. One of your villains would do that, am I correct?"

He cocked his head to the side as he considered her. "Thank you," he said.

"Thank me? For what?" Cassie asked as she opened the tea sack to get the rich black tea inside.

"For being accepting of what I do," he said.

"More of not letting my imagination run away with me and seeing parallels in my life."

"From what your brother told me, there are a great many parallels."

"Yes. It is unnerving, but I now know you were not here. It is a strange coincidence, but I can live with that."

Agnes came into the kitchen. "Oh, my lady, what be ye doing? You shouldn't be here."

"Nonsense. As I told the Viscount, I am a clergyman's daughter and used to being in the kitchen. I checked the basket, and there wasn't much food left from last night, just a bit of ham and cheese. No bread, though."

"I heard chickens out behind the stables yesterday. Perhaps there are eggs," Lakehurst said.

"Yes, we always had chickens there. I never expected there to still be any. That is good news if there are and if they are layers."

"I'll go check," said Agnes.

"If you see an old man out there, that is Carlyle. Don't bother to call him, he won't hear you. Stand in front of him to talk to him; no need to shout. He will read your lips. He will help you gather eggs."

"Do you regret coming here?" Lakehurst asked her after Agnes left.

"To Baydon? No. I think the Duchess had the right of it. Coming here has been cathartic, and more so, I think, because of the castle's condition and how the Gallaghers have acted! It has pulled me out of myself. Having spent so long with everyone doing things for me and not having to think for myself, this has been refreshing! And a reminder that I am not weak."

"No, you are not. I think we should go to the village together. The villagers need to see you," Lakehurst said.

She nodded. "I do wish to go; however, I'm not certain the shopkeepers in Baydonton will have all that we need. They will need to place orders."

"Hopefully, with the supplies the Malmsby staff will bring and what we can get in the village, we can get provisioned before others arrive."

"Once they know we went ahead, how long before they will be on their way?" she asked.

"Two days, I'd guess. Maybe longer knowing Grandmother. She might want to delay them to ensure the servants have time to arrive first. At least I'm hoping the staff arrives before they do."

"I want to find out what the Gallaghers have been up to and what is happening with Mr. Browning before the Tidemarks arrive. I want to ensure I can present to Edmund exactly how much the Gallaghers have cost the marquessate since he chose not to return here."

He laughed. "On our return from the village, I'll go through the account books to look for any irregularities. What do you say they will show a salary paid to Carlyle that hasn't been?"

Her lips compressed. "I'm certain of it."

~

LAKEHURST, his jacket off and shirt sleeves rolled up, looked up from the letter he was reading when the door to the study opened.

Cassie pushed the door open wide so Gwinnie could enter carrying a coffee service. She walked slowly and carefully—a feat difficult for his boisterous twin—and placed the heavy tray on the sideboard in the study.

"Agnes and Rose are putting their heads together to plan a dinner for everyone," Gwinnie said. "Carlyle butchered a couple of chickens, so to have enough for everyone, we will have a chicken stew tonight. I shall certainly be glad when the cook from Malmsby House gets here!"

Lakehurst nodded acknowledgement.

Cassie poured the coffee. "I'll let you fix your coffee to your liking and I'll watch to learn your preferences," she said. She added cream and sugar to her own and stepped aside.

"Have you discovered anything interesting yet?" Cassie asked Lord Lakehurst.

"I was just reading a letter from this Mr. Browning you mentioned," he said as he stirred his coffee.

"The estate steward."

He nodded. "Judging by this letter, I would hazard that Mr. Gallagher told him he was only needed for the intake of the quarterly rents, which he was to report directly to him, not to Mr. Tidemark or yourself. Mr. Browning objected, saying he disagreed with this arrangement, that he should have visibility to the accounting for both profit and expense, especially as he had been told to raise the rents by ten percent."

"Ten percent!" objected Cassie. "There are tenants

that would break! Edmund never mentioned raising the rents."

"I'm not certain he did. I have found no correspondence from Mr. Tidemark that suggests that. What I have seen is an admonishment to guard expenses, and at this time, he saw no reason for a raise as their daily tasks had gone down with an empty castle," Lakehurst said.

He sipped his coffee. "I'm sure that did not sit well with the Gallaghers. And maybe what set them on the path of dishonesty?" Lakehurst suggested.

"I think they were dishonest before that," Cassie said drily.

Gwinnie snorted inelegantly. "That I would believe. So, brother, what have you gone through so far, and where should we begin to canvas the study?"

"I am concentrating on the desk. Cassie, do you know if one of the desk drawers has a false back or bottom?"

"No, I don't. I rarely came into this room. Richard preferred it that way."

"Interesting," Lakehurst mused.

"Did you find something that might show that?"

"Possibly. I'll look more closely when I've finished seeing what I can find after going through the drawers."

"The account books should be in the bookcase to the right of the desk," Cassie said. "I do remember that from the few times I was in this room."

"Let's start there," Gwinnie said. "What should we be looking for?"

"I don't know, precisely. I think we should discover what books are from the last two years—from six months before Richard died to the present."

"I'd also suggest quickly going through the other

books to look for loose papers or pamphlets stuck in places they don't belong," suggested Lakehurst.

"I'll start with that task, and I'll organize the ledgers by date, as I know nothing about the estate," Gwinnie said, crossing to the bookcase and looking up at the volumes in the shelves.

"I'll look through the more recent ledgers," Cassie said. She picked out a few books with newer appearances and set them on a chess table under the window. The later afternoon sun streamed across the books and the floor, illuminating the rug pattern's rich red, gold, and brown threads. "Though I can't imagine Mr. Gallagher would make records pointing to embezzlement in the official estate books."

"No," Lakehurst agreed, "However, he would have to record something if he wrote nothing down that would be suspect in itself if someone came to look at the account books."

"True.—Here is a record from just last month for the purchase of beeswax candles."

"Beeswax, not tallow?" Gwinnie said from where she stood in front of the bookcase.

"Yes, beeswax."

A muffled laugh came from Lakehurst, his head bent over one of the bottom desk drawers. "As we have surmised, they did like their comforts," he said, standing up and pulling an account book out of the drawer as he did so. "Cassie, this looks like a recent account book, so I'll give this to you to go through with the others."

"Thank you," she said, taking it from him.

"I've found some pretty pressed flowers," Gwinnie said.

"I'll wager that was thirty years ago," Cassie said.

Gwinnie looked at the frontispiece. "Yes. 1785."

Cassie nodded. "That would make sense. Richard's mother liked to press flowers and then frame them. There are pictures she made hanging in my sitting room."

"That is sweet," Gwinnie said, returning the flowers to where she found them.

THEY WORKED TOGETHER SILENTLY for an hour—only an occasional snicker, or groan punctuating the silence—until Rose came to tell them dinner was ready.

"Thank you, Rose," Gwinnie said to her maid. She stretched her arms above her head, then folded over to touch the floor. "Ah, to stretch feels good."

"I've set aside documents I think we should take a closer look at," Lakehurst said, as he rolled his shoulders.

"I, also, have found a couple of notations to share that are questionable. And we were right, Lakehurst, in our thinking they recorded paying a salary to Carlyle when they never did. The most recent record was from the first of June."

"After dinner, let's share notes on discoveries and perhaps continue this effort tomorrow if we feel it needful," Lakehurst suggested. He escorted the ladies out before he shut and locked the door afterward.

"With the Gallaghers no longer here, do you still think you need to lock the door?" Cassie asked.

"I had John and Henry lock and blockade the door the Gallaghers used to leave the castle. However, if there is another secret door, what prevents them from coming in through it?"

"I only know of that one as unblocked; however, you raise a good point. I don't believe I know all the secrets of Baydon, though I lived in the castle for four years," she admitted.

"It is a massive, rambling place," said Gwinnie as they entered the dining room. "How does one get up to the ramparts? I think I should like to play my violin up there if the wind is not too strong."

"From the next floor above the bedrooms, if you follow the hall to what would be the front of the castle, there is a door leading to another set of stairs to the ramparts," Cassie said.

"If you play from up there, it should be a dramatic piece, filled with fire and fury," Lakehurst suggested.

Gwinnie grinned as she sat down. "Of course!... What is that delightful smell?" she said as Rose brought in a large tureen of a chicken and vegetable stew.

"Country fare, my lady," Rose said as she ladled stew into the bowl she set before Gwinnie. "Agnes suggested it, said we could feed more with less."

Cassie laughed. "She would know. She comes from a large family with ten children. Her father is a tenant farmer on the Earl of Galborough's estate.—But there are also herbs in this?" she asked.

"Yes, my lady, we found the cook's garden. Agnes says it needs a good gardener's hand, but some of the herbs have done all right, like the rosemary and thyme. Agnes used them for the stew. We don't know how to cook fancy meals, but betweens us, we can keep yous fed."

"We don't need fancy meals," Gwinnie said. "This is perfect."

"You and Agnes have served us well beyond the duties of ladies' maids. We won't forget that," Lord Lakehurst said.

Cassie and Gwinnie agreed.

Rose blushed as she curtsied, then scurried to leave the room.

They ate in silence, savoring the rich chicken stew.

"Today, when I visited with Mr. Fortesque, the vicar, I asked about villagers coming to the castle to set things to right after being empty for so long. He said he would put the word out to his parishioners. He thought we would get some maids of all work and some laborers coming here tomorrow. I'd like to get the other outbuildings set to rights if that is agreeable to you, Cassie," Lakehurst said as he finished his stew and pushed the bowl away.

"Yes. Thank you for thinking of those matters. I'd like the dairy to be one of the priorities so we can have fresh milk, cream, and butter if there is a dairymaid available," Cassie said before eating her last bit of bread.

"How long do you intend to stay here?" Gwinnie asked, startled.

Cassie laughed around the bread in her mouth. She held her serviette to her mouth for a moment as she swallowed. "Only a few weeks," she admitted. She grew serious. "But I want the castle property to function as it once did. Being left alone with only a caretaker couple who did nothing to upkeep the property was not good! I can see deterioration that shouldn't be! This is my son's inheritance. If I need to, I will lease it out until he reaches his majority to have someone living here and keeping it safe."

"I think it could pay for itself in estate goods," Lakehurst said.

"We did while my husband was alive. I don't think Edmund understood that."

"Most likely not," Lakehurst said. He stood. "Shall we return to the library?"

The ladies agreed. Cassie requested brandy to be brought to them in that room.

"I found a stack of receipts stuffed into the back of one of the drawers we should compare against the ledger books you have been studying Cassie."

"I also found some newer receipts stuffed between old account books," said Gwinnie.

"Bring them to the table where I have been going through the ledgers.—Lakehurst, if you would be so kind as to pull up another chair, I think we can sit here comfortably," Cassie said. She pulled the most recent ledger to her. "This ledger starts in January, so let's look at the receipts for this timeframe," she suggested.

They read off the items and the amounts spent. Cassie checked off their entries and noted the amount on the receipt in a column next to the amount listed. When they finished, every receipt they matched was for less than the amount in the account book. There were also entries in the account book for which they didn't have receipts, like Carlyle's wages.

Lakehurst leaned back in his chair when they were done. "They have been systematically embezzling funds. And they have been smart about it. The amounts range from 20 to 100 guineas and fluctuate based on the season."

"Amazing," Gwinnie said. She rose. "I know it is not late; however, I am tired. I'm going upstairs to my room."

Cassie and Lakehurst wished her a good night.

Lakehurst refilled their brandy glasses, and they returned to reviewing the documents, the only sound in the room the scratching of their quills on paper.

Lakehurst finally laid his quill down and finished his brandy.

"I like working with you like this," he said. "You're

a restful woman to work alongside, not chattering about this or that."

She smiled as she laid her quill down and turned toward him. "Thank you. I could say the same of you —not the woman part," she jokingly clarified and he laughed with her. "The restful part. It is just nice to know someone is near, even if we don't say a word."

"That is precisely what I meant." He leaned forward, resting his forearms on his thighs. He looked down at his hands clasped between his legs, then back up at her.

"I can't imagine not having you in my life."

"Please—No."

"No, what?"

"Don't think there might be a future for us. I've quite decided. I will not marry again."

"Why do you say that?"

She turned her head to the side, away from his piercing gaze as she considered how to answer him. It had been well known in society that the Marquess of Darkford had possessed a passionate nature. His passions ran high for many things and many people.

Just not for her.

She'd come to believe there was something in her nature that depressed strong feelings for her. There was something fundamentally missing in her. And she thought it went both ways. She wasn't sure if she was capable of strong feelings for a man any more than a man could have strong feelings for her.

Viscount Lakehurst might think he liked her now, but with time, Cassie feared those feelings would evaporate.

She turned back to him. "I disappointed Darkford. I fear I should disappoint you, as well. There is something lacking in me."

"What?"

"I don't know," she said sadly. Tears ran gently down her cheeks.

Lakehurst rose and pulled her from her chair. He wrapped his arms about her, gently pressing her head against his chest. "I don't believe you could ever disappoint me; however, I respect your fears," he murmured. "And I have fears, too," he said.

She gave a watery chuckle. "You with your size, strength, and position in society? You are bamming me, my lord."

"I could wish that were true. No matter. My intent was not to make you cry. But I do want you to know, I like being around you. How about we leave it at that for now and see what happens?"

She nodded against his chest.

"It has been a long, tiring day. Sometimes emotions get the best of us when we're tired."

She stepped back, and he let his arms fall to his sides. "I should retire."

"We both should," he said.

Cassie started for the door, then stopped and turned to look back at him, the mammoth man with the gentle manner. He stared at the rug on the floor.

"Thank you," she said.

He raised his head. "For what?"

"Just for being who you are," she said with a warm smile before she left the room.

CHAPTER 11

COME TOGETHER

The next morning, while Lakehurst was meeting with John, Henry, and Carlyle to discuss the day's tasks, they heard wagons roll into the yard before the castle. The men came out of the stable to see who'd arrived. Some locals from the village climbed out of the wagons, pulling out tools and cleaning supplies with them. On horseback came the Reverend Mr. Fortesque dressed in solemn black, wearing a high white stock and cravat, a low-crowned black beaver hat and a multitude of shiny gold buttons down the front of his jacquard-patterned black waistcoat.

This was a moment Lakehurst wished he could raise one eyebrow in the way his grandmother did. Mr. Fortesque had more the image of a Mayfair clergy than a country clergy. For Lady Darkford's benefit, no doubt, Lakehurst mused.

Lakehurst sent Henry into the castle to tell the ladies while he walked forward to greet Mr. Fortesque and the newcomers he'd brought with him.

Mr. Fortesque dismounted and tossed the reins to Carlyle.

"As you can see, my lord, I spread the word that

the marchioness would like assistance in putting the castle to rights. The villagers always liked Lady Darkford, so many are happy to see her returned and welcome the work." He frowned slightly. "The village has not been as prosperous since the Marquess died," he added.

There was something about the way Mr. Fortesque spoke that had Lakehurst feeling like the man read from a script.

"No, I don't suppose it has not, judging by the condition of the castle when we arrived."

"The Gallaghers didn't tend to the castle properly?"

Lakehurst laughed shortly. "Hardly. They were taking the funds sent for the castle upkeep for deposit in their own pockets."

Mr. Fortesque's brows drew together in surprise. "Embezzling?" he asked. It was the first thing he said that sounded unscripted.

"Just so. They secretly left early in the morning the day after we arrived. No doubt they knew it would not take long for us to discover their thievery."

"Always thought they was slimy," a man who came in one of the wagons said. Others around him muttered agreement.

Mr. Fortesque looked at them disapprovingly. They looked down at the ground, avoiding his eyes.

"Norton," Lakehurst called out. "Please see these gentlemen started on the tasks we discussed this morning."

"Right away, my lord. With this many hands we should have the buildings serviceable quickly, I'd say." He looked at the men, then gestured for them to follow him. "Lady Darkford wants a dairy again, so's that will be our first task. There's also a pantry to clean out, a chicken house repaired, and the stable roof repaired. That's what I knows so far fer a start." They followed him as he led them back toward the stable.

Cassie and Gwinnie came out of the castle, followed by Agnes and Rose. Lakehurst almost laughed. Cassie and his sister looked much like the ladies from the village with aprons over their dresses and old cloths wrapped around their hair to keep the worst of the dust and cobwebs away.

"Reverend Fortesque," Cassie said, "It's been a long time. I'd say welcome, however, the interior of the castle is not fit for entertaining at the moment." She looked at the women gathered. "Thank you all for coming! I'm ever so grateful to you. This is Gwinnie. If you can't tell, she is Lord Lakehurst's twin sister. And over here is Agnes and Rose. They came with us from London and have been doing the best they can. We certainly welcome you all! Half of you will accompany Agnes, who is working in the kitchen, dining, and other ground floor areas, and the other half, please follow Rose to work on the bed chambers. We are expecting company in a day or two and need the house ready! You will be well compensated for your efforts. If anyone would wish to stay on for the house party, please let Agnes or Rose know. I expect to be here a month for this visit. I can't stay away from my son longer than that!"

The women murmured their thanks and followed Agnes and Rose.

"The young master did not come with you?" Reverend Fortesque asked.

Lakehurst thought he saw consternation in his eyes.

"No," Cassie said with a sad smile. "He has gone on holiday with Lord Lakehurst's and Gwinnie's—I mean

Lady Guinevere's grandmother, the Dowager Duchess of Malmsby," she said.

"Lady Guinevere?" Mr. Fortesque repeated. He cocked his head to the side as he looked about.

"Yes, that would be me," Gwinnie said, bouncing on her toes.

Lakehurst grinned as he looked at his sister. With an old cloth wrapped around her head to tie up her hair and a stained apron over her dress, she did not look like a duke's daughter.

Mr. Fortesque stared at her. "Your father is..."

"The Duke of Malmsby," she cheerfully supplied.

Mr. Fortesque looked at Lakehurst. "And you are the Duke's heir?" he asked. "You didn't mention that when we met yesterday."

"I have that privilege and penance," Lakehurst admitted, shrugging. He wondered at Mr. Fortesque's reaction to knowledge of their societal position. It seemed... odd.

"Ah," Mr. Fortesque said, nodding.

Lakehurst saw him look toward Cassie, his expression changing, smoothing out to unctuous pleasantry and curiosity. "I am gratified to see you have fallen in with good friends, my lady."

"It wasn't me, it was my brother, Miles. He is marrying a cousin of Lord Lakehurst and Lady Guinevere."

"I see... Well, my felicitations on everything working out so well," he said heartily. "Right now, I must get back to the church."

"Thank you again for coming to our rescue with the workers. You must come for a visit when our other guests arrive."

"Guests?" he asked politely.

"Besides my brother and his fiancée, Mr. Tidemark, Lord Darkford's uncle, and Mr. Stillworth are coming."

"Raymond Stillworth?" Mr. Fortesque clarified.

"Yes."

He smiled. "Mr. Stillworth recommended me to Lord Darkford after the unfortunate death of the previous vicar, I was much appreciative as I had just returned from India where I served ministerial duties for the East India Company employees and needed to secure a new position upon my return to England."

"Is that where you met Mr. Stillworth? In India?"

"Yes."

"I remember when you came," Cassie said. "Everyone was excited to have a permanent vicar living in the rectory again."

He smiled. "Everyone was most welcoming."

Lakehurst thought it was a perfunctory smile for it did not reach his pale eyes.

"After they arrive, you must come to dine with us," Cassie said.

"I would like that. I shall look forward to the invitation," he said, formally with a bow. He turned to Lakehurst and his sister. "Lord Lakehurst, Lady Guinevere," he said, bowing deeply, "I look forward to seeing you again in the future."

"Of course," Lakehurst said. He motioned to Carlyle to bring the Reverend Fortesque's horse back.

Carlyle brought the reverend's glossy, dark brown horse out of the stable and led him to the mounting block near the castle entrance. He held the horse steady as Mr. Fortesque swung his leg over his saddle and settled in his stirrups.

The horse was a beautiful animal, Lakehurst thought, studying his conformation. He stepped up beside Cassie and Gwinnie onto the flat stone slab stoop before the great castle oak door. He wondered how the reverend came by such a fine animal on a clergy salary. A gift, perhaps?

Standing with Gwinnie and Cassie, they waved congenially after the reverend as he rode off.

"So what do you think that was all about?" Lakehurst said out of the side of his mouth as he continued to smile at the reverend when he turned to wave at them.

"I have not the slightest idea; however, I should tell you the reverend is not an innocent in Richard's former games. Once he arrived in the village, he became a frequent guest," Cassie said grimly. Smiling and waving as well.

"I'd guess he is into it up to that fancy waistcoat he wears," Gwinnie said brightly. "Interesting days ahead."

Cassie shuddered. "I hate to think of the ramifications of our thoughts."

"Then don't, at least not yet. We shouldn't make assumptions," Lakehurst said.

Gwinnie laughed. "You already have, so don't get all sanctimonious on us now! Well, I've more work to do. There is a parlor I am claiming for my music practice room. I'm cleaning it to make it usable. I'll see you at luncheon."

BY THE END of the day when the wagons left, all the workers had committed to returning the next day, and four had agreed to become house staff through the month of July. With the staff they were expecting from Malmsby House, they should be well acquitted for the arrival of their guests. Throughout the day, more foodstuffs and supplies arrived from their orders placed the previous day. The big, delightful surprise was the milk cow and dairymaid who came together. They were effectively leasing the cow and the services of the dairymaid for the duration of their stay at Baydon. The cow was a good producer, too. They might even have a surplus, depending on the milk and butter needs of the guests.

Cassie collapsed into a chair in the front parlor. Lakehurst brought her a small glass of sherry. "Thank you," she said softly. She balanced the glass in her hand on the sofa arm as she leaned her head back for a moment and closed her eyes. In the silence, the first she'd been able to listen to all day, she heard the soft strains of a violin. She smiled.

Gwinnie.

She raised her head. "Where do you think she is? It sounds too far away to be the parlor she intends to make her music room while she is here."

"I think she is playing into the wind," Lakehurst said softly as he listened.

"From the ramparts?"

"Yes. But don't worry, she won't be up there long. Her stomach will have her coming down. She is so active that if she missed meals, she could easily die of starvation."

Cassie laughed.

"How do you feel about all we have accomplished today?" she asked him.

"I feel good about it. I do wonder what Mr. Tidemark will say about all the funds we have promised."

"I know it is odd, but I don't care. This is my son's property, and Edmund has let it go to near ruin. I shall take his mismanagement to court if need be."

"You do realize they will not give you the purse

strings. They will pass them on to another man," Lakehurst said.

She made a face. "Yes, I do know. Truthfully, I would prefer Mr. Stillworth was in charge of the marquessate."

"Your husband's cousin?"

"Yes. They were good friends and went into business ventures together."

"Like the tea growing in India."

"Yes, just like that."

"I don't know much about him; however, he did seem the steadiest of those in your circle."

"It would be hard not to be," she said drily.

He swallowed a laugh.

They suddenly realized the music had cut off, and footsteps were clattering down the stairs.

"Here comes Gwinnie," Lakehurst said with a smile.

"Is it dinner yet?" Gwinnie said as she burst into the room a moment later.

"Soon. Would you like a preprandial?"

"Yes, thank you." She put her violin in its case on the sideboard and accepted the glass. "It was a good day today."

"We were saying the same thing," Cassie said.

"Excuse me, my lady," Agnes said from the doorway. "There's a gentleman at the kitchen door as says he's a friend of Mr. Martin and wantin' to speak with you all."

"A Mr. Liddle?" Lakehurst asked.

"Yes, my lord," Agnes said.

"Excellent!" He rubbed his hands together delightedly. "And we have the proof he needs to go after Mr. and Mrs. Gallagher."

"Please show him in here and then set another

place for him in the dining room. He will join us for dinner," Cassie told Agnes.

"Yes, ma'am."

A man as dark-haired as Mr. Martin was fair entered the parlor from the servants' entrance.

"Forgive my visit without forewarning, and at this hour," he said in a deep voice as he bowed to them all. His black hair was shoulder length and pulled back in a queue. He had intelligent gray eyes below thick dark brows that observed each of them in turn. His appearance was entirely nondescript until he smiled. Lakehurst found himself liking the man instantly.

"I imagine not giving forewarning is a benefit in your vocation," Lakehurst said laconically.

"It is," Mr. Liddle agreed.

"Please sit down, Mr. Liddle. You will be joining us for dinner. I have already requested a place setting for you," Cassie said.

Mr. Liddle's brows rose; however, he merely murmured a thank you for including him. "I have made some local inquiries around the circumstances of the Marquess of Darkford's death over eighteen months ago. What I got were multiple scrambled interpretations of the event. The only consistent facts I could ascertain from all the stories is they knew the Marquess gave wild parties for which you, Lady Darkford, were not present, and the servants were sent away; however, that night, you and your son remained at Baydon."

"That is true," Cassie said, nodding.

"And that the Marquess's cause of death was a knife wound, which some say you inflicted."

"No!"

He shook his head and held up his hand to tell her to calm down. "Others disagree and say it was..." He ticked off the stories he'd heard on his fingers. "A fight among partygoers," he held up a second finger, "the work of Satan's demons, or three, a jealous lover who wanted you for himself."

"The man who murdered Richard tried to carve a symbol on my chest, so Richard attacked him."

"What symbol?"

"He called it the mark of Satan."

Mr. Liddle frowned, his face going dark.

"Who suggested Satan's demons murdered him?" Lakehurst asked.

"A former groom here at Baydon," Mr. Liddle said thoughtfully, "who was let go after the Marquess's death. He works in Wells now."

"Mr. Liddle, the man who killed my husband had some form of control over him, I'm certain of it."

"What do you mean, my lady?"

"At first, Richard acted like he wasn't aware of what was happening around him. He was like one of those wind-up little automatons. I kept screaming at him to help, to make the man stop. It was like he didn't hear me. Then, all of a sudden, it was like he'd been set free. He started yelling at the man, and they fought over the knife the man had been using to cut my shoulder. I honestly don't know if whoever stabbed him meant to do so, or not."

"What did the man look like?"

Cassie shrugged helplessly. "They were all masked and cloaked, and they poured some foul draught down my throat that made everything go in and out of focus. I can't even be sure if what I remember is complete or not. Or even real."

Lakehurst frowned at hearing this part of her story. Ellinbourne hadn't mentioned someone had drugged her. It made sense, given she thought someone drugged the other men or put them in some trance.

"How many men were there?"

"Three besides Richard and the man with the knife."

"So five total."

"That I saw. But the cave where all this happened is large, and the torch lights did not light it up completely. Large areas were in deep shadows."

"A cave under the castle?"

"Yes."

Lakehurst squirmed in his chair and leaned forward. "Though all this is important to solve, we have a more pressing need for your services, sir."

Mr. Liddle tilted his head as he observed Lakehurst. "And what would that be?"

"Since the Marquess died, the estate's caretakers have been systematically embezzling from the estate. They did not expect us when we arrived and fled the castle in the early morning hours."

"Do you have proof of your charges?"

"Yes!" Cassie said emphatically. "And I want them caught. I fear the estate may have drastically decreased in value, if not be on the verge of bankruptcy due to their actions. This is my son's inheritance. I can't just sit back and see it destroyed."

Mr. Liddle's lips kicked up at the corners. "No, my lady, I see you cannot. And the needs of the living are more important than those of the dead."

Lakehurst nodded. "We'd like you to make capturing the Gallaghers your first priority."

Mr. Liddle's brow furrowed in thought as he nodded.

"Dinner is served," Rose said from the doorway.

"Whatever you have made this evening smells even better than last night!" Gwinnie said.

"It is a beef stew made with burgundy and root vegetables."

"Excellent." Gwinnie tossed back the rest of her sherry. "Lead on!"

~

THEY'D ALMOST FINISHED dinner when someone pounded on the castle door. Cassie, Gwinnie, and Lakehurst looked from one to another. Lakehurst threw his serviette down on the table and rose from his chair.

"I'll see who it is. Stay here."

"I'll take my dishes and exit through the kitchen," Mr. Liddle said. "Best no one know of my connection to you yet."

Cassie also rose and followed Lakehurst as far as the dining room door. From there, she had a view of the heavy oak entrance door. Gwinnie assisted Mr. Liddle in removing signs of his presence.

"*Mr. Stillworth!*" Cassie heard Lakehurst say loudly in surprise. She ran toward the door.

"Forgive the late hour; I pressed ahead of the others to warn you," he said.

"Come in, come in," Lakehurst said.

"Mr. Stillworth!" Cassie said. "What's this about a warning?"

Walking in the door of Baydon, he looked so much like Richard, her late husband, it nearly took her breath away. They could be twins if it weren't for his darker blond hair. She might have called him Richard if Lakehurst hadn't said his name first. The thought unnerved her, putting her on edge.

With Mr. Liddle safely gone, Gwinnie followed her out into the hall.

Mr. Stillworth quickly removed his high-crowned beaver hat and came into the hall. "Beg your pardon. Uncle Edmund thinks I decided not to come and have returned to London; however, I thought I should tell you he is in a temper. I have never seen him as angry as he was when he discovered you'd gone on ahead to Baydon."

"I'm certain he is not as angry as I have been to discover how poorly he has managed Alex's patrimony," she said, placing her hands on her hips, her breathing faster. "You shall hear me ring a peal over his head, I can tell you that!" The shock of first perceiving him as Richard lingered.

Gwinnie placed a light hand on her shoulder. Cassie let out her breath on a sigh at her friend's gentle touch.

"I'll bet you have forgone dinner to ride to us," Gwinnie said. "Let's get Mr. Stillworth some dinner, and we can sit back at the table to hear what he has to say."

Cassie relaxed. "Yes, an excellent idea, Gwinnie," Cassie said, recovering. "Thank you. I have been suppressing my anger at Edmund, and like a covered boiling water pot, it has been waiting to boil over! My apologies for you getting the effects of the boil over. Please, join us in the dining room."

"I would like that, but my horse—"

"I'll see your horse is taken to the stable. Either Henry or Carlyle will see he is fed and cared for," Lakehurst said.

"Thank you," he said, bowing. He followed Cassie and Gwinnie into the dining room.

Cassie was relieved to see no sign of Mr. Liddle's

presence remained. Gwinnie winked at her. She smiled conspiratorially back at her.

"I'll tell Rose and Agnes we have another for dinner," Gwinnie said, heading toward the butler's pantry.

"Would you like the local ale or wine?" Cassie asked.

"Ale, I think, thank you. But you shouldn't be serving me!" he exclaimed.

She laughed. "Under the circumstances, until we have servants here, we all do what needs to be done. Even Lord Lakehurst and Lady Guinevere. Or I should say, especially them, for you know my upbringing was not one of privilege."

"Uncle Edmund and Aunt Vanessa are concerned about your being here with Lord Lakehurst."

"Why?" she asked, pouring ale from a pitcher on the sideboard into a mug.

"It is not seemly. It could ruin you."

"Piffle, first, I am a widow. Second, Lady Guinevere and our ladies' maids are here." She handed him the mug. "They provide chaperonage enough—if I were worried about such things. Which, I tell you plainly, I am not."

"They do not understand why they are inserting themselves in your business. Aunt Vanessa has wondered if they are secretly impoverished and thinking of recovering their funds by a marriage to you."

Gwinnie laughed. Mr. Stillworth glanced at her but turned back quickly to Cassie.

Cassie sat down across from him. "Vanessa wants to think the worst of everyone with a higher societal position than her. A few days ago, she tried to spread the rumor that Lord Lakehurst and Lady Guinevere were not the Duke of Malmsby's children. She decided this was the case based on their size. She was certain their father was some Highlander or some such thing. Then she tried to make a to-do about Gwinnie taking money for the concerts she provides, that it was unseemly, and that made her an unseemly person. If there is no scandal that Vanessa knows of about a person, she will make one up."

He winced. "I'll own I have seen that a time or two."

"Precisely. Then you should know how we disabuse her of those notions."

He frowned and nodded.

"But that doesn't seem like enough to have Edmund furious at me, as you say he is."

"The second thing Uncle Edmund is furious about is your allowing Alex to go with the Dowager Duchess of Malmsby without consulting him."

"We discussed this at the dinner party," Cassie protested.

"He remembers it being discussed. He says he hadn't agreed to that idea yet. He thinks this is enough to wrest him from you and have you committed."

"What?" said Gwinnie from the butler's pantry doorway. She had a place setting in her hands. Behind her stood Rose with another tureen of beef stew.

"He wouldn't dare," she continued as she set the things on the table. "My family would support Lady Darkford, and we are not without respect in London."

He looked doubtful. "He says the Duke of Malmsby has a reputation for being an academic with his head in the clouds."

Gwinnie snorted in an unladylike manner. "Part of that is his little joke. He takes after his mother. He regularly does his duty in Parliament and is a quiet leader

—a word here, a word there—that is how he gets things done without putting himself forward."

"Why wouldn't he want anyone to know his role? That makes little sense. He is a duke, after all."

Gwinnie laughed. "And that is precisely why! You'd have to know the Duke to understand. He enjoys being a behind-the-scenes person."

"Regardless," Cassie cut in, "when it is known how poorly the estate has been managed under him, I would have an argument to present as to why he should no longer be the executor of the marquessate and that role be given to another. Like yourself, perhaps."

"Me! I don't understand."

Lord Lakehurst returned to the dining room, carrying Mr. Stillworth's portmanteau. "Did you know your horse is limping?"

Stillworth finished his stew and pushed away from the table to turn and look at Lord Lakehurst.

"Yes, I think he picked up a stone on the way up the road from the village," he said.

"And you continued to ride him?" Lakehurst asked. He tossed his portmanteau to the side of the room.

"What else should I have done? He already had the stone, and I knew we weren't far from here."

"Is he your horse?"

"No, no. I rode mine hard to get well ahead of the Tidemarks. He was exhausted by the time we reached Wells. The innkeeper suggested the exchange for the rest of the journey."

Lakehurst inhaled deeply. Cassie could see him struggling to contain his anger.

"I gather you have not much experience with horses."

Mr. Stillworth frowned. "I have ridden horses my entire life."

"Ridden," Lakehurst said flatly. "Have you spent much time in the stables with them and the grooms that care for them?"

"Egad, no. Why should I?"

Cassie frowned.

Lord Lakehurst walked to the sideboard to refill his mug with ale before he answered. Though he stood with his back to them, Cassie could tell he was angry.

He turned to face Mr. Stillworth. "In the future, Mr. Stillworth," he said with feigned calmness, "dismount the horse and try to get the stone out. Whether you get it out or not, walk him slowly to your destination or to the nearest inn where they might see to him. With your weight on him, the stone became deeply embedded and bleeding. We shall have to be careful against infection. I have seen horses being put down for a small injury that becamed abscessed." He looked over at Cassie. "We have removed the stone, cleaned the wound, and applied a poultice."

"Good. Thank you for seeing to that." Cassie knew her late husband would never have ridden a limping horse. If a stone were caught in the frog, he would try to get it out and walk the horse to where someone could take care of the animal. Though her late husband and cousin looked more like brothers than cousins, they were vastly different. Perhaps she didn't wish him to be the executor of the estate instead of Mr. Tidemark!

"Can we return to our original discussion, cousin?" Stillworth asked.

Cassie had never liked being called *cousin* and he knew it. She ignored the form of address.

"With regarding..." she trailed off, waiting for him to continue.

"The Tidemarks, of course. What's he done? The castle is still standing," he said as a joke.

Cassie stared at him. She'd never seen this cavalier manner in him, yet he said he rode ahead to warn her. She compressed her lips. She reminded herself she had seen little of him since Richard died; still, his manner concerned her. "I wonder for how long," she finally said.

She picked up her unfinished glass of wine and took a drink. "The caretakers he'd left here were robbing the estate."

"Surely you exaggerate. How can you know this?" he asked, leaning back in his chair.

"We have examined the estate books," she said, her hand sweeping before her to include Gwinnie and Lakehurst in her statement. "They'd enter ten guineas in the ledger book if they received a bill for five guineas. Reports sent back to Edmund would show an expensive place to run, and he continued to try to create economies. Never once did he come here. My brother came to Baydon to get me and Alex after Richard's death, not Edmund."

Mr. Stillworth's lower lip jutted forward. "I thought Uncle Edmund was hoarding funds, increasing the estate's value. I find what you are saying hard to believe," he said, shaking his head.

"You remember Carlyle, don't you?"

"The deaf stable hand? Yes, I do. Good with horses."

"Richard provided for him in his will, promising room and board for his life. It didn't specify a salary for work done, so the Gallaghers fired him as a stable hand and grudgingly gave him food and a place to sleep, that is all."

"Sounds more like the fault of the estate manager than the Gallaghers," he said offhandedly.

"We have found, for reasons I cannot fathom yet, Mr. Brownings only responsibility to the estate is in collecting rents that Mr. Gallagher took from him. I have no idea where Mr. Browning is now; however, I can tell you I wish to speak to him."

"You know why Uncle Edmund didn't want to come here, don't you?" Stillworth offered.

"No, I don't," Cassie said emphatically.

"Because the old Marquess never let him bring Vanessa here."

"Vanessa has never been here?"

He shook his head. "Never. And that hurt both of them. Edmund did not receive much in the way of money from his father. Vanessa Farrow came from a wealthy merchant family. Her dowry was large. And strangely, they fell in love with each other." He shook his head, his expression displaying wonder over that fact.

"And remain devoted to each other," Cassie added in mutual wonder.

"I know! It's unfathomable. When Edmund announced he would marry Vanessa Farrow, his father cut him off, saying he'd smell too much of the shop to be welcomed at Baydon any longer. After he died, Edmund thought he might be able to come here; however, his brother was like-minded to their father and refused their visit. Quite embarrassing for Uncle Edmund after they travel to get here following his father's death. His sister, my mother, tried to intervene on his behalf. However, the new Marquess was as much of a curmudgeon as his father had been. From what my mother told me, they only saw a softness in him when his wife, Richard's mother, died after childbirth."

"How sad," Gwinnie said.

Stillworth nodded. "After his father died, Richard determined to heal the breach, and I think did; however, Edmund refused to come here. He said he saw no reason to."

"But he's coming here now," said Gwinnie.

"It is a sad tale; however, it doesn't answer the question as to why Tidemark didn't take more of an interest in the estate; after all, following years of neglect by the family, he suddenly had his nephew honoring him with his trust," Lakehurst observed.

Stillworth shrugged. "I agree. It makes little sense."

"We are not going to solve that mystery tonight. Now that there are four of us, shall we adjourn to the parlor for a game of whist?" Gwinnie suggested, bouncing up out of her seat.

Cassie laughed and rose as well. "I'm up for it."

Lakehurst and Stillworth followed them out of the dining room.

CHAPTER 12

BATS

Lakehurst rose early the next day. He hadn't slept well during the night, his mind thinking about all that he'd learned the day before... and what he still didn't know.

Along with his concern for Cassie's well-being and safety expanding, his admiration grew, his heart considering possibilities he hadn't allowed his mind to consider.

He closed the castle's front door softly behind him. The castle faced west, so he did not see the rising sun; however, the sky before him shifted from the dark of night to the gray of dawn. He walked toward the stables. He heard Carlyle talking to the chickens behind the stable, coaxing the hens to move aside so he might gather their eggs for Cook. He walked around the stable to see Carlyle. He waited for Carlyle to spot him. When the man did, he walked toward him.

"Mornin', m'lord," Carlyle said. "Ye be up early."

"Yes. I couldn't sleep."

Carlyle nodded his head in understanding.

"Can you tell me how to find the cave?" Lakehurst asked him.

Carlyle compressed his lips. "Aye, but best I show ye." He set the egg basket on the ground.

Lakehurst touched his arm to draw his attention back. "Go take those to the kitchen first," Lakehurst told him. "I'll wait."

"Aye. I will be quick," Carlyle promised. He picked the basket back up again and trotted off toward the castle kitchen entrance.

Lakehurst walked back to the path that ran along the cliff edge. He probably could find the cave himself if he tracked the worn path, but he wanted to talk to Carlyle away from others. It was challenging enough as it was to remember always to face Carlyle when he spoke to him. The man seemed to read lips well. He wondered how he learned.

He walked toward the cliff edge. The morning fog had settled into the crevasse. Maybe he should wait to explore the cave until the fog burned away with the rising sun. But if he waited, no doubt others would want to come as well, which would not allow him to absorb the setting for himself and question Carlyle as he wished. As they had used the cave at night, surely there were torches or oil lamps in the cave to light their way.

When Carlyle returned, he carried two lit lanterns and a handful of punks to light other lanterns or candles. He handed one lantern to Lakehurst.

Lakehurst told Carlyle to lead him to the cave and was surprised when the man turned back toward the castle. They went behind a large stack of gray limestone at the other side of the castle forecourt and then down a trail made into a rough-cut limestone stairway. Lakehurst looked back. The cave must be directly under the castle! That was a surprise. Did the cave also have one of the hidden entrances to the castle? He imagined it did.

If so, that will need to be blocked, he thought grimly.

They followed a switchbacked path until they came to a large opening in the cliff face. As Ellinbourne had told him, carved into the rock at the top of the entrance were the words: *Do what thou wilt.*

Lakehurst wryly wondered what sybaritic pleasures that entailed!

They first stepped inside a small room, like a receiving chamber or anteroom. A thick layer of dust covered everything. Once elegant red velvet upholstery had turned brown and showed the depredations of small animals chewing through the fabric. Nude marble statues now appeared as clothed in brown cloth from the dirt and dust that had blown into the chamber. The rug underfoot showed paws, claws, and hoofprints of various creatures.

Carlyle lit torches at either side of the entrance.

"This way, m'lord," he said, pointing to a narrow opening in the back wall.

Lakehurst followed him. Immediately, their lantern light became insufficient to see the scale of the room they entered. He instinctively ducked when something flew by his head.

Bats

The cave smelled of damp, must, and ammonia.

Carlyle lit more torches around the room, and as he lit each one, Lakehurst's wonder at the space increased. More bat wings beat the air. He ducked again quickly. In a wild flurry of beating wings and odd cries, hundreds of bats flew about the room as they found their way out of the cave, disturbed by their intrusion.

Bat droppings littered the floor, and roaches,

feasting on the droppings, glinted in the torchlight as they skittered about. Lakehurst conceded he'd not considered this aspect of caves in his novels. Perhaps he should in future books.

The furniture set about the room was in better condition than the entrance area, but were covered in more bat droppings than dust. A large stone slab had had a bowl shape carved out of its center. Remnants of spent charcoal lay under the bat droppings. A large crystal chandelier hung from the ceiling on a pulley to allow it to be raised and lowered to have its candles lit and extinguished. Below the chandelier stood an altar with iron rings embedded in the rock, much like he'd described in his novel. Around the room, situated between the chairs and more marble statues, were tented beds. Some tents still hung, two had fallen to drape over the bed beneath it and across the floor.

When he'd finished lighting the torches around the room, Carlyle went over to the altar.

"Here," he said, his voice echoing slightly. He laid his hand on the altar.

Lakehurst walked across the room to join him by the altar.

"Here I find them."

"Lord Darkford and Lady Darkford?"

He nodded, then looked back at the altar. Lakehurst followed the man's gaze to see the traces of blood on the side of the thick stone and on the floor.

"I pulled m'lord off of m'lady, and lay him there," he said, pointing to a place near the fire pit. "He were not dead yet."

Lakehurst looked at him in surprise. "Cassie—I mean, Lady Darkford said he was dead."

He nodded sadly. "I told her that."

"Did he say anything?" When Carlyle didn't answer, Lakehurst realized he had not talked directly at Carlyle. He touched Carlyle's shoulder, and the man turned to him. "Did he say anything?" he asked again.

Carlyle nodded. "But I don't see his lips. Part I see looks like he says My, my bro—or bra..." He shook his head. "I could not see!" he said, agitated.

"I understand," Lakehurst said. "But you took care of Lady Darkford."

"Aye, back to the castle," he said, pointing to the back of the large room.

"Is there a way into the castle from here?"

"Was." His face took on a hard expression. "I pegged the door closed, then blocked the passage."

"Show me," Lakehurst said.

Carlyle led him to a tapestry hung on the stone wall. When he pushed it aside, Lakehurst saw a narrow passage. He held his torch high, then entered the passage. About twenty feet in, he could see the path blocked with furniture Carlyle had dragged into the space. It was all jammed in tight, and would take time for anyone to dismantle his blockade. The makeshift solution caused Lakehurst to smile. Something else for his fictional stories.

As they made their way out of the cave, Carlyle doused every torch. Outside, the sun had risen, and the fog burned away. Lakehurst touched Carlyle's shoulder. "You are a good man, Carlyle. Thank you."

He shrugged, dipped his head down, and turned to ascend the trail, embarrassed to be recognized.

As Lakehurst climbed the trail back up to the castle forecourt, he thought about Cassie tied to that stone altar, the flickering torchlight, the slight echoes of voices, and the masks and cloaks the men wore. And worse, the knife against her fair shoulder. He flinched as he imagined it, and a cold hand clenched his heart.

THE CARRIAGES with the Malmsby London servants rolled into the forecourt in the early afternoon.

Mr. Harold, the butler, and Mrs. Pritchet, the upstairs housekeeper from Malmsby House—eager to prove her ability to be a full housekeeper—together inspected the castle. They praised the village locals who had come to the castle to work for all that had been done, then immediately got to work changing everything.

"I guess that puts me in my place," Gwinnie said sourly to Cassie as they sat together in the parlor, banished there by Mr. Harold and Mrs. Pritchet.

Cassie laughed. "They don't know what we have done over the last few days."

Gwinnie squirmed where she sat, then agreed. "I was actually rather proud of us."

"I know. And we did a great deal, which I assume they will learn as they talk more to the villagers and Rose and Agnes. What has me concerned is I haven't seen a cook with them."

"Mr. Harold told me the cook is coming with a wagon of provisions purchased in Wells. He thought he and the food should be here in the next hour or so."

"I'm certain Agnes and Rose will be relieved to hear that."

"We were lucky that they had some experience with cooking from their lives before becoming ladies' maids," Gwinnie said.

"I know Agnes's background as we come from the same village. What is Rose's background?"

"Rose's father owned a public house. She worked there, and he protected her from the more importuning of his clientele. But her father died, and her uncle inherited the business. He wasn't so nice about protection. Fact is, he thought he could make extra coins off of her servicing customers laying on her back instead of serving food and drink."

"Disgusting," Cassie said.

"That is life in the city for many women," Gwinnie said. "She was lucky to end up at Mrs. Southerlands'. That's where we met. I fortuitously taught her how to go on as a ladies' maid so when my maid married a local haberdasher and gave notice, Rose was able to come work for me."

Gwinnie twirled a ribbon from her gown around one finger. "So," she said, "what do you think of my brother?"

"What do you mean?" Cassie said, deliberately evading. She wasn't sure she wanted to look too closely at her feelings for Lakehurst. At least not yet.

Gwinnie bounced up and flounced over to the fireplace. She fiddled with a candlestick on the mantle. "Don't be obtuse. You know what I mean."

Yes, Cassie did know but didn't know what she wanted to say. "He is a caring man, he appears to take what happens around himself and others quite seriously. And there is no naysaying he is intelligent and handsome."

"You see he is caring?" Gwinnie asked eagerly. "I think he is. He tries to hide that, you know."

Cassie looked at her curiously. "Why? It is one of his most endearing traits."

"I think because of that word *endearing* Men don't like to be thought of as having *endearing* traits. Just not masculine enough, I suppose," she said. "As a child, Lakehurst was bullied for his large size, but more strongly admonished by our father to not take out anger on anyone physically, as he could easily hurt someone without meaning to. And of course, this led to more bullying because it appeared he would not stand up for himself."

"I've heard those boarding schools can be quite ruthless. I worry for Alex when it is time for him to be sent away to school," Cassie said.

Gwinnie nodded. "I can well understand that! Because of his size, Lakehurst withdrew from the other boys, spending much of his time alone reading or scribbling his own little stories if he couldn't find a story he wanted to read." She drew her green wool shawl higher up on her shoulder.

"I'm surprised that Lord Lakehurst has not wed yet. He's handsome, wealthy, kind; I would think the debutants would be falling all over each other for his attentions."

Gwinnie snorted. "You'd think so, wouldn't you? I know I do. I discovered recently why they don't."

"There is a reason?"

Gwinnie nodded, "A reason only a naïve, young debutant would believe, but there is a reason." She shook her head. "I wonder if I was ever that naïve," she said pensively.

"Well, what is it?"

"He is too large for intimacy."

"What?"

Gwinnie nodded. "They are afraid that his size would make the act of procreation too painful."

Cassie blinked at her. A sudden, unbidden image of him nude and in her bed flashed through her mind. She shivered inside. "I would hate to tell you anything of what is going through my mind at the moment; however, fear is not there," she admitted.

Gwinnie snorted.

"And he knows this?" Cassie asked.

"He overheard a conversation."

"But did he rightly hear?"

Gwinnie shrugged. "He says he did. It has thrown him in a dither."

Cassie stared at her for a moment. "He is not—forgive me—a virgin, is he?" she suggested tentatively.

Gwinnie laughed. "Hardly! No, no. He's had his share of youthful indiscretions in the past. No. No," she said, continuing to chuckle.

"Then why..."

Gwinnie shook her head. "I don't pretend to understand the workings of his mind."

"No, I don't suppose one would." Cassie frowned.

"I told him his best prospects for a bride were either a bluestocking who is too intelligent for such idiocy, or a widow such as yourself."

"Oh, not me," she immediately said, then wondered why she said that, for she could see herself wed to him, contrary to what she'd told him.

Gwinnie tilted her head. "Why not?"

"I'll not marry again," she said stoutly, pushing her other wayward thoughts away. "I found marriage totally unsatisfying. I had thought Richard and I could have at least been friends, for he'd told me before the marriage he wanted a biddable wife who would not complain about anything he did. No. He was nice enough, but we were never friends and if he came to my bed after Alex was born, I think of it as trying to relieve an itch, and I was the only scratching post around."

Gwinnie grimaced. "Oh, that is coarse."

Cassie nodded slowly. "Yes, but it was how I felt and still feel."

"Not every man is like the Marquess was," Gwinnie said gently.

"I know. I just... I just don't want to chance it. I was so miserable." Tears filled Cassie's eyes.

"But you were even more miserable after his death! You said your depression was so deep they wanted to send you to an asylum."

"The depression was not caused by losing Richard. The depression was due to what I experienced that night. And it was a depression fraught with fear, fear that it wasn't over yet and, as we have determined, it's not," she explained.

"But what of yourself?" she countered to Gwinnie. "You are older than I and are not wed. And you are a duke's daughter!"

Gwinnie sighed, her habitual ebullience falling away, and Cassie felt the veriest lowlife for saying what she did. "Lakehurst asked me that same question not long ago. Look at me," she said, standing straight, holding her hands away from her sides. "I am large."

"You are not fat," Cassie protested.

"I didn't say I was fat. I am large. Large boned. It is the way I am built."

"But you have the curves men love."

"On a smaller woman, they do. I am taller than most men in society or of a height. They do not want to look directly into a woman's eyes or look up to her. It is that masculine thing again. They want a woman shorter than them, who can lay their dainty heads on their manly chests as they enfold them in their embrace, the big strong, *'I'll take care of you'* man," she declared, throwing her chest out and her head up like a warrior accepting his due honor.

Cassie laughed at Gwinnie's play despite the seriousness of Gwinnie's fears.

"Not one of them could pick me up should I swoon," she said dramatically. "However, I am certain I could throw them over my shoulder and climb a flight of stairs," she said, mimicking the actions.

"Gwinnie, you could tread the boards!" Cassie exclaimed, laughing harder. Though she laughed with her, inside her heart cried for her.

"What part should I play? Oh, I know, I could play the male roles when it calls for a manly man."

Gwinnie collapsed onto the couch, biting her lip as tears spilled from her eyes and traced down her cheeks. "I am so lonely," she said, her voice breaking.

Cassie put her arms around her and drew her close. "I am so sorry. I had no idea. I did not think... That is the problem. No one thinks." She pushed Gwinnie's hair away from her face.

"We all assume we know everyone else from what we think we see. But we don't know their lives or the lies they might have lived."

They were silent together as Gwinnie gently cried. Cassie thought her heart would break for her. The bouncy, ebullient Gwinnie hid a lonely young woman.

Was she hiding, too? Was the truth of her dismal marriage part of her depression and the fear she wasn't worthy of love? She'd often wondered what was wrong with her that Richard did not love her. In her thoughts, she knew it wasn't about her, that the fault lay within Richard; however, that did not help her heart, which cried against her unworthiness. Her declaration not to marry again was part of the fortifications she had built and was continuing to build around herself.

Women were so at the mercy of men.

Gwinnie straightened, wiping the tears off her cheeks. "Well," she said with pseudo brightness, "enough of that now."

"Has there ever been someone you would like to marry?"

Gwinnie laughed shortly. "Oh, several times," she declared flippantly.

"That you thought you could love?" Cassie asked.

Gwinnie took in a deep breath and looked away. "Yes," she said, "but we are so far apart in our backgrounds and lives, it would never work."

"How can you say that? You are not a naïve debutant like those who fear your brother. A handsome face or purse does not sway you. You wouldn't feel the way you do if there wasn't some commonality."

Gwinnie laughed slightly. "At least he is slightly taller than me."

"Don't let society dictate," Cassie implored her.

"Easy to say. In our world, it's difficult to do," Gwinnie said with a long, drawn-out sigh.

MR. STILLWORTH LOOKED DOWN at the wrapped and tied bandage about the horse's hoof and frowned. "How long will it take to heal?" he asked.

Lakehurst shook his head. "I don't know. We will have to ask Carlyle."

"Ask Carlyle? Don't you know he's deaf?" Mr. Stillworth exclaimed, disgusted.

"Yes, I do," Lakehurst said placidly. "I also know he reads lips."

"What?" His astonishment had him looking from Lakehurst to Carlyle and back.

Lakehurst was surprised he did not know this if

he'd been to the castle before, which Lady Darkford indicated he had. He tapped Carlyle on his shoulder to get his attention.

Carlyle straightened and looked at Lakehurst, nodding to indicate Lakehurst had his attention.

"How long will his hoof take to heal?"

Carlyle scratched his balding head. "Hard to say, m'lord, but if no abscess sets in, I'll make a leather shoe to strap on when we takes off the bandages, and he ken be turned out to pasture. A couple more weeks afore he ken be ridden."

"He needs to go back to the innkeeper in Wells, and I need to get my horse!"

His agitation confused Lakehurst. He saw no reason for it. He frowned at him. "I was intending to send Henry to Wells to pick up some things. He can take a note to the innkeeper explaining the situation and retrieve your horse at the same time. It is not a big issue. These things happen."

"When can this Henry of yours go?"

Lakehurst crossed his arms over his chest. "By tomorrow I should have a list from the staff of what is needful that is not available in the village."

"Tomorrow!"

"What is the issue with tomorrow?" Lakehurst asked. "Were you planning to leave today?"

"No, of course not. I just don't like being without a horse," Stillworth grumbled, looking down at the horse's bandaged hoof.

"If you wish to go riding, I can lend you MacKenzie, my horse," Lakehurst offered.

"No—well, maybe. Sorry, I'm just rattled at how severely the horse is hurt. I had no idea," he said, smoothing out his irritated features into a semblance of caring.

It was the rapid change from irritation to caring that caught Lakehurst's attention. It did not strike him as authentic. What else about Mr. Stillworth might also be inauthentic?

"Let's go back to the castle. I want to show you some of the financial chicanery we found."

"Yes. That is a splendid idea. I should like to see this evidence to corroborate your statements to Uncle Edmund, or else I know he'll refuse to believe. Isn't there a bird from Africa or Australia or someplace like that that hides its head in the sand?" They walked out of the stable and crossed the forecourt.

"I believe you are referring to an ostrich," Lakehurst offered.

"Yes, that's the one. Sometimes I think Uncle Edmund is like that bird, hiding his head in the sand."

"From what I have come to know of Edmund Tidemark, that is most likely true," Lakehurst said with a slight laugh as they walked into the castle. He led the way to the study where he stopped to unlock the door.

"You keep the door locked?"

"Yes."

"Why?"

"First, in here is proof of the Gallaghers embezzlement. Second, we want to make sure all the records are available for the estate steward or whomever they deem appropriate, to audit the financial records of the marquessate. It could be in serious financial difficulties or healthy and profitable. An accountant needs to make that determination."

"You're serious, aren't you? About the potential for financial difficulties?"

Lakehurst looked at him solemnly. "Very."

"What are Cassandra's—excuse me, Lady Darkford's thoughts?"

"I don't know. I haven't shared my concerns with Lady Darkford as I don't wish to worry her needlessly."

Mr. Stillworth followed Lakehurst into the study and looked around at the books and papers piled about.

"I wonder," Mr. Stillworth said softly.

"I beg your pardon?" Lakehurst said.

Mr. Stillworth waved his hand negligently. "Nothing. Just musing if Uncle Edmund had a hand in the Gallaghers actions. Doesn't seem like he'd have the stomach for it, but it was a passing thought."

"Everything should be a consideration until we know what has happened."

"So why have you taken such an extreme interest in Lady Darkford and her affairs?" Mr. Stillworth asked, looking suspiciously at him.

"Because she threw a book across the room."

"She threw a book?"

"Yes, a new gothic novel called 'The Game' by Anonymous."

"I read about it in the newspaper. It's causing quite a stir."

"She claims chapter seventeen is like what she experienced the night the Marquess died."

He frowned. "What do you mean?"

"I'll lend you a copy, and you can read for yourself."

"Why can't you just tell me? I ain't much for novels."

"It will make more of an impact, and you might understand better why Lady Darkford threw the book across the room."

"Well, show me this proof about the Gallaghers,"

he snapped, his tone eloquent in his vexation with Lakehurst.

Lakehurst ignored his attitude. "Right here," he said, leading him to the round table where Lady Darkford had been working the previous day. "Here are receipts for expenditures. Note the date, amount, and vendor. Now we will look at the ledger book for that same time."

Mr. Stillworth looked like he would protest the effort but instead sat down at the table to better look at what Lakehurst showed him.

He was silent a moment as he studied the entries, and then he looked up at Lakehurst. "The amounts recorded in the book are higher!"

Lakehurst nodded as he sat down opposite him. "Exactly, and there is a pattern of this occurring."

"That was rather bold."

"They either didn't think they would be caught or that anyone would care."

"A bit of both, I'd say. Now I understand your concern for the marquessate coffers. What about the estate steward? I met him once. I think his name is Brown, or Browning, or something like that. Isn't he going over the books?"

"From correspondence we found, it appears your uncle limited his involvement to the income half of the ledgers and let the Gallaghers handle the expenses to save money."

"No wonder Lady Darkford is incensed with Uncle Edmund," he said disgustedly.

"It would be difficult not to be in the face of this evidence," Lakehurst said, pointing to the books and papers. "It will be interesting to see what he says in the face of all this. And until he does, this door will stay locked."

Mr. Stillworth turned to stare at him. To Lakehurst, he appeared like he wanted to argue, but he didn't.

"Shall we join the ladies in the parlor? It should be time for afternoon tea—or, if you would prefer, a stronger libation."

"Yes, let's do that. I need to think more about what the evidence in this room means to the overall estate, particularly Baydon Imports."

Lakehurst raised his eyebrows. "I had forgotten about that endeavor with your cousin. I can understand your concern. Much to ponder in this situation."

He wondered if he should tell him about the man following Lady Darkford in London. No, he didn't understand the ramifications of the man's reactions. Best to wait.

CHAPTER 13

THE TIDEMARKS ARRIVE

"Why are you in here?" Lakehurst asked Cassie from the study's open doorway early the next morning. "The more you find, the more distressed you will become," he said as he walked into the room. "You will not be able to greet Mr. Tidemark with any equanimity."

"That is precisely the point," she said.

He looked askance at her. "What do you mean?"

"I want to be angry with him. I want to keep up my disgust for the condition of the estate accounts and the extent of the Gallaghers' thefts."

He sat down in a chair at the other side of the round table where she worked, paper and ink beside, her documenting her discoveries. She ignored him as she finished the notes she'd been taking when he entered.

The morning sun streamed in the windows, the heavy dark blue drapes pushed open as far as they would go to allow the most light to enter. It fell across her as she worked. She looked beautiful. He wondered if she knew how striking she looked, her dark, abundant hair in slight disarray, wild tendrils curling about her face. There was an air of maturity in her face that debutants lacked, and with that maturity, a serenity in her expression as she worked. She smiled slightly as she turned the page of the account book open before her.

"What are you smiling about?" he asked, entranced by how her lovely lips curved up at the sides.

"What? Oh, forgive me. This is all rather fascinating to me. I have to laugh when I see what the Gallaghers got away with. And I am beginning to suspect they were in league with someone else."

"Mr. Browning, perhaps?" he suggested as he leaned back in his chair and crossed one boot-shod leg over the other.

She frowned. "I had considered him, but I don't believe so. At least not wittingly. In one of those letters you found the other day, he appeared to question the instructions they gave him that they said were relayed to them by Edmund."

"Perhaps someone from the village to sell the extra goods they purchased?"

"That is what I'm wondering," she acknowledged, her lips twisting.

He doubted many society women would allow their features to twist into quite that expression of distaste. It made him smile. He pondered a moment on how to describe it in a book.

He pulled his wayward thoughts back from the hole they'd fallen into, a hole they fell into with increasing ease.

"We should ask Carlyle if someone visited them fairly regularly or if they took a wagon with crates in it away from the castle at any time," he said.

She nodded. "That's a sound plan. Do you think they will arrive today?"

"Mr. Stillworth seemed to think so. On the way here, they met up with Ellinbourne. If they want to travel with him, I don't think he would allow them to tarry unnecessarily."

She laughed outright. "So true. My brother can be easy going, but not when he is traveling. He can't sketch while traveling, so he will push on to get where he means to go as quickly as possible."

"And I do not think the Tidemarks would nay say a duke," Lakehurst observed.

"Not the way Vanessa fawns," Cassie said. She pounced her notes, then pushed the pen, ink, and paper to the side.

She sat back in her chair, staring at the ledgers momentarily. "I am concerned for all of this," she said, waving a hand toward the piles of books and papers.

He tilted his head. "In what way?"

She folded her hands in her lap. "I am afraid that we are not as wealthy as I believed. And haven't been since before Richard's death."

"Why do you say that?"

"I looked at a few books from the years before Richard died. It appears he sold off an unentailed property to finance Baydon Imports. Raymond Stillworth's forty-nine percent investment share has been calculated by the value of his work in India to set up their business."

Lakehurst frowned. "Forty-nine percent! That sounds generous. More generous than would typically be seen between cousins. Where did you discover that?"

"I knew Gwinnie had looked in the account ledger bookcase and you looked all through the desk. I wondered what we might find in other parts of the room." She rose from her chair and crossed to another bookcase, painted blue to match the drapes, with a cabinet in the lower half.

Curious, Lakehurst followed her.

She pulled the cabinet doors open. Inside were folders of papers, other ledger books, and bunches of correspondence tied up with string.

"From what I can tell, everything in this cabinet is related to his business venture with Raymond. I didn't dig into everything in here. I am anxious to do so; however, as this does not relate to the Gallaghers' thefts or Edmund's inattention to the marquessate finances, I felt this investigation could wait."

He nodded, thoughts and possibilities racing around in his head. He wondered if Mr. Stillworth knew the Marquess sold property to fund their venture. He leaned down to shut the cabinet for her. "Let's keep this to ourselves for now," he suggested.

She looked at him quizzically.

He took her arm to lead her back to the table. "As you say, one mystery at a time, and should Mr. Stillworth learn of these papers, he would most likely want to investigate them, as they are the most import to him."

"I do feel for Mr. Stillworth. I think Edmund has given him short shrift."

"On the other hand, Mr. Stillworth has allowed it. I wonder why?"

"You suspect something?"

"I don't know. Could be my author's imagination," he said with a deprecating laugh. At the moment, he didn't wish to focus on some of the ideas flitting through his thoughts.

"Nuncheon, anyone?" Gwinnie asked from the doorway. "Cook has prepared a cold collation for us in the dining parlor. Mrs. Pritchet said it was so we don't bother the kitchen staff too much. As we will have more people for dinner, they are in a flurry of activity cooking while still cleaning and setting up the kitchen appropriately."

"Do you know if anyone has addressed the state of the larder yet?" Cassie asked. She smiled, though she shivered dramatically at the thought of all the rats and bugs inside that little room.

"Oh, that was done two days ago by a couple of the men from the village. They are only now putting supplies back in that space. They waited to ensure more vermin didn't come." Gwinnie looked at her brother and grinned. "Would you believe Cook has requested a kitchen mouser?"

He laughed. "After all the times she would yell about Oscar invading her domain. I hope Oscar is all right with so many of us away."

She nodded. "Grandmother will ensure he is. But come on. I am starved, and I have hardly done anything today. Mr. Stillworth is in the dining room before us. I want to make sure he doesn't consume everything before we get there!"

"HENRY SHOULD RETURN with your horse this afternoon, Mr. Stillworth," Lakehurst told him as he sat at the table.

Mr. Stillworth nodded. "Excellent. I'd like to do some riding around the estate. I don't think I've been all over it. As children, Richard came to our estate more than I came to the castle. Irritated my mother a bit as she grew up in the castle, but her brother was a taciturn, unfriendly sort. Mother said he became that way after his wife died. Loved her apparently and never got over her death shortly after Richard's birth. He was so distraught over his wife's death he refused to see Richard until he was a year old, and it became clear Richard resembled him more than his mother. Leastwise, that is what my mother always told me. Odd duck."

"How did you come to be in business with the Marquess?" Lakehurst asked, thinking about Cassie's discoveries in the study.

Mr. Stillworth's eyes took on a faraway look, obviously remembering another time. "It was strange," he said slowly. "Richard approached me on our birthday."

"You were born on the same day?" Gwinnie asked.

He laughed as he looked over at her. "Unusual, isn't it? And my mother and his mother were close schoolgirl friends. My mother often told me she was devastated when Roxanne—Richard's mother—died."

Lakehurst saw the confusion on Cassie's face.

"I wonder why I never knew that?" she mused.

Mr. Stillworth shrugged. "Possibly because we were seldom together when our birthdays came around. Anyway, shortly after our twenty-first birthday, he sought me out. Said he wanted to discuss a potential business venture with me. He was doing coffee trading then but wanted to expand. He saw no reason why China should dominate the tea market, charging whatever they wanted. He suggested I travel to China to see about a trade agreement for tea or, failing that, learn their secrets of tea and spirit away some cuttings for experimental plantings in India."

"At his expense," Lakehurst clarified.

"Yes. He thought India had the right climate to grow tea."

"So, did you do that? Grow tea in India?" he asked.

"Yes, though not as successfully as Richard envisioned. I told him we needed to look at other areas for tea growth. The area he wanted to plant was too hot. I thought some mountainous areas, like the Assam region, would have done better. There is a native tea grown there by the Singphos tribe. The only difference in that tea that I could see, or anyone I talked with could see from the tea grown in China, was the leaves are thicker. I started investing in this area without waiting for any reply from Richard. The time required to send a message to England and get a response back was nigh on a year, so I went ahead with plans, not waiting for a response. I assumed he would be in agreement."

"But he wasn't," Cassie said.

He shook his head. "No. He said the Assam region was too well known. He wanted to find someplace new, where the land would undoubtedly be much cheaper and the native population more eager for work in their region. I couldn't face all the work I'd done getting a position in the Assam market being for naught."

"What did you do?" Lakehurst asked, contemplating the Marquess' motivation. Why send Stillworth to India to research the opportunities then suddenly take a stance of disagreement. Did he not trust his cousin?

He shrugged. "What could I do? I left a manager in charge of the estate I'd purchased in the Assam region and returned to England to talk to Richard, to reason with him."

"When did you return?"

"About six months before he died."

"Had you ever attended one of his parties?" Lakehurst asked.

"I did. I thought joining in his entertainments would open his mind to listen to my reasoning," he explained.

"I take it, it didn't," Lakehurst said drily.

He shook his head, "Kept saying he had his reasons and would laugh."

"Laugh?" Lakehurst queried.

"That would be Richard. He could be highly secretive when he chose," Cassie said wryly.

"But he was always so nice about his secrets," Mr. Stillworth said.

Cassie laughed. "True!"

"I wish I knew why he cooled to our venture. I hoped to use our venture to make my fortune," Mr. Stillworth said sadly.

"We believe he may have been having money problems," Lakehurst said.

Stillworth shook his head vehemently. "No! Never!"

"Did you know he sold an unentailed property to fund your India venture?"

Mr. Stillworth frowned. "Surely there is another reason he did that."

"We don't know," Cassie said with a sigh. "But what with the thefts by the Gallaghers and what we believe he did to finance your efforts, I intend to hire an accountant to go over the marquessate finances."

Mr. Stillworth looked troubled. "You are serious."

"I am," she said.

"That does put a different light on things." He laughed shortly, "I have heard from the tea estate manager that things are going well in India."

"That could be a saving grace for the estate."

"Yes," he said softly, his frown evidence of his deepening thought.

"Well, on that melancholy bit of revelations, and since it is nice outside, I think I will go practice my violin on the ramparts," Gwinnie said, rising from the table.

The others rose as well, and they all left the dining parlor, more subdued than when they entered.

CASSIE THREW a wool shawl about her shoulders and left the castle following their meal. She had no destination in mind, just the compulsion to leave the castle and walk. As Gwinnie had said, it was a nice day. She walked past the stable and Carlyle's hen house down a faint path through the wild grasses and plants. She was surprised the path still existed after little use in the past years. The path led to the cliffs, a crack in the earth. If she followed the path far enough, the cliff's two sides merged. Up ahead, she saw sheep grazing near a dry-stack stone wall that cut across the landscape. She wondered who the sheep belonged to. Baydon didn't have any sheep she knew of, though she granted the estate should. Or cows. Or both. That was Baydon land. Had Edmund leased the land out? Or had the Gallaghers, and then kept the funds for themselves. She would ask Edmund if he had done so. She had not seen anything in the papers she'd examined to indicate he had. Another mystery for later.

The cheddar-pinks still bloomed among the rocks and among Somerset grass's long, needle-like clumps. She mused the unfortunate rains and cooler weather of the year had been a fortunate event for wildflowers typically spent by late June.

The even gray of the sky matched the limestone outcroppings in the earth. The sameness of color made time non-existent until darkness descended again. The temperature was more akin to early spring than summer.

She drew her wool shawl higher up on her shoulders, clutching it at her chest.

Her mind tumbled in turmoil. The marquessate was an enormous responsibility. People depended on it. Could it really be suffering financially? What had Richard actually left his son? It was obvious Edmund was not the person to oversee the holdings. Cassie knew she would have to ensure it gained proper management before there was nothing left for Alex. She did not have the knowledge for such an undertaking, nor she admitted to herself, the interest as it would be a time-consuming task. Thoughts of all the columns of numbers in ledgers made her head hurt. Perhaps Lord Lakehurst or her brother could recommend a gentleman to review the estates' finances, though she truly feared what they might find. However, despite her fears, she would rather know than not know. If they needed to live simply, they could do so. She didn't grow up with an abundance of wealth.

Thinking of Lord Lakehurst made her smile. A gentle giant, and—she thought—a bit shy. If any man deserved happiness, he did. She could not believe the silly gossip passed among the debutants. She considered him a moment and smiled. Those silly girls had no idea of the pleasures that could be found with a man of his size. She could imagine being enfolded in his arms at night, protected from life's storms.

A shiver ran through her.

Gracious! What was she thinking? She wasn't alone. She had Alex, and he must be her priority.

She was not interested in a second marriage. She'd told Gwinnie that. She was certain that was true. Her first marriage, despite her hopes, had quickly become a cool marriage. Two pleasant enough people sharing a living space and a child without any emotional connection between them. Sterile, dry, empty. In these hills, she'd often felt inordinately alone. Is that what she wanted to go on feeling for the rest of her life?

The wind picked up, rustling the long grasses and tugging wisps of hair out of the neat bun Agnes had put her hair in that morning. She turned her face into the wind. She hadn't put on a bonnet before she came out. She'd reasoned that the uniform gray sky hid any sun that might darken her complexion, though in truth, she wanted the freedom. If it had been warmer, she would have also abandoned the shawl, spreading her arms wide to welcome the wind.

"*Cassie!*" she heard faintly.

She turned. Lakehurst came up the path she'd walked.

"Cassie," he called again, his pace quickening.

She waited for him to catch up to her, her feelings mixed on the interruption to her solitude.

"Henry has returned with Mr. Stillworth's horse. He says your brother and the others should be here in less than two hours."

"Thank you," she said. She inhaled deeply and turned to look back over the undulating hills and valleys. "And so it begins," she said.

"Are you afraid for this meeting with your uncle by marriage?" Lakehurst asked.

"Afraid? No, that is not the right word. Apprehensive, perhaps. I do not like discord, and there will be much discord in the conversations we need to have."

"Yes; however, you know you will have the support of Gwinnie and me, and perhaps Mr. Stillworth as well."

"Yes, Raymond as well. I'm afraid he had all his hopes for his future tied up in the Baydon Imports Company."

"I fear you are correct."

They turned to walk back toward the castle.

"Edmund will become defensive and not listen if I display anger immediately. We will need to see he is relaxed."

Lakehurst nodded. "Wise. Ask him what he knew of the Gallaghers, then bring up your concerns after listening to him."

"I agree."

~

ELLINBOURNE, his fiancée Ann Hallowell, and her stepmother, Ursula Hallowell, arrived shortly after Lakehurst and Cassie returned to the castle. They said they thought the Tidemarks were a good half hour behind them.

"Mrs. Tidemark demanded the coachman slow down as the ruts and rocks of the roads leading to the castle made her uncomfortable," Ellinbourne told them.

Cassie nodded. "I believe that. She has never been a good traveler."

"She is an awful traveler," Ursula Hallowell put in. "And a worse traveling companion," she groused.

"Now Ursula," protested Ann.

"You know I am right."

Ann sighed.

Cassie laughed. "Let me show you to your rooms so you might wash the traveling dust away."

"That would be lovely," Ursula said.

"We'll serve tea in the parlor as soon as the Tidemarks arrive, for I'm sure that will be more important to Vanessa than washing up first. The parlor is right here," she said, pointing to a room on the left, "for whenever you feel like coming down."

"Oh, oh! I swear I shall have bruises atop of bruises," they heard Mrs. Tidemark wail as her husband assisted her from their carriage forty-five minutes later. Her hand rubbed her generous backside for a moment before she accepted Tidemark's arm to lead her to the castle door.

Lakehurst noticed his sister looking down and compressing her lips tightly against a smile or laugh.

Cassie left his side to approach Mrs. Tidemark. "You poor dear. Let's get you in the castle and make you comfortable. Would you rather go to your room first or relax on a sofa in the parlor with tea and cakes?" she asked.

"Tea sounds wonderful," she said weakly, leaning on her husband's arm. "And... and maybe a little cake?"

"Of course, this way," Cassie soothed.

Mrs. Tidemark's response had been exactly as Cassie predicted, Lakehurst mused.

"It's quite large, isn't it?" Mrs. Tidemark said, staring up at the castle.

Lakehurst noticed apprehension in her eyes. He remembered that Cassie said the woman had never been to the castle before.

"Jolly grand!" Mrs. Tidemark's brother, Harrison Farrow, said jovially, swinging down from his horse and handing the reins to Henry. The London dandy swaggered toward them as they stood on the broad stone steps before the castle. "I'll go to my room first, if you don't mind. Can't visit in all my dirt, you know," he said.

"The housekeeper will show you to your room," Lakehurst said, inviting the man to proceed before him into the house.

"Excellent! Excellent!" crowed Mr. Farrow.

In the hall, Mr. Farrow paused to look around. The entrance hall retained much of its medieval decor with banners and crossed spears and swords on the dark wood-paneled walls. "I say, those small windows up there throw more light during the day into this hall than one would think, eh?" he said, pointing to the line of square windows high on the front wall.

Lakehurst watched him follow after the housekeeper, his eyes darting everywhere. Lakehurst looked over at his sister. "Have you seen Mr. Stillworth recently?" he asked.

She shook her head. "Not since nuncheon, but I believe I heard him saying something about taking your horse and going out for a ride."

"My horse?"

"You did offer," she reminded him.

He grimaced. "So I did. I just thought he wouldn't want to ride until his horse rested since the horse just arrived today. Didn't know he'd be that impatient to ride. Perhaps it is just as well that he is not here for the initial conversations with Mr. Tidemark."

Gwinnie grinned. "I think I'll head to the small parlor to practice. It was getting too windy up on the ramparts earlier."

"You don't want to come observe?"

She shook her head. "Might be too windy in there, too. Don't think I could keep a straight face."

"True. I saw you when the Tidemarks arrived. Not good to laugh at guests, Gwinnie."

"I know, but no need to get stuffy about it. You know it was like watching a play. That's why I shall return after the comedic conclusion, else my face would betray me."

He shook his head at her insouciance, then turned to follow the others into the main parlor. Ellinbourne, Ann, and Ursula had come back downstairs and were before them. They had hurried through their ablutions when they heard a brief summary of what the castle conditions were when Cassie and the Nowltons arrived. They didn't want to miss the Tidemark's reactions.

LAKEHURST WATCHED Cassie settle Mrs. Tidemark on the sofa with the plumpest cushions and encouraged her to slip off her shoes and bring her legs up on the sofa. She draped a throw over Mrs. Tidemark's legs.

"Thank you, dear. That is so sweet of you, isn't it, Edmund?" the woman said, looking over at her husband.

"Yes, yes, very. But I am extremely vexed with her!" he stated, throwing out the first salvo.

Lakehurst grinned as Cassie looked at Edmund Tidemark with feigned equanimity.

"How well do you know the Gallaghers?" she asked.

"Well enough. Why are you asking? They have nothing to do with my unhappiness with your actions. How dare you allow Alex to go with the Duchess of Malmsby without consulting me first!"

"Would you have forbidden it? We discussed it at the dinner party."

He squirmed, his lips working. He pushed his glasses up his nose. "That is not the point!" he finally said.

"Tell me about the Gallaghers," Cassie countered again.

Lakehurst leaned back in his chair. The formerly timid Marchioness had become a virago.

"I know them only through letters," he admitted.

"Ah. Why did you cut Mr. Browning's responsibilities?"

"Why are you asking these questions? This is no concern of yours, nor anyone else's. Mr. Gallagher suggested the estate didn't need him full-time. With him paying the bills, all Mr. Browning needs to do is collect the rents."

"Did you tell Mr. Browning to raise the rents?"

"No, of course not. I don't communicate with Mr. Browning. There is no need. I let Mr. Gallagher do that. Mr. Gallagher said that would make for cleaner communications, and I have found that to be true. I have absolute faith in the man. But again, I say, that is not the point!"

"On the contrary, Edmund," Cassie said serenely. She sipped her tea. "I think it is precisely the point. You do not know, nor did you ask, for an estate accounting. You have no idea as to the condition of the marquessate, do you? Have you hired an accountant to balance the books?"

"Of course not. I get reports from Mr. Gallagher."

"You won't get them any longer." She set her cup down on the table.

"What have you done, woman? If you have fired him to the detriment of the estate, you are crazy, and that gives me grounds to assign you to a sanitorium, and don't think I won't!"

"You would have to go through me and my family to do that," Ellinbourne growled.

"Mine as well," said Lakehurst, staring Mr. Tidemark down.

Mr. Tidemark stared at Ellinbourne and Lakehurst and squirmed under their regard. "The Gallaghers have been good caretakers of the property," protested Mr. Tidemark in a whine.

"Are you sure of that?" Cassie asked calmly.

He stared at her for a moment, his lips tightening, loosening, and tightening again as he ran through what he would say. "Yes, I am, dammit," he finally said, the words bursting from between his lips. "Where are they? I demand to speak to them!"

"They ran away," Cassie said complacently. She smiled as she picked up her cup of tea again and took another sip.

"If they did, you threatened them! You are piling on the reasons why you need to be institutionalized. You are erratic and unsafe, and I shall also report this to the magistrate."

Lakehurst rose from his chair. He crossed to the fireplace and leaned against the mantle behind Mr. Tidemark. The man glanced up at him nervously.

Lakehurst grinned. For perhaps the first time in his life, he deliberately used his size for intimidation.

Cassie's eyes lit up as she laughed. "Please do report this," she said earnestly. "And I will show all the receipts and books that do not match and the letter from Mr. Browning protesting a ten percent rent increase Mr. Gallagher informed him you requested."

"I did no such thing," he bristled.

"Precisely my point," she said, now glaring at him.

Color rose up his neck and through his face. "What are you saying, madam?" he demanded.

"Edmund, you have callously ignored this estate. You have even denied Mr. Stillworth the ability to proceed with the plans he and Richard had begun for their venture. You have withheld my money and reduced my staff to a bare minimum. I'd like to know why?"

"But Edmund was saving the estate!" Mrs. Tidemark said, her expression pulled tight in confusion. "Isn't that right Edmund? You told me everything is in funds," she stated. "Just as my brother, Rupert, instructed you to do."

Mr. Tidemark shifted in his seat. "Not precisely, my pet," he admitted.

"Well, however, it was, I'm sure my husband has made the best decisions for you," Mrs. Tidemark said airily. She reached for another cake from the tray at the end of the sofa.

"My brother started a new venture growing tea in Assam, India, you know," Mrs. Tidemark rattled on.

"Vanessa, you know your brother said that is not for general knowledge," Mr. Tidemark said. "Mustn't speak of it."

"Like Richard and Raymond's venture?" Cassie asked.

"Yes, and better!" Vanessa said. "Edmund, this is not sharing in society. This is family," she explained. "He said—"

"Vanessa!" Mr. Tidemark yelled at his wife.

"What?" she cried out, her expression crumbling. "I understand more than you think I do. I am not stupid." Tears slid down her cheeks.

Mr. Tidemark rose from his chair to sit next to his wife. He put his arm around her ample shoulders. "I'm sorry, my sweet, I shouldn't have yelled. It's just... It's just..." he trailed off.

"It is just what?" Cassie asked.

"Rupert convinced me he was more likely to succeed than Richard and Raymond. It would be better to invest money in his venture than sink any more funds into Baydon Imports."

"But you have never told Raymond this, you merely ignored him whenever he would speak of it with you."

He glared at her but reluctantly nodded.

"You undermined what could have been a profitable venture for the marquessate."

"Rupert convinced me Richard's plans wouldn't be profitable. I was doing what I saw as right to protect young Alex's inheritance," he declared pugnaciously. "The estate has not been particularly profitable, quite the reverse. I have been worried for its solvency."

"Problems caused by you and the Gallaghers," Lakehurst said from behind him.

"Were you in league with the Gallaghers in their embezzling?" Cassie asked.

"Embezzling?"

"Yes. The Gallaghers, who you think were doing a good job, would get a receipt for goods at one price and enter a price twice that in the ledger books."

"What? No! That's daft. You know nothing about money and accounts. I am sure you are misinterpreting the entries."

Cassie's eyes flared. "We have proof. I, Lady Guinevere, Lord Lakehurst, and Raymond have all seen the falsified entries. They are quite easy to discern."

Stillworth's name seemed to bring him up short. Tidemark frowned. "Stillworth is here?"

Cassie nodded. "He is out riding the property right now."

Mr. Tidemark frowned. "I didn't think he'd actually come," he said. "Too rustic, he always complained about Baydon, so I tried to dissuade him from coming. I thought when he left us he was returning to London. Didn't even have his valet with him, you know."

"Too rustic? Odd for you to say that. Yet he came here for the Marquess's parties."

Tidemark compressed his lips. "Unfortunately, he and Richard were quite close."

"*Unfortunately?* Why would you say that?" Cassie asked.

"Because they weren't supposed to be!" he ground out.

"What? Why not? I'm not understanding you, Edmund," Cassie said. "You seem to be tied in knots."

He appeared to collapse in on himself. He put his head in his hands. "I can't talk anymore. I'm tired. I can't think straight. It has been a long trip, a trip I never thought to make again. I hate this place!" he said vehemently.

Mrs. Tidemark clung to her husband. It was obvious she didn't understand what was going on. "Can we go to our room?" she asked Cassie tentatively.

Cassie realized there was no getting any more from Edmund at the moment. "Of course. I'll have Mrs. Pritchet show you to your room. Please don't hesitate to ask her for anything you require."

Mr. and Mrs. Tidemark rose, leaning on each other.

"Thank you, thank you," Mr. Tidemark said on a great sigh. They walked to the parlor door. Suddenly, Mr. Tidemark stopped and turned back to the others in the room. "Let's not discuss the tea venture in front of Mr. Stillworth," he asked plaintively, then they left the room.

When the door closed behind them, everyone looked at each other.

"What just happened?" Ellinbourne asked.

Cassie shook her head. "I don't know; however, I feel there is more going on than we ever thought."

"Excuse me, my lady," Mr. Harold said, coming into the parlor from the servant's entrance. "There is a gentleman at the kitchen door to see you."

"Who is it?" Cassie asked.

"A Mr. Liddle. Says you know him."

"Mr. Liddle? Here already? Yes, please show him in," Cassie said.

"But do not let anyone else into this parlor while he is here," Lakehurst said, thinking quickly of Mr. Tidemark's possible reaction to any news Mr. Liddle might bring.

Cassie nodded. "Excellent suggestion," she said. The smile she directed at him threatened to addle his brain.

"Very good, my lord," bowed Mr. Harold.

"Who is Mr. Liddle?" Ellinbourne asked.

"He's a friend of Mr. Martin's. Mr. Martin sent him a letter asking him to contact us. When we met two days ago, we asked him to go after the Gallaghers," Lakehurst explained, pulling his thoughts back together as the back door to the parlor opened.

"And I have apprehended them. They are in the magistrate's custody in Wells," Mr. Liddle announced as he entered the room.

"Amazing!" Cassie said, clapping.

"Did you recover stolen goods?"

Mr. Liddle's grin went lopsided. "Goods and cash," he said as he pulled a leather pouch out of the deep pockets of his coat. He crossed the room to place it in Cassie's lap.

Cassie's eyes went wide. "It's heavy!"

He nodded. "The goods will arrive tomorrow by cart."

"There was that much?" Cassie asked. She turned to look at Lakehurst. "I thought Henry only saw them load luggage into their carriage."

Lakehurst shrugged.

Mr. Liddle smiled. "The goods were in a storeroom at The Bristled Hound coaching inn, ready to be transported to auction. Thanks to the good offices of the magistrate, they were induced to provide me with this information."

"Induced, you say?" said Ellinbourne.

"Oh, Mr. Liddle, this is my brother, the Duke of Ellinbourne," Cassie said.

"Your Grace," Mr. Liddle acknowledged, making his bow.

"Let me introduce you to the others—You will stay the night, won't you?"

"I should be delighted, my lady," he said. "But most people would prefer to see a thief-taker leave as soon as possible after they are paid," he told her seriously.

She squeezed the pouch that lay in her lap. "Mr. Liddle, I am not most people. But, to keep things in accordance with expectations, you may leave as soon as possible after you have been paid.—Tomorrow.—After breakfast," Cassie said, drawing it out.

"Or later," Lakehurst added. "We still need to discuss the death of the Marquess of Darkford."

"Oh! Yes! The Gallaghers were only part of our requirements," Cassie said.

Mr. Liddle laughed, and held up his hands before him. "All right!"

"Excellent. You have met my brother, now let me introduce you to the others. This is Miss Hallowell, my brother's fiancée, and her stepmother, Mrs. Hallowell."

"Charmed," he said in a deep, rumbling voice as he bowed over their hands.

"Also staying with us is Mr. Stillworth, and Mr. and Mrs. Tidemark, and of course, Gwinnie, who you met the other night. Most of the servants are from the Duke of Malmsby's household."

"In his letter to me, Lewis mentioned that would be the situation."

"How long have you known Mr. Martin?" Ellinbourne asked. "We had the pleasure of working with him at the Duchess of Malmsby's estate."

"We met at school," Mr. Liddle said, "And have kept in contact over the years."

Lakehurst nodded, and would have liked to ask him more questions about his association with Mr. Martin, but not in a group. Perhaps over a pint of ale, or a brandy, later.

"I'm going to put this money in the study," Cassie said, standing up. "It will be an hour and a half before dinner. You all may want to rest or take a walk. Please don't roam the castle without one of us or the servants, it would be easy to get lost and I fear not all of it is in the best of repair. Mr. Liddle, Mrs. Prichett will show you to a room."

He inclined his head. "Thank you, my lady."

Lakehurst followed Cassie as the rest of the party dispersed. "I'll help you count the money, if you like," he told her. "We will need to determine how much to pay Mr. Liddle."

"Thank you for offering. I believe it is quite a sum. The bag is heavy," she said, passing it to him.

He chuckled as he hefted it. "So it appears to be. This should go a long way to pay for repairs."

She unlocked the door to the study.

Lakehurst crossed to the desk to set the bag down while Cassie found the tinderbox and lit candles in the room, as the afternoon had turned gray and the sun no longer penetrated into the room.

They sat across from each other, neither speaking as they sorted the coins and counted them into stacks. Cassie liked working with Lakehurst across the desk. They worked methodically, the only sounds disturbing the afternoon quiet were the clinking of coins and the distant strains of Gwinnie on her violin. When Cassie put her last coin on a pile, she sat back in her chair.

"I put the total value to 478 guineas," Lakehurst said.

Cassie nodded. "That is what I count as well. That is a large amount to have robbed from the estate. If that is just what they had in the castle when we arrived, how much else have they taken away or spent over the past eighteen months?"

"At least double that, I would guess," Lakehurst said, "judging by the discrepancies in the receipts and ledger books."

Cassie shook her head. "I wonder why they even kept the receipts?"

"Most likely to ensure the merchants they purchased from were not cheating them and asking for more money on an invoice," Lakehurst drawled. "Thieves fear being robbed more than we do."

Cassie laughed, then stood up and crossed to the window. She saw her brother and Ann walking the same cliff path she'd walked the other day. It looked like Ann was pointing at the sheep she'd seen the other day, for her brother nodded and they walked in that direction along the cliff edge.

She sighed. She envied her brother's happiness. He'd found the perfect woman for his wife. Ann was gentle and sweet, but intermixed with intelligence and a sense of fun. Her brother needed her sense of fun. He'd become far too serious since becoming the Duke of Ellinbourne. And with Ann, he did not have to deny his art for his title. She loved who he was, as he was.

She turned to look back to where Lakehurst stood by the desk, staring at her. She smiled.

"I see my brother and Ann, sketchbooks in hand, walking down the cliff path."

"I don't think I've ever seen Ellinbourne without a sketchbook," Lakehurst said.

"Not often," Cassie admitted. She turned to look back out the window.

Lakehurst came up behind. He gently pulled her back against him. She allowed her head to fall back to rest against his chest as he wrapped his large arms gently around her. She felt the steady beat of his heart.

"Thank you," she said.

"For what?" he whispered.

"As I said the other day, for being who you are," she answered simply.

"And who is that?" he asked with a low chuckle. He brushed his chin across the top of her head.

She took a deep, relaxing breath, then let it out slowly. "A caring man," she said. "A man who uses his size for protection, not intimidation. I feel safe, something I haven't felt in a long time," she said with a curious lilt to her voice. She wondered when during her marriage to the Marquess of Darkford she'd stopped feeling safe. He'd always been pleasant and respectful to her; however, she'd never felt safe, that she could recall. Odd to think of that now.

"I've fallen in love with you," he said.

She stiffened again, then turned in his arms, placing her hands against his chest. "Please, don't..." she said, her voice hurting.

"Why not?" he asked. He kissed the top of her head. "I can't help that I fell in love with you when you threw my book across the room."

Cassie felt a shiver run through her body. She closed her eyes as she wanted to melt into him. She laid her forehead against his chest.

"I don't know that I am ready. Or that I ever shall be," she wailed. "If only I'd met you instead of Richard six years ago. We might have had a chance."

"Why do we not have a chance now?" he asked gently. He brushed a thumb against the side of her cheek. She leaned into his hand without thinking, savoring his touch.

He bent his head down to touch her lips with his. She looked up into his eyes with wonder.

Shouts and the clattering of boots running down the hall broke them apart.

The door to the study burst open.

"Carlyle's dead!" said Henry, gasping for breath.

"Dead!" repeated Cassie, stunned.

Henry nodded.

"Where?" Lakehurst demanded, coming toward the man.

"Down the cliff."

Lakehurst ran out of the room. Cassie gathered her skirts in her hand and ran after him.

CHAPTER 14
CARLYLE

Lakehurst ran to where Ellinbourne, Ann, and his coachman, John Norton, stood at the cliff edge, Ann's face buried in Ellinbourne's jacket.

"Where?" he asked.

"Right down there, my lord," Norton said, pointing. "Landed on a ledge. From 'ere it looks like the fall broke 'is neck."

Lakehurst nodded, but something made him doubt it was that simple. "Norton, go back to the castle and ask Mr. Liddle to please join us."

"I'll do that," Ellinbourne said before Norton could leave. "I want to take Ann back to the house. You can stay here to help Lakehurst with whatever he needs," he said as Cassie reached the group.

She walked up to look over the cliff edge. Lakehurst pulled her away. "You should go with Ellinbourne. It's no sight for a lady."

"That may be," Cassie said, "however, I am his employer and as such I need to see all that is going on," she said, pulling out of Lakehurst's restraint.

Carlyle lay on a ledge a third of the way down the crevice, his head bent at an odd angle.

Lakehurst frowned. "Norton, get a rope from the stable and have Henry harness a horse to the farm cart. We'll need it once we bring Carlyle up."

Norton pulled on his forelock and trotted toward the stable as Lakehurst studied the terrain to determine the best way to get down the cliff to reach Carlyle. With a rope, he could descend the cliff to the right of him where the ledge appeared wider. He'd have to carry him over his shoulder. He squinted his eyes. Maybe he could tie him to himself as he climbed back up.

"What are you thinking?" Cassie asked.

"How to get him out of there. With a rope, I can get down there."

"Why you? Shouldn't that be something Norton, Henry, or Mr. Liddle should do?" she asked.

"It would take more than one of them to get him up, but that ledge is too small to have two men down there. I can put him over my shoulder, tie him in place if need be, and climb back up."

"But—" she started to protest.

He placed his large hands on her shoulders. "Cassie, I'd like to use my size for more than filling out a coat," he said with a rueful sad smile.

She closed her eyes for a moment and nodded. "But it's dangerous!" she blurted out when she opened her eyes again.

He wanted to kiss her for her concern. Instead, he dropped his arms from her shoulders and stepped away.

"I'll be careful. I have a lot of new plans for the future that I promise I will not jeopardize," he said, looking at her intently, at the incessant wind pulling her dark hair out of its neat confines and blowing her skirts close about here. She looked vulnerable yet strong as she stood resolute against the wind, her eyes wide, her gaze intent on him.

She bit her lip and nodded.

He nodded in return and smiled. Something precious had just passed between them. He couldn't name it, yet it made him feel complete.

Mr. Liddle approached them as Norton drove the farm cart out of the stable with Henry beside him.

"YOUR MAN SAID SOMEONE FELL?" Mr. Liddle said when he approached them.

"Dead, so it appears. Whether he accidentally fell remains to be determined," Lakehurst said.

Cassie looked from one man to the other. "It's Carlyle," she said. "He's been on the estate since the Marquess was a child. He was deaf due to mumps as a young man."

"So he was extremely familiar with the property and its cliffs," Mr. Liddle clarified.

"Very much so," she said. "But if someone came up behind him and pushed him, he would not have heard them."

"Is that what you think happened?" he asked, crossing his arms over his chest. He looked around them, studying the area.

"I don't know what to think," she said honestly. "Just that he should not be dead," she said, looking back over the cliff at his body sprawled below.

"I am going to climb down to bring up the body," Lakehurst told him.

Mr. Liddle looked at him, then nodded. He uncrossed his arms. "Let me go down first to inspect the scene, to see if there are any other marks on him that might let us know if he fell or someone pushed him. Those signs may not be clear once he is brought up," Mr. Liddle said.

Lakehurst scowled but agreed. "We'll tie the rope around this large rock," he said.

Mr. Liddle looked at the area and nodded. "That looks strong enough not to pull out." He pulled gloves out of his pocket, then removed his coat before putting the gloves on.

Cassie thought gloves were an excellent idea. "Henry," she called out. "Please return to the castle to fetch Viscount Lakehurst's gloves."

With the rope in place, Mr. Liddle eased himself over the side of the cliff and slowly climbed down, avoiding scrubby bits of bushes and grasses growing from cracks in the rock. He squatted down next to Carlyle's body when he reached the ledge. He examined his hands and head and pulled his shirt away from his neck. Then he carefully turned the man over. Carlyle's body was near to tumbling further down the rock face. He checked him over, then rolled him back, away from the treacherous edge. He stood and stared down at the body for a moment longer, his hands on his hips, then grabbed the rope to climb back up.

Lakehurst reached out a hand to him as he got near the top and pulled him up the rest of the way.

"As I believe you suspected, my lord, the man did not accidentally fall; but he was not simply pushed, either." He slipped his coat back on. "There are signs on his neck that show someone strangled him first."

"Strangled!" Cassie repeated.

Mr. Liddle turned toward her. "Yes, my lady. And I'd say the person approached him from behind and used their bare hands. There are bruises in the shape of finger marks on the front of his neck."

"But why kill Carlyle?" Cassie said. "He was a gentle, faithful soul."

"He was also the only person from the castle staff here that night," Lakehurst said grimly.

"That night?" prompted Mr. Liddle.

"The night of the Marquess of Darkford's death," Lakehurst said.

"It was Carlyle who removed Richard's body from on top of me and brought me out of the cave," Cassie explained.

Lakehurst looked at Cassie. "Carlyle told me he wasn't dead yet, though he expired shortly after he moved him," Lakehurst said.

"Did he say anything else?" Mr. Liddle asked.

"Carlyle said the Marquess tried to tell him something; however, the light was dim and his head was turned slightly away. Carlyle tried to understand. He thought he said something like *my bra* or *my bro*, he couldn't tell what he was trying to say as he was fading fast, his lips barely moving."

"But Carlyle told me Richard was already dead!" cried Cassie.

"He told you that to help ease your mind. If you had known he was alive while he laid across you and you could do nothing to help it would have destroyed you."

Tears filled her eyes. "He might have thought right."

"Someone thinks he knew something. And perhaps he did," Mr. Liddle said grimly.

"I'll bring him up," Lakehurst said.

"I suggest taking your boots off. I wished I had," Mr. Liddle said.

He looked down at his heavy boots and nodded. "Excellent suggestion." He sat down on the rock they'd wrapped the rope around, removed his boots, then stood and removed his jacket. Looking at Cassie a moment, he draped his coat over her shoulders. "You forgot your shawl," he said softly.

She nodded and pulled his coat close around her shoulders. It was warm and smelled of him.

Lakehurst put on the leather gloves Henry brought him.

Cassie reached out to touch his arm. "Be careful," she whispered.

He nodded.

Grabbing the rope and loosely wrapping it around himself, he climbed down the rocks. Once on the ledge, he stooped to pick up Carlyle. The poor man's body was stiffening, the smell of death rising. He'd been dead for a while.

He hefted him onto his shoulder, then using a knife Mr. Liddle had handed him before he descended, he cut off a length of rope to secure Carlyle to his chest, for once grateful he was a large man.

He thought grimly that he would tell his man to dispose of these clothes after this. He couldn't imagine wearing them again.

He started the climb up the rock wall, his toes finding crevices as a foundation to hold him against the rock as his arms pulled one hand over the other on the rope, his shoulders burning. Dead weight was dead weight.

"Let us help," Mr. Liddle called down. "As your feet find purchase, Norton, Henry, and I will help pull you up. Wrap your hands around the rope," he suggested.

Lakehurst tried what Liddle suggested and found that easier. He walked up the wall to each tug on the rope. Near the top, Mr. Liddle grabbed on to Carlyle's body, easing some of the weight off his shoulder so he could pull himself up the rest of the way. He collapsed at the top of the cliff, Carlyle's body still tied to him.

Mr. Liddle swiftly cut the rope loose and he and Norton carried Carlyle to the wagon and heaved him into it.

Lakehurst laid there a moment, his muscles quivering. "Thank you," he said when they returned.

With Cassie on one side and Mr. Liddle on the other, they got him to his feet.

"I never want to do that again," he said, huffing, bending forward, his hands pressed against his knees.

Next to him, Cassie and Mr. Liddle laughed tightly. There were tears in Cassie's eyes. "And I pray you won't either," she said.

"What's going on?" demanded Mr. Stillworth as he rode up to them on MacKenzie, Lakehurst's horse.

Lakehurst frowned and straightened. Sweat glistened on his horse's body. He looked blown. He had been ridden hard. Lakehurst ground his teeth in silent vexation.

Stillworth looked in the farm cart. "Is that Carlyle? Is he dead?" He dismounted and tossed the reins to Henry.

"Yes," Cassie said, tears coming to the fore again. She pulled Lakehurst's jacket more snuggly about her.

Lakehurst stepped away from Liddle's and Cassie's support and stomped over to his horse. Without a word to anyone, he took the reins from Henry and walked MacKenzie to the barn, his jaw rigid.

"I say, what's going on?" Stillworth asked, staring after Lakehurst. He turned to Cassie and Mr. Liddle. "And who are you?" he demanded, looking Mr. Liddle up and down.

"Harry Liddle," Mr. Liddle said, offering no other information.

"Where have you been all day?" Cassie asked Stillworth.

"Riding around the estate, checking on the tenants, the mines, that sort of thing. I say, did you know the Graymore mine is no longer worked?"

"No."

His brow furrowed in thought. "Well, it isn't. Surprised me, as Richard always spoke about the popularity of the stone from that site for its color."

"Edmund," Cassie said angrily. "I'm sure of it—Oh, no! The study door is unlocked, and we left all that money on the desk!" She ran toward the castle.

"My lady!" Norton called after her. "Where do we take Carlyle?"

Cassie stopped and turned, thinking for a moment. She pushed wind-tossed hair strands away from her face. "To the old castle chapel!" she yelled back at them, then turned and continued running down the path to the castle.

~

CASSIE RETURNED to the study in time to find Edmund hurriedly stuffing the last of the coins back in the leather pouch.

"Put that pouch down!" she ordered, her hands on her hips, her eyes flashing fire at him.

"This is not yours," he said sternly.

"Correct. It is the estate money which means it is not yours to take."

"I am executor of the estate and in that role I shall take charge of the funds," he declared, pushing past her.

He was stopped at the door by the presence of Mr. Liddle who had followed after Cassie.

"No, you will not," Mr. Liddle declared calmly.

"Whoever you are, get out of my way!" Edmund blustered.

Mr. Liddle smiled at him. "No. I am a thief-taker, hired by Lady Darkford and Lord Lakehurst to recover the funds and the goods stolen from the castle. Right now, you look to me like a thief, so I will take that pouch from you and turn you over to the magistrate as I have turned over the Gallaghers," his voice low, dark, and menacing.

Cassie's eyes opened wide at Mr. Liddle's change in manner. He looked like a feral wolf, quite unlike the man she'd had dealings with. She blinked. This must be why he was a successful thief-taker.

"You wouldn't dare!" Edmund said.

"Oh, but I would," declared Mr. Liddle softly.

Cassie could see his shoulders bunching under his jacket.

"Would you care for proof?" he asked silkily in his dark, rumbling bass voice.

"I will be discussing this with the magistrate," Edmund declared, handing him the pouch.

Mr. Liddle bowed his head. "From you, I would expect nothing less. But remember, the magistrate is local. You are not."

"Are you threatening me?"

"I thought I'd already done so," Mr. Liddle told him. "Did I not, Lady Darkford?"

"I believe you did, Mr. Liddle."

Mr. Liddle stepped aside and allowed Edmund to leave the study.

"Best lock this away, my lady," Mr. Liddle said.

She nodded. She took the pouch from him. "Thank you," she said.

He waved her thanks aside. "I know his type," he

said. "That would-be lion possesses neither teeth nor claws, just weight to throw around, and not even much of that."

~

LAKEHURST HELD the bucket of oats for MacKenzie after rubbing him down. His Uncle Griffin gifted the horse to him the last time he'd been in Scotland. He snorted as he thought of that. It was eighteen months ago, about the time of Darkford's murder. The chestnut had the size and stamina of a war horse. His uncle had claimed he was a horse well up to Lakehurst's size and weight. Lakehurst agreed.

MacKenzie could take the abuse Stillworth had shown him; however, that was not what Lakehurst wished for him to endure. Stillworth was a handsome ass, not worthy of Cassie.

What had made him admit he loved her? He did, but he knew his timing was wrong. That he loved her surprised him. He didn't know when it happened. It had caught him off-guard.

He wanted her for his wife, his future duchess, and for him to be a father to Alex and to however many other children they might be blessed to have. She certainly fit in with his eccentric family and never batted an eye at their machinations. His grandmother already loved her—not that Grandmother's approval mattered.

He knew Cassie was afraid. Not like the debutants were afraid. She wasn't afraid of him.

She was afraid of herself, afraid she had somehow been the reason Darkford had not loved her. That there was something about her that was ultimately unlovable.

The fool idiot man.

He needed to prove to her he loved her and would always love her. The fault in her first marriage had been with Darkford, not her.

With the bucket of oats empty, Lakehurst patted his horse's neck and left the stable.

UPON HIS RETURN to the castle, Lakehurst asked a footman to find his valet and send him to him and went immediately upstairs to the rooms he'd been assigned. He'd just removed his waistcoat and shirt when Gwinnie barged into his room.

"Gwinnie!" he protested.

"Lake, where have you been?"

"Tending MacKenzie. Don't you know how to knock? A moment more and I'd been undressed, fool woman."

She waved her hand dismissively. "You're just my brother; besides, I've seen you skinny-dipping at Versely Park. I know what you look like in the altogether."

"What?" Lakehurst protested. "And it doesn't matter if you are my sister or not. A lady does not barge into a man's rooms. It just isn't done."

"Well, it's done if she has something important to tell him."

"And what is so important?" he asked, calming down. Gwinnie was Gwinnie, and he loved her dearly.

"Mr. Tidemark tried to steal the money Mr. Liddle gave Cassie yesterday. Mr. Liddle stopped him, but Mr. Tidemark is angry and threatening everything he can think of, greatly distressing Cassie. She is putting on a brave, calm face; however, I've seen her hands shake.

She is near breaking, I swear it. I know I would be if I had to deal with an idiot like Mr. Tidemark," Gwinnie said, pacing his room.

"No, you wouldn't," her brother contradicted. "However, I understand the strength of your concern that you would say so. Let me get cleaned up, and I'll be down."

Gwinnie paused, her brows knitting together. "She needs you, brother of mine."

"I hope for more than just dealing with Darkford messes," he groused.

His sister stopped and visibly relaxed as she smiled at him. "She does. She may not realize it yet, but she does."

COMING DOWNSTAIRS TWENTY MINUTES LATER, Lakehurst heard loud voices coming from the parlor. He winced. While he'd enjoyed a few moments of solitude with MacKenzie in the stable, his sister's words raised guilt in his chest, for Cassie had not had any time alone, time to think through all that had been happening. Now his gentle love was caught in the middle of irate gentlemen. Gwinnie was likely correct in her assessment of Cassie. She needed support.

He pushed open the parlor door.

Mr. Tidemark glanced in his direction, then turned and marched toward him. "You! You! This is all your fault!" he declared repeatedly, poking at his broad chest with his forefinger.

Lakehurst caught the man's hand. "Enough," he said. "Unless you wish to temporarily—if you are lucky, only temporarily—lose the use of this hand," he said with equanimity as he squeezed Mr. Tidemark's hand slightly, then let go.

Mr. Tidemark scowled and then sneered. "You don't frighten me; I have the law on my side," he said, pulling on his coat lapels as he backed away.

"Mr. Tidemark," Lakehurst said tiredly, "since last I saw you, I have climbed up a cliff with a dead man on my shoulder, curried and fed my lathered horse as the stable hands were called to other matters, gone to my room to get cleaned up, come downstairs to hear acrimonious voices coming from this room that could be heard by anyone in the hall, and walked in only to have you accost me on my entrance. I strongly suggest you sit down next to your wife and calm down lest I have you thrown out of the castle."

"You would not be so presumptuous," Mr. Tidemark huffed defiantly.

"Tidemark," Lakehurst said, his eyes narrowing as he looked down on him. "You do not know me well enough to make that statement with any measure of certainty, so I suggest you sit down."

"Edmund," wailed Mrs. Tidemark softly.

Mr. Tidemark glared at him, but returned to his seat by his wife.

"Well done, brother of mine!" crowed Gwinnie, smiling and rocking happily while Mr. Liddle clapped, and Ellinbourne tilted his head and nodded.

"Thank you," Cassie said. She sat on a sofa facing the Tidemarks. Ann and Ursula sat on either side of her, holding her hands.

Mr. Stillworth sat in a chair by the fireplace, looking bored. Lakehurst studied him. To merely ride about the estate would not have taxed MacKenzie. He would know where Stillworth went and what he did with his horse. But he would deal with him and the matter of MacKenzie, later.

He walked over to the sofa where Cassie sat. Ann smiled at him, gently released Cassie's hand, and stood up. She went to stand by Ellinbourne, linking her arm through his. Lakehurst took her seat next to Cassie. Though he didn't touch her, he sensed the tension in her lessen.

"Has the coroner been sent for?" he asked the others in the room.

"I sent a note to the coroner and the magistrate," Mr. Liddle said. "As they are in Wells, we likely won't see them until tomorrow."

Lakehurst nodded.

"I sent a note to Mr. Fortesque," Ellinbourne said. "I felt that only proper." He looked at Cassie. "I asked him to come here," he told her.

"Thank you," she said softly. She looked up at Lakehurst, concern in her large brown eyes.

Lakehurst reached over to squeeze her hand reassuringly. He thought it unfortunate they hadn't had an opportunity to relay to Ellinbourne their misgivings about the man.

"Fortesque?" Stillworth said, sitting straighter in his chair, the air of ennui gone. "Why would you send for him?"

Ellinbourne frowned at him. "He is the local clergy. They always notified my father of a death in our church area, no matter the soul or the circumstances."

Cassie nodded. "That is proper," she said.

"I saw you today in the village when I passed through," Mr. Liddle said, crossing his arms over his wide chest while he cocked his head to look at Mr. Stillworth. "You were coming out of the rectory, arguing with Mr. Fortesque."

"Arguing with the vicar? What were you arguing with him about?" Lakehurst asked.

"That's none of your concern," snapped Stillworth. "And who the bloody 'ell are you, anyway?" he said, looking at Mr. Liddle.

"Raymond!" Cassie said crisply. "You will watch your language in my home."

"Your home!" protested Mr. Tidemark.

"Yes, more so properly than the London townhouse is yours!" she snapped back, recalling him to the day of the Duchess's visit.

"I," Mr. Liddle began after he was sure there would be no more rebuttals, "am Harry Liddle, at your service," he said with a bow. "I work closely with the area magistrate on various matters," he said.

"A thief-taker." Stillworth's lips curled into a contemptuous sneer as he looked him up and down.

Mr. Liddle smiled.

"Oh, my," Ursula Hallowell said, looking up at Mr. Liddle, her eyes widening.

Lakehurst held his hands up. "Everyone stop. Please. We have two concerns before us. Possibly three, and possibly related."

"Related?" Ellinbourne said. He looked at his sister, concern etched across his face.

"We came to Baydon for two reasons. First, to help Lady Darkford dispel the lingering nightmares she's had since the night they killed her husband. To resolve the mystery of why he died and who did it. The castle and surrounding properties and ventures are her son's patrimony. She could not allow her fear to prevent her from ensuring his inheritance remained secure for him. Second, a man had been following her in London and asked a local street urchin to notify him whenever she went out and who visited her."

Mr. Tidemark straightened. "Why was I not told of this?" he asked.

"Why should you be?" Cassie asked. "You wouldn't have believed it if you were told. You would use it as another reason to send me to a sanitorium," she said sourly.

"How did you find out about the follower and the boy?" her brother asked, his dark brows drawing together.

"We saw him follow her out of the park and we had him followed," Lakehurst said.

"And I know the boy the man asked to spy on Lady Darkford through my charity work," Gwinnie supplied, "so he was happy to earn coin from two sources."

"Enterprising young man," Ellinbourne murmured. Gwinnie grinned at him.

"Mr. Martin said Lady Darkford would be hard to protect in London. He encouraged the trip to Baydon for her safety," Lakehurst explained.

"Doesn't seem safe now if someone's been murdered here," Tidemark protested. "Don't know why you would listen to this Mr. Martin."

"Mr. Martin is a senior agent with Bow Street." said Gwinnie.

"What! You told me when we met him he was a friend of your family's."

"He is," Lakehurst said. "And he is with Bow Street."

"Mr. Martin wisely recommended Mr. Liddle to us," Cassie said.

"A thief-taker." Tidemark scowled.

"Yes," Cassie said.

"Which became fortuitous when we arrived and discovered the Gallaghers were stealing from the estate. They knew we would discover the theft. They had done nothing to hide their activities," Lakehurst continued.

"Why should they when they knew you, Edmund," Cassie said, "would not come here. Plus, you told them to fire the staff! There was no way for the castle and the estate to be maintained. You even had them close down one of the limestone quarries that was lucrative for the shade of stone it produced."

"Graymore?" Mr. Stillworth clarified as he straightened in his chair, now attentively listening.

"Yes, Graymore," Cassie said.

Mr. Stillworth turned to his uncle. "Why?" he asked. "Why close a profitable mine?"

Tidemark's face had taken on a choleric hue. His lips worked back and forth. "Because I want to beggar the estate!" he decried. "I want to destroy Darkford!"

"Edmund!" Vanessa exclaimed.

He turned toward his wife, clutching her pudgy hand tightly in his. "Because Father looked down his aristocratic nose at you, my darling Vanessa, and disowned me when I married you," he told her. Reaching out to tenderly stroke her hair. He turned back to look at Cassie and Lakehurst. "My brother George was no better, hateful, bitter, manipulative man."

From across the room, Harrison Farrow snorted. "You're a great noddy; that's what you are. Of all the buffle-headed things to do, this takes the prize. Rupert won't be happy to hear this," he said, rising from his seat. He stuck his thumbs in his flowered waistcoat pockets as he sauntered toward them.

"Rupert and the Marquess had plans together, you know," Harrison declared.

"What are you talking about?" Mr. Tidemark asked testily.

Harrison grinned. "If the Marquess could get his unentailed properties profitable, Rupert would buy from him what was profitable, and then the Marquess could use the funds to invest in other ventures."

"Rupert Farrow ventures?" Ellinbourne asked sardonically.

Harrison shrugged slightly. "There was that aspect," he agreed.

"That was a sweet arrangement for Farrow!" Lakehurst said. "He acquires a profitable property, then gets the money he spent back to use in investments."

"Yes, but the Marquess did get a percentage of interest in the new venture investments," Harrison defended. "And he did invest in other things with some of the money, like Baydon Imports with Mr. Stillworth."

"It has been eighteen months since the Marquess died. Mr. Farrow is certain to know Mr. Tidemark is the executor of the estate. Why hasn't he said anything to him?" Ellinbourne asked.

"Could one of Richard's investments with Mr. Farrow be highly profitable?" Cassie asked. "If no one knew of the investment, Mr. Farrow could keep the all funds. Perhaps he does know of Edmund's desire to destroy Darkford, and it is to his benefit to say nothing," she suggested.

Harrison Farrow's lips twisted as he scratched his head. "You could have the right of it and I could be the buffle-headed fellow. Rupert will not be happy with me showing his hand," he said with what Lakehurst thought was a surprising grasp of understanding coming from the dandy.

Mr. Tidemark stood up. "I must return to London immediately."

"But Edmund," whined Vanessa. "We just got here. I can't, I can't get in that carriage again today."

"I know, my darling. But we must. I must speak to Rupert as soon as possible! Certainly, you see that! If I have done something he does not like he can cut us off!"

"You may be able to go; however, your horses won't be," Lakehurst said. "I won't allow them to be harnessed again today and we have no other horses available. You will have to wait until morning."

"That sounds soon enough," Vanessa offered, looking up at her husband pleadingly.

Mr. Tidemark's mouth worked back and forth. "All right," he said to her, gently. He looked back at Lakehurst and Cassie. "We would go to our rooms now and have a tray brought to us. My darling will need to rest as much as possible if we are to leave tomorrow."

Mrs. Tidemark nodded, now smiling brightly up at her husband. He offered her his hand to help her to her feet. She lumbered up out of the nest of pillows Cassie had made for her.

Cassie and Lakehurst stood, and Cassie crossed the room to open the parlor door. "Mrs. Pritchet we'll see to your comfort. She is quite good at ensuring guests are comfortable in their rooms," she told them.

CHAPTER 15

A BLESSING

"Lady Darkford, would you take it amiss if I did some searches in the cupboards in the study and library for any additional papers like you discovered?" Mr. Liddle asked.

"Not at all, please do. After discovering those property sales papers and items relating to Baydon Imports, I am curious as to what else might be found." She pulled the key off her chatelaine and handed it to him.

"Thank you. I will get on that, then," he said, bowing, then striding out of the room.

"I am off to the ramparts to play my violin," Gwinnie announced, bouncing out of her chair and grabbing her violin case from where she'd left it on the sideboard.

"I'll join you up there if you don't mind. Your music is soothing," Ann said.

"Not at all! I always like an audience. It improves my playing," Gwinnie said with a grin.

"I'll come with you," Ellinbourne said. "I have done no sketches from up there."

"Yes!" Ann said. "Excellent idea. Ursula, will you join us?"

"No, you know I do not do well with heights," she said with a laugh. "I'll see if I can assist Mr. Liddle in his search."

"Lord Lakehurst, might I borrow your novel? I should like to read the infamous chapter that Lady Darkford likened to her experience." Mr. Stillworth said.

"Yes. I have a copy in my room. I'll get it for you," he said, rising.

"I'll come with you and take it to my room to read until dinner," he said, following Lord Lakehurst from the room.

Cassie looked around the suddenly empty room. What should she do? What did she want to do?

She sighed. Nothing. She didn't want to do anything. She kept seeing Carlyle sprawled on the narrow ledge down thirty feet from the top of the cliff path. She felt guilt for Carlyle's death. If she hadn't returned to Baydon Castle, he wouldn't be dead.

That pain would remain in her heart forever, this she knew. But Baydon Castle also did not deserve to die, and it was surely dying. Already the closing of a mine and the letting go of staff there and at the castle had affected lives and livelihoods.

Where did she stand in all of this? Where should she stand?

She'd never liked Baydon Castle. Its remoteness had isolated her. It hadn't helped that Richard had remained coolly nice.

Nice. What a word. There was no love, no affection from her husband; however, he was *nice* to her to the extent he was able. He did not take her to London or Bath or any other location where she might mingle with other people other than an occasional trip to Wells to see the Loftbridges. He had his friends come to Baydon; however, he'd instructed her not to mingle with his guests.

Sometime between her marriage to the Marquess of Darkford and now she'd become a veritable wraith, a shade that floated through life, a remnant of the past.

She frowned. She did not see how Lord Lakehurst could believe he loved her. There was nothing here to love but a ghost.

She closed her eyes and laughed at herself. She was becoming maudlin and ridiculous, and the absurdity of her emotions penetrated her thoughts. A slight smile pulled at the corner of her lips. It was time for self-pity to be left behind and time to step into the future.

From the ramparts, she could hear Gwinnie playing a stirring piece full of action and emotion. Vivaldi?

A maid entered to remove the tea things. "Beg pardon, my lady," the maid said, curtsying when she saw Cassie on the couch. "I didn't think anyone was still in here."

"It's quite all right," Cassie told her. She leaned her head back against the sofa and relaxed.

Lakehurst entered while the maid was finishing up.

"That is how I like to see you," he said, "relaxed and smiling."

"I was considering what a goose I've been," Cassie said, straightening and removing her feet from the sofa.

"Goose?" he said, coming to sit beside her.

"I have been indulging in self-pity for months—nay years!" she said.

He cocked his head to the side. "Years? I request you explain that to me."

"It's not a self-flattering realization to admit I have quietly pitied myself for my marriage to Darkford not being the marriage of my dreams. He was *nice* to me. That is the best I can describe our relationship. I should have been content with that; however, I wasn't."

Lakehurst frowned, then pulled her onto his lap. "I can promise you," he said as he pulled her closer, lowering his head to hers, "our marriage will not be nice," he said softly before his lips descended on hers.

Cassie's eyes flared wide at the rush of tingling feelings that flooded her, then her eyes closed as she gave herself up to his kiss, a kiss unlike anything she had felt before.

She felt so safe, secure, loved, and perhaps most importantly, wanted. Lakehurst wanted her, she felt it in his kiss and the way he held her. She thrilled at the sensations running wild through her. She raised her hand, her fingers spearing his thick dark red hair, pulling his head closer. Never had she felt, nor imagined the feelings he roused in her.

He lifted his head and she looked at him in wonder.

"Nice will not be a word to describe our relationship," he told her. "Passionate, enthralling," he said, kissing her after each word, "captivating, loving, ardent, enchanting, and," he said, pausing as he looked at her, his eyes on her lips, "—*lustful*," he finished softly with a wry, promising smile.

The parlor door burst open. "Cassie! He's coming,"

Gwinnie said running into the room before she saw them together.

"Oh! Pardon! But about time, brother of mine," Gwinnie said severely, stopping and placing her hands on her hips. "But now isn't the time for dalliance," she continued. "That vicar is on his way here. I saw him from the ramparts."

Lakehurst lifted Cassie from his lap and sat her back on the sofa. He rose. "How far away is he?" he asked as he ran a hand through his disheveled hair.

"Now? Probably ten minutes at the most."

"I'll go upstairs to freshen up," Cassie said, rising to her feet as Ann and Ellinbourne came into the parlor.

Her brother looked her up and down. "That is a well-advised idea," Ellinbourne said with a wink.

Cassie felt color flood her cheeks as she fled the room.

LAKEHURST MET Mr. Fortesque in the great entrance hall. The man had dressed in somber clerical black, no bright waistcoat buttons on this day. He clasped his hands in front of him.

"I received a message from the Duke of Ellinbourne?" he said. His voice rose in a questioning tone. "He said Carlyle was dead, and he had been murdered?" Again, he spoke with that doubting, questioning tone in his voice.

"I am Ellinbourne. I sent you the note as was proper in our village. Without knowing, I assumed it was proper here as well and took it upon myself to send it for my sister, Lady Darkford."

"You are Lady Darkford's brother?" Mr. Fortesque

frowned and leaned forward a little. "I was under the impression she was the daughter of a clergyman, that her sister is a governess in Boston I believe she told me one time, and that her brother is an artist."

"That is all true. Our father was third in line to inherit the Ellinbourne dignities. When he and his brothers passed, as did their male issue, the title and properties landed on an artist's shoulders, much to the dismay of several family members, including me."

"Fascinating," he said slowly. "And where is your sister, our Lady Darkford?"

"She is in her room, freshening up," Lakehurst said. There was something about Fortesque's manner that he couldn't like; however, he couldn't identify what aroused his displeasure.

"If you gentlemen will excuse me, I will go upstairs to freshen up before dinner, as I am quite windblown," Gwinnie said.

"I as well," said Ann, following Gwinnie out of the room.

Mr. Fortesque smirked. "I'm sure they were aware my next request would be to see the body and had no wish to accompany us on that regrettable task."

Lakehurst did not like Fortesque referring to Carlyle as *the body*. Surely he knew the man. "He is in the castle chapel," Lakehurst told him. "This way," he said, turning to lead him to the chapel.

They entered the chapel through the south door's direct entry to the castle. Henry and Norton had left Carlyle in what had been formerly the west entrance narthex before the public entrance had been moved to the north side of the chapel. The massive entrance door which would have been on the west side in earlier times had been replaced with two gothic styled windows with trefoil arches supplanted by a cinquefoil design at the top using beveled clear glass in place of stained glass as used in original windows in the rest of the chapel.

The late afternoon sun shone on Carlyle's still body. Lakehurst could see dust, like fairy glitter, sparkling in the moving sunlight. The man lay so still and peaceful. Lakehurst wondered if he'd ever felt peace in his life.

Mr. Fortesque walked up to where they'd placed Carlyle, then turned to look at Lakehurst and Ellinbourne.

"You say he was murdered. How did you determine this?" he asked.

Lakehurst pulled Mr. Carlyle's shirt at his neck aside. "See the bruise pattern on his neck? It matches in pattern to the shape of a man's hands. They must have grabbed him from behind. Carlyle would not have heard them approach. Someone strangled him, then pushed him off the cliff. He fell thirty feet to a narrow ledge. The fall broke his neck. If strangling him hadn't killed him, the fall would have finished the job."

"I see. How did you deduce all of this?" he asked.

"I'm a writer. We notice details as they might be useful in a book at sometime," he answered with a wry smile.

Mr. Fortesque frowned. "Of course."

"The coroner will be here tomorrow to confirm his manner of death," Ellinbourne said.

Mr. Fortesque nodded as he pulled a book of prayer from his pocket and began to read. "*O God, who...*"

Ellinbourne frowned. He tapped Lakehurst on the arm to show his wish to speak away from Carlyle's body and Mr. Fortesque.

"My father never had to read those words. Everything in that prayer book was also in his mind for recitation," he whispered.

Lakehurst nodded.

When Mr. Fortesque finished his prayers and lightly touched Carlyle's brow, he joined Ellinbourne and Lakehurst.

"Carlyle was a good man. Do you know if Carlyle was his given name or surname?" he asked.

Lakehurst and Ellinbourne admitted they did not know as they walked back toward the castle entrance.

"I'll check the church records. He may be listed there. He'd served the Tidemark family for many years."

"Lady Darkford mentioned in conversation that Carlyle taught the Marquess how to ride a horse."

Mr. Fortesque nodded. "He certainly did care for the man. I understand he was the only member of his staff allowed to stay on the property when he threw his parties, and the only reason he could stay was because he was deaf. I've known the man since I came to the village of Baydonton two years ago, and knew he was deaf, but only learned recently he could read lips."

"Yes, he could, however, only if you talked directly at him. I have the unfortunate habit of looking around while I'm talking to people. Sometimes, Carlyle would tap my arm to get me to look at him while I was speaking. I could tell I frustrated him; however, he always remained respectful," Lakehurst said.

"Fascinating," Mr. Fortesque said in the same manner he'd had earlier.

Lakehurst looked at him.

~

Cassie and Gwinnie were in the parlor when they returned.

"Lady Darkford," Mr. Fortesque said, quickly crossing the room to take her hand between his. "I am so sorry for your loss of a loyal retainer," he said, squeezing her hand between his.

"Thank you," Cassie said as she tried to pull her hand free.

He released her hand, then sat down in an armchair angle to the sofa she sat on. Soon, Mr. Stillworth entered the room. Mr. Stillworth visibly stiffened when he saw Mr. Fortesque, however he nodded his head in recognition and took a seat across the room, as far from Mr. Fortesque as there was a chair available. Lakehurst pursed his lips on seeing Mr. Stillworth's manner; however, he didn't comment.

"Pardon, my lady," Mr. Harold said from the doorway. "Cook advises dinner will be ready in forty-five minutes."

"Excellent, then we have time for a preprandial," Lakehurst said.

"Mr. Harold, please let Mr. Liddle and Mrs. Hallowell know. I believe they are in the library."

"Immediately," he said. "Lord Lakehurst, you will require more glasses for your drinks. I shall bring them around, directly."

"Thank you."

Fifteen minutes later, Mr. Harold returned with a tray of cut-glass crystal glasses. Ursula Hallowell, Ann Hallowell, and Mr. Liddle followed behind him into the room.

"Just in time for a before dinner drink," Lakehurst said as he walked to the sideboard cabinet where the alcohol was kept and Mr. Harold placed the glasses.

"We should have our preprandial in honor of Carlyle," Mr. Fortesque said. He rose and walked toward Lakehurst. "I shall assist you, my lord," he said.

"Lord Lakehurst," Mr. Stillworth said from his seat across the room.

Lakehurst turned to Stillworth while Mr. Fortesque continued organizing the glasses and pouring the aromatic liquor.

"Have you gone to look at the cave since you arrived here?" Stillworth asked.

"Yes," Lakehurst said. "Carlyle took me there. Evidence remains that Lord Darkford had it kitted out elegantly; however, over the past eighteen months, bats and other vermin have taken over. Bat guano covers the floor and leaves a most unpleasant odor."

"That is unfortunate," Mr. Fortesque said.

"Why do you say unfortunate?" Lakehurst asked. He glanced back at Mr. Fortesque.

"I believe I should bless the cave."

"Bless the cave?"

"Yes. To dispel whatever lingered." He looked at Lady Darkford. "I believe a blessing will ease your mind."

"I don't believe anything could ease my mind about that cave, Mr. Fortesque."

"Hmmm. We shall see." He handed a small tray of drinks to Lakehurst. "Would you do the honors to pass these to the ladies while I finish pouring the rest of the glasses?"

"I can do that," Lakehurst said, accepting the tray from him. He passed the drinks to the ladies and accepted a glass from Mr. Fortesque as he passed the rest of the glasses around to the men.

"I should like," Mr. Fortesque said, "to bless Carlyle for his Tidemark family loyalty. Such dedication is rare. And to call a blessing down upon all of us in this sad time," he said. He raised his glass and then drank it. The company followed his lead. Cassie whispered, "Amen."

Mr. Fortesque confused him. Lakehurst could understand a blessing for Carlyle, but why would he want to bless the cave?

The company was quiet for a moment after the blessing toast, then Mr. Harold came to the doorway. "Dinner is served," he intoned.

CHAPTER 16
THE CAVE

The shallow, first chamber of the cave was not anything Cassie remembered. She held her lantern up and turned slowly to look about. Old bits of vermin-chewed red velvet upholstered furniture layered with limestone dust sat in companionable arrangements. Along one short wall stood a bookcase filled with gray and moldy books. The room could have been an abandoned gentlemen's club room if not for the stone walls, floor, and ceiling. At the back left corner was a narrow opening in the cave wall. Mr. Stillworth led them to that doorway. A strong smell of bat guano wafted through the opening. She pulled out a handkerchief from the hidden pocket of her gown and held it to her nose.

Suddenly she wondered why she was here? Why had she wanted to return to her nightmare? Where was everyone else? Her brother, Ann, Ursula, and the others from dinner? Why weren't they here? Lakehurst followed behind her; however, he was the only one.

She vaguely remembered Mr. Fortesque suggesting the visit after dinner, and she remembered agreeing, thinking, of course, she would go. Now she wondered why? It had felt somehow right to agree. There had been no thought associated with her agreement.

As she stepped forward into the grand cavern, her lantern light became pathetically inadequate for lighting the area and seeing more than ten feet in front of her. Mr. Fortesque took a torch from a bracket on the wall and lit it with his lantern, then lit several others on one side while Mr. Stillworth lit the other side.

She followed Mr. Fortesque without questioning why until she saw the stone altar. The sight of it jarred her. She stopped, frozen in place, and watched Mr. Fortesque walk ahead to finish lighting the torches. Lakehurst came up beside her.

Shouldn't it seem odd to her that Mr. Fortesque and Mr. Stillworth knew where the torches hung in the dark cavern? Her thinking felt muddled, a combination of accepting and questioning. She reached out for Lakehurst's lantern-bearing arm and clasped onto it.

"You're coming out of it, too," he whispered.

She looked up at him with confusion.

"The drink before dinner." He spoke with a bare whisper, his head leaning toward hers.

She looked up at him, her eyes wide. "Drugged?" she mouthed.

He nodded.

Finished with lighting the torches, Mr. Fortesque came toward them. "You look quite comfortable with one another. I hadn't expected that," he said.

"I beg your pardon," said Cassie.

"Come here, Lady Darkford," Mr. Fortesque commanded.

Cassie found herself wanting to obey him. She

would have pulled her hand free from Lakehurst's arm, but he caught her hand and held it in place.

"I—" She shook her head and closed her eyes briefly as if that could help clear the muddle in her mind.

"Lord Lakehurst, let her go," commanded Mr. Fortesque.

"No," Lakehurst said.

Stillworth laughed. "You didn't use enough *burundanga,* Fortesque, you didn't account for his size. You made a mistake. Imagine that, you making a mistake. The same mistake that got you kicked out of the East India Company and sent back to England. The same mistake you made with Darkford."

"Shut up, Stillworth," Mr. Fortesque snarled as he pulled a small, two-barreled revolver from his coat pocket.

Lakehurst gently pushed Cassie behind him.

"I should never have introduced you to Darkford," Stillworth said.

Cassie thought she heard sincere regret in his voice. She peeked around Lakehurst's broad chest, calmed by his even breathing, though she could feel how tense his muscles were under his jacket.

Mr. Fortesque's mouth quirked up at the side. "But you did, and together we have started down a path I intend for us to finish!"

"And what path is that?" Lakehurst asked calmly, as if he were asking about the weather.

"I will have his power!" Fortesque declared.

"Power? Whose power?" Lakehurst asked.

"Our lord, Satan!" Fortesque proclaimed. "And Lady Darkford will give it to me," he said.

"Satan!" Lakehurst repeated. "I've read of *burundanga* or *Devil's Breath,* as it is sometimes called, being used in devil worship rituals in South America, not India."

"His disciples have spread the word worldwide of the *Devil's Breath* and its uses," Fortesque said smugly. "Lady Darkford, your marriage bed awaits," he said, pointing to the stone altar.

"No!" she screamed.

Lakehurst held her behind him and urged her to walk backward to put distance between them and Fortesque.

"You're too late, Fortesque," Stillworth said. "The drug has worn off. Just like it wore off Darkford."

"Stillworth, how did you get involved with Mr. Fortesque?" Lakehurst asked as they inched backward.

Stillworth laughed. "Over mugs of ale. I told him my sad tale of being the rightful Marquess of Darkford. I am Darkford's brother. Did you ever guess that, Lady Darkford? Richard told me he was my brother, and dear, helpful Uncle Edmund explained to me that his brother took Richard for his heir as his hair was blonder, though he was the second born. Imagine losing a title because of hair color." Stillworth laughed again, harshly and a little hysterically.

"After hearing my sad tale, to cheer me up—Fortesque kindly said—he took me to an Indian gentlemen's club that catered to gentlemen with boys. I am ashamed to say I indulged, and he has never let me forget that. I even *dispatched* Carlyle on his orders when he discovered Carlyle could read lips."

"I told you to shut up!" Fortesque yelled as he raised the gun and fired at Stillworth.

Cassie screamed as Stillworth crumbled to the floor, clutching his side. His lantern shattered on the stone floor, the oil mixing with the bat guano to whoosh the small lantern flame into a fire that followed the piles of excrement on the floor.

Panicked, Stillworth scrambled backward, then stood up, still clutching his side as he tried to escape the fire.

Lakehurst plowed into Fortesque as the man retook aim at Mr. Stillworth. The shot went wild as Lakehurst and Fortesque fell to the floor, and the torch Mr. Fortesque carried ignited the pile of dung the men lay in.

Cassie screamed. Fire ran across the floor, now jumping from pile to pile.

Lakehurst scrambled backward and pulled Fortesque with him, but the man's coat had already caught fire.

Mr. Stillworth escaped out of the large cavern.

Fortesque pulled away from Lakehurst. "My Lord Satan has come for me! Praise be Lord Satan!" he cried joyfully as he ran toward the fire just as a small explosion brought down a wall of rock closing off the entrance to the cavern. Fortesque's death screams were nearly drowned out by the falling rocks.

Lakehurst backed away from the conflagration. He grabbed Cassie's hand and pulled her further into the cavern, behind the tapestry, and toward the blocked tunnel Carlyle had shown him.

Cassie cried out at the blockage, but Lakehurst immediately began to pull the tangled pieces or furniture loose and toss them behind him. Cassie, seeing what he was doing, began to help.

"Carlyle said," Lakehurst grunted as he pulled a heavy trestle aside, "the tunnel leads to the study."

"I didn't know of that tunnel entrance. That must have been how they got me in the cavern that night," she said as she pulled a chair away.

"Watch yourself," Lakehurst said as the pile began to tumble.

Smoke had begun to seep around the tapestry that hung over the tunnel entrance. They coughed and rubbed smoke-filled eyes. Through the stinging smoke, they could see the other side.

Now working feverishly together, they managed to clear Carlyle's barrier. Lakehurst helped Cassie over the last of the fallen items and they clung to each other as they made their way up the dark passage. Behind them, they heard another explosion and cave-in.

"I think the bats have lost their home," Lakehurst said.

Cassie started laughing, soon she was laughing so hard her sides hurt. Laughing as much in relief that they were alive as to Lakehurst's weak humor.

Lakehurst pushed her along farther into the darkness.

"I love you, Lakehurst," she said into the black void ahead of them.

"I love you, too, sweetheart," he replied. "And since we are going to be married, you need to start calling me Lancelot or Lance. That is my name, you know."

She giggled. "My heroic knight, Lancelot."

"I try. I will always try to be your knight."

"You are and you will be," she said simply.

The tunnel narrowed. Cassie leaned into Lakehurst, and he wrapped his arm around her.

The tunnel and its gentle climb upward seemed endless. It was so dark Cassie nearly ran into the wall at the end of the tunnel. She pushed against the wood barrier, but it didn't move.

Lakehurst found the pegged closure near the floor that held the door in place, but not the lever to actuate the door. "There should be a lever somewhere," Lakehurst said.

"Is someone there?" they heard muffled through the wood.

"Yes!" Lakehurst shouted back. "It's Lady Darkford and Lord Lakehurst. Who's there?"

"Liddle and Mrs. Hallowell," came the muffled reply through the thick wood.

Cassie grabbed on to Lakehurst's arm, almost wanting to bounce like Gwinnie did.

"Liddle, see if you can find a lever that will open the door to the tunnel," Lakehurst yelled back.

They heard pounding and scratching from the other side as Mr. Liddle searched for the lever. Lakehurst pulled Cassie into the circle of his arms and kissed her. She wrapped her arms around his neck, pulling him closer, her fingers threading his hair.

Suddenly, the door swung outward. But they didn't jump apart.

"I'd say they're fine, wouldn't you, Ursula?" Mr. Liddle said.

"Exquisitely fine," Ursula agreed.

THE NEXT MORNING, before Mr. Tidemark could hustle his wife back into their carriage to leave Baydon, Cassie demanded they tell her the truth about the Marquess and Mr. Stillworth.

Lakehurst thought she looked quite fierce, standing in the entrance hall, her arms akimbo as she stared Mr. Tidemark down.

He nervously pushed his glasses up his nose. "I don't know what you are talking about," he declared huffily.

"I will not allow your carriage to leave until I am satisfied with the truth. Please, into the parlor," she said sternly, gesturing to the open parlor door.

"Ask Mr. Stillworth," he said instead.

"We don't know where he is or if he even made it out of the cave alive. Lord Lakehurst and I almost died last night escaping Darkford's cave. I'd like to know why."

Mr. Tidemark's mouth moved back and forth, as was his habit, before blurting out some piece of information. He pushed his glasses up his nose again. "It is all my brother, George's, fault," he declared.

Mr. Liddle came up behind the couple and gently touched their shoulders to encourage them to go into the parlor.

Mr. Tidemark sneered at him. He walked into the room with ill grace. Vanessa clung to his arm, tears beginning to puddle in her blue eyes.

Cassie saw everyone seated comfortably, then turned to Mr. Tidemark again. "Explain," she said sternly.

He sighed. "Roxanne, the Marchioness of Darkford, gave birth to twin sons she named Richard and Raymond. Everyone thought the births were fine; however, she contracted childbed fever and soon died. My brother was distraught. He didn't want to have anything to do with his sons since he'd lost his wife. He told me to get rid of them. Bernice, our sister, had just lost her babe. I suggested she could take them. Bernice agreed.

"After a year, when his grief lessened, he decided he needed to have his heir. He came to Bernice and took the baby known as Richard away with him. But Richard was not the firstborn, and once Raymond discovered they were brothers, I made sure he knew he was the elder and that he should be the rightful heir to the Marquess of Darkford."

"Part of your revenge against your brother?" Lakehurst said, his arms crossed over his chest as he glared down at the man.

"Yes."

"Stillworth said he chose Richard due to his hair color?" Cassie said.

He laughed. "He felt Ricard looked more like himself."

"But they were twins!" she exclaimed.

"Not identical twins. Richard's hair, for example, was a lighter blond."

"Why didn't he take both babies?" she asked.

"After Roxanne died, he didn't even want one! But he needed an heir and did not want to remarry. Truthfully, Raymond had it better than Richard, for our sister loved him as if he was her own. She and her husband gave him everything. Discovering Richard was his brother after their twenty-first birthday was the worst thing that ever happened to him."

"What was your role in all of this?" Lakehurst asked.

He laughed. "George and Bernice's arranger.— Until I met Vanessa, then George tossed me aside as if I were an old piece of boot leather."

"Arranger?" Lakehurst said.

"When he needed something to happen, I quietly made sure it did."

"Including switching children," Cassie said.

He nodded. "I didn't care. I was a younger son. To me, one baby was like another."

"The magistrate and the coroner are coming up the drive. Behind them there is a carriage with a ducal shield," Mr. Liddle said from his vantage point by the narrow window.

"What?" said Lakehurst. He crossed to the window.

"It's Grandmother!"

"Mama! Mama!" cried out Alex from the carriage. He jumped down when the door opened, landing on all fours in the dirt. He scrambled to his feet and ran to Cassie who'd come out of the castle at the news of the carriage arriving.

He threw himself at her. She might have fallen backward if Lakehurst hadn't been at her back. "I missed you, Mama! I missed you so much!" he said, clinging to her.

"I missed you, too," Cassie said, tears of happiness streaming down her cheeks as she bent down to pick him up.

Henry assisted the Dowager Duchess of Malmsby and her good friend, Lady Oakley, out of the carriage while John Norton took the reins of the magistrate's and coroner's horses to lead them to the stable.

Gwinnie bounced out of the castle and ran up to her grandmother. She hugged her and tucked her arm in hers. "You have missed everything! Come in! Come in!" she said, taking Lady Oakley's arm on her other side.

Lakehurst and Mr. Liddle went to the magistrate and coroner and led them to the chapel by the outside entrance to where Carlyle's body lay.

"He missed you so much," the Duchess told Cassie, "I decided we would come surprise you."

Cassie laughed. "You have! But as Gwinnie said,

come in! Did you travel from Wells this morning? You must have left quite early."

"We did," the Duchess agreed. "When I discovered from Mr. Martin that he had apprehended the man responsible for stalking you and sending the letter, I knew I had to come here as quickly as possible. When we stopped in Wells for the night, I heard the magistrate and coroner were coming here early today. I decided I must come with them. What has been happening? Who died that has necessitated a magistrate and coroner?"

Cassie and Gwinnie stopped in the hall when they recalled the Tidemarks were in the main parlor.

"Let's go to the parlor where I practice," Gwinnie suggested.

"Yes," Cassie agreed. "Mr. Harold, tell the Tidemarks they are free to leave." She looked at Gwinnie, "I think the sooner they are gone, the better."

"Agreed. Alex, are you hungry?" Gwinnie asked Alex.

"Yes!" Alex exclaimed.

"Come with me then," she said, taking him from his mother's arms. "Let's go visit Cook and see what she has." She looked at Cassie. "I'll leave you to explain the goings-on."

Cassie laughed, but nodded.

"You must tell me of the stalker and the letter!" she said to the Duchess as she led her and Lady Oakley into the smaller parlor.

"It is most extraordinary. It was Mr. Stillworth's valet! Acting on Mr. Stillworth's behalf! Is Mr. Stillworth here? The magistrate will be arresting him."

"So that's why he didn't have his valet here," Cassie said. "The magistrate is here because one of Baydon's long-time servants died yesterday. Murdered. By Mr. Stillworth!"

The Duchess and Lady Oakley exclaimed at the news. The Duchess squeezed Cassie's hand in hers.

Cassie told the Duchess and Lady Oakley about the events of the past few days, starting with the embezzling caretakers and ending with discovering Mr. Stillworth should have been the marquis.

"This is not what I would have wished you to encounter here," said the Duchess with a long sigh.

"What did you hope for?" Lakehurst asked from the doorway. But before she could answer, he looked over at Cassie. "The magistrate and Mr. Liddle have gone in search of any sign of Mr. Stillworth." He sat beside Cassie on the couch and threaded his fingers through hers.

The Duchess grinned. "Now that is exactly what I wished for you," she said, indicating their clasped hands.

"She could talk of little else on the journey here," Lady Oakley said drily.

"Of course! I've planned this since Ann and Ellinbourne's betrothal ball," the Duchess declared. "This makes four matches I've had a hand in arranging in less than three months! You all were helpless until I took a hand in the matter."

"Oh dear," Gwinnie said from the doorway. She had a hold of one of Alex's hands. In his other hand, he held a large slice of cake.

Lakehurst laughed. "You're next, sister of mine. You're next."

EPILOGUE

VERSELY PARK – LATE OCTOBER 1816

Cassie sat on the terrace of Versely Park watching Alex with his new tutor, Mr. Murdoch.

It was a crisp fall day, but sunnier than all of summer had been.

Alex and Mr. Murdoch had a target set up and Mr. Murdoch was teaching Alex archery. Not typically a subject for tutor and pupil, but they had developed a schedule for academic lessons in the morning and other gentleman lessons in the afternoon.

Mr. Murdoch was a veteran of the wars. He'd been a young lieutenant in Wellington's army and came away from the war with a desire to live a quiet life. Though a young boy's tutor might have seemed beneath the younger son of an Irish earl, the role suited Mr. Murdoch. She and Lakehurst considered themselves lucky to have his services for Alex. Dulcie remained as Alex's maid until such time as she would be needed again as a nursemaid. Soon, Cassie hoped.

She and Lakehurst had married a month ago at the Michaelmas holiday in a small ceremony at Versely Park. While she and Lakehurst would have preferred a quick and private special license ceremony, the Duchess of Malmsby had protested loudly. With good humor, they'd agreed to be wed at Versely Park. She wished her brother and Ann could have wed at the same time; however, her brother stubbornly awaited news from Boston if their sister, Margaret, or Maggie, as she was known in the family, would return for his nuptials. She didn't know how Ann had remained so patient! At least her brother had finally conceded to wed before year's end, regardless of Maggie's attendance.

Suddenly, Mr. Peabody jumped on her lap, startling her. She laughed, then began to pet the Versely Park resident mouser. They'd brought Oscar to Versely Park before the wedding, and he and Mr. Peabody had a guarded relationship, at best. At least there had not been any loud catfights. That Oscar was not out here on the terrace meant her husband was writing. He'd taken over the old Abbot's office in the monastery portion of the estate as his writing room. Oscar had been so insistent he be allowed to be in there that they had to create a cat door for him to come and go between the manor house and the old connected monastery at his leisure.

Lakehurst, or Lance, as she now called him, gave her his novel's tour of Versely Park, the secret passages he'd described, and the ruined chapel where the devil's disciple had wanted to brand the heroine. Seeing the exact locations he'd described had helped alleviate any lingering unease she'd felt with his book. She'd gone back and read it cover to cover, and it no longer gave her any nightmarish thoughts of similarities. Now she saw more differences! Her husband was a talented writer. There was no mistaking his abilities. And society still did not know who *Anonymous* was, though Lance thought he might put his name on the next one.

Perhaps.

Maybe.

He waffled back and forth on that decision.

It could stay a secret as far as she was concerned. If his authorship were known she'd have to share him with the world, and she wasn't ready to do that.

Marriage to Lance was so different from her marriage to Darkford that she scarcely considered that marriage to have been a marriage. Lance enjoyed her company and would rather spend his evenings with her than with other people. They laughed together and cried together. It was glorious.

And those poor debutants, they certainly did not understand the joys a man like Lance could bring into the bedroom. She blushed just thinking of their lovemaking.

She heard the terrace door open. It was Lance and Oscar. Oscar bounded forward, then stopped when he saw Mr. Peabody.

Lance sat in a chair close enough to her to thread his fingers through hers. Oscar jumped into his lap, looked over at Mr. Peabody, then circled in Lance's lap to lay down with his back to the other cat.

Cassie and Lance exchanged amused glances.

"How did your writing go?" Cassie asked.

"I got to the end of that troublesome chapter. It will need a rewrite edit; however, it got my hero where I needed him to be, so that's good."

She nodded. "Good. Do you think it will be finished before the holidays?"

"I'm fairly confident. Why?"

"I've received a letter from Ann. She says Miles has agreed to a wedding before the end of the year, regardless of Maggie's presence. Since Ursula Hallowell and Harry Liddle have wed and moved to Wells, Ann's lived with Lady Oakley. That has been pleasant enough, but not quite comfortable."

Lakehurst laughed. "I can see how that would be the case. As one of Grandmother's cronies, she's nearly as bad as her. The renovations to The Knight's House will be completed this week. We could return to London and have her live with us."

Cassie nodded. "There is merit to that idea." *The Knight's House* was what they named their new London townhouse, their private joke from their time in the tunnel. Lance bought the unentailed Darkford House from the Darkford estate to remove that property from the marquessate liabilities and provide them a home in London. But Cassie insisted it be renovated and redecorated first to make it a lighter, brighter home.

Mr. Liddle and the magistrate found Mr. Stillworth's body outside the cave entrance. It appeared the large stone with the quotation from Rabelais that encouraged a person to do as they wanted had fallen and hit him on the head.

Back in London, they'd met with solicitors for the marquessate and, with Mr. Tidemark declaring he no longer wanted to be executor and guardian for Alex, it was arranged for Lance to take over those duties.

Rupert Farrow purchased Baydon Imports' assets and signed a lease on Baydon Castle for fifteen years. The castle was to be the center of his merchant empire, and he was delighted to have a real castle to live in.

Much to Cassie and Lance's surprise, Harrison Farrow asked to be the new Darkford properties steward. He granted he had no experience, but he had his brother Rupert for advice. He'd become bored following in the prince's wake. He wanted to do something. He wanted to see if he could turn the marquessate fortunes around. He didn't need the money. He needed the challenge.

After a brief discussion with Mr. Rupert Farrow, they gave Harrison Farrow the position. His first endeavor had been to reopen the Graymore limestone mine.

The Farrow brothers wanted to see the damage done by Edmund Tidemark mitigated, and the marquessate prosperous again—so long as that helped their pockets as well.

Edmund and Vanessa Tidemark had retired to Bath. Cassie said that Bath had suddenly become a city she never wanted to visit. Lance laughed.

"I don't think Alex should grow up an only child," Lance said as they sat in companionable silence, watching Alex with Mr. Murdoch.

Cassie was silent a moment, though a slow smile curved her lips. "I think we should take advantage of our opportunities to see that doesn't happen," she said.

They looked at each other, then grinned and shooed cats off their laps.

Lance put his arm around Cassie as he led her into the house.

THE END

CONNECTIONS

My characters come from a "connected" world. Many know each other and appear in more than one book. Sometimes they rise to the level where they need their own story.

Here are some of the connections within *Artful Deceit.*

Lord Candelstone was first mentioned in *The Waylaid Heart* as a spymaster, a behind the scenes person. He then appeared in *Rarer Than Gold* and it was his activities within that story that "encouraged" his retirement.

Mr. Lewis Martin first appeared in *Heart of a Tiger.* He has been slowly relating to me his back story – how an obviously educated man became a well-regarded Bow Street agent. We will have to see when he makes his move for center stage.

Lady Oakley was introduced in *A Grand Gesture* and has also appeared in *Heart of a Tiger.*

The Marquis who learned woodworking in order to build his daughter a rocking horse is in *The Rocking Horse – A Christmas Regency Novella.*

SCRIBBLINGS BY HOLLY NEWMAN

A Chance Inquiry series

The Waylaid Heart

Rarer Than Gold

Heart of a Tiger

And coming soon

Murder of a Dead Man

Murder on the Downs

The Art of Love series

An Artful Deceit

An Artful Compromise

An Artful Lie

An Artful Secret

And coming soon

An Artful Decision

An Artful Practice

An Artful Trade

Flowers and Thorns series

A Grand Gesture

Honor's Players

A Heart in Jeopardy

Heart's Companion

Other works

Gentleman's Trade

Reckless Hearts

A Lady Follows

The Rocking Horse (novella)

Perchance to Dream (short story)

ABOUT HOLLY NEWMAN

I decided to be a writer when I was in the fifth grade. I filled notebooks with stories—until a mean-spirited high school teacher told me I had no talent for writing. Crushed, for several years I stopped writing, but writing was an itch that wouldn't go away.

My interest in the Regency period came while in high school when I volunteered to re-shelve returned books at the community library. Every week there were Georgette Heyer novels to be shelved. I finally checked one out and became immersed in the world of the Regency.

Fast forward ten years. When attending Science Fiction Conventions, I met people who read science fiction, but also enjoyed the works of Jane Austen and Georgette Heyer, just as I did! They liked these books so much that they wore Regency costumes at the science fiction conventions. They even had Regency era dancing on the convention program. These science fiction readers and writers knew a lot about the Regency era. Intrigued, I did research on the era and quickly went from casual Regency reader to a Regency history buff. Woo-hoo!

After that, with encouragement from science fiction authors, it was just a small step to writing Regencies.

After living thirty years in the Arizona desert, I now live in Florida, seven miles from the Gulf Coast, with my husband, Ken, and our *clowder* of cats. (I don't dare say a number of cats. My husband has developed a habit of collecting strays.)

Subscribe to my newsletter to learn about books and other writings I'm working on. You can sign up here to subscribe and get *Perchance to Dream*, a Georgian fantasy short story.

And be sure to follow me on Bookbub, to be notified about new books and book sales.

Here are other ways to connect!

Website
Facebook
Pinterest
Goodreads
Instagram
Etsy

9 781648 395161